Moonlight Encounter Ebook Edition
Copyright © 2024 by Nina Jarrett. All rights reserved.
Published by Rogue Press.
Edited by Katie Jackson

All rights reserved. No part of this book may be used or reproduced in any form by any means—except in the case of brief quotations embodied in critical articles or reviews—without written permission.

This is a work of fiction. Names, characters, places, and incidents are products of the author's imagination or are used fictitiously and are not to be construed as real. Any resemblance to actual events, locales, organizations, or persons, living or dead, is entirely coincidental.

This e-book is licensed for your personal enjoyment only. This e-book may not be re-sold or given away to other people. If you would like to share this book with another person, please purchase an additional copy for each reader. If you are reading this book and did not purchase it, or it was not purchased for your use only, please return to your favorite retailer and purchase your own copy. Thank you for respecting the hard work of the author.

For more information, contact author Nina Jarrett. www.ninajarrett.com

MOONLIGHT ENCOUNTER

NINA JARRETT

To my father, for encouraging every artistic tendency he found in his kids.

Miss you, Dad.

PROLOGUE

"Fear is pain arising from the anticipation of evil."

Aristotle

* * *

AUGUST 1, 1821

Lord Aidan Abbott, the honorary Baron of Abbott and heir to Viscount Moreland, carefully wiped his riding boots before entering the family townhouse from the back garden. Riding Valor had been a boon to his recent turbulent thoughts, and his spirits had been lifted by the invigorating air.

Striding down the hall, and contemplating if he needed to change before he went out again, he entered the entrance hall. Where he found Lord Moreland frozen and staring at the letter in his hand while an unknown footman awaited a response.

Aidan frowned in consternation. His father was a composed gentleman of the highest order, and little could shake his exemplary demeanor, but his pale complexion spoke to troubling news.

"Father?"

The sound of Aidan's voice seemed to jolt Lord Moreland from a trance. Drawing a deep breath, his father looked up at the waiting servant. "We will be arriving at Ridley House as soon as our carriage is readied."

The servant nodded. "Yes, milord. I shall inform Mr. Michaels of your arrival."

Once they were alone, Lord Moreland turned to Aidan. "It is your sister. One of the footmen at Ridley House held Lily hostage and attempted to abduct her after she uncovered his involvement in the late baron's murder."

Aidan's knees went weak, and he grabbed for the banister. "Is she ..." He could not bring himself to complete the sentence, overcome by the nightmarish images racing through his head.

Is she dead?

"Their butler informs me that she is well, but the servant is ... no longer with us." Lord Moreland waved the page in his hand, but despite his reassurance, he was still pale and distracted. His concern for his young daughter was evident.

Aidan drew in a shaky breath at this news, not realizing until that moment that his lungs had stopped working at the thought that his little sister might be harmed—all because he had been a selfish cad and left her alone when he had promised his parents to take care of her.

"This is my fault!"

Lord Moreland shook his head as if to gather his own wits. "Nonsense. This is the fault of the man who murdered Lord Filminster. I ... must find your mother, so we may depart for Ridley House."

Aidan nodded, but he was unconvinced. His selfish behavior the night of the King's coronation was the reason that Lily had been alone in their home. It was the reason she had witnessed Brendan Ridley entering the widow's home across the street. Why she had fallen asleep in the drawing room window seat, and then later witnessed Ridley's departure from the widow's home in the early hours. It was Aidan's neglect that was the reason she had felt it necessary to step forward and provide a scandalous alibi to save Ridley from the hangman's noose when the young man had been suspected of patricide. There was no denying that Aidan's actions had forced Lily to marry Ridley to save herself from scandal.

"I am not waiting for the carriage. I shall see you at Ridley House."

His father raised his brows in surprise, but Aidan ignored him to run out of the Abbott townhouse, leaving the door ajar to head down the street away from Grosvenor Square with his long legs eating the distance. He did not care if he appeared a lunatic running as if the hounds of hell were chasing him. He must confirm for himself that Lily was unharmed. This entire situation was his fault, and it was time he took responsibility for his part in the risks that his innocent sister had undertaken to save another.

This is my fault, this is my fault, this is my fault.

The litany in his head beat in time to his pumping heart as he reached Ridley House. Bounding up, he raised a fist and pounded loudly on the wooden door. Soon it swung open to reveal the butler, Michaels. His eyes flickered in disdain over the sweating Aidan, who had no time to worry about his appearance.

"Where is she?" he demanded.

Michaels sniffed before standing aside. "The drawing room at the top of the stairs."

Ridley House was a behemoth, stuck in the mists of time. Faded carpets and wallpaper framed looming furniture darkened by lacquer and the patina of age while austere barons and their wives glared down from moody paintings.

Aidan made for the dim stairs, not bothering to acknowledge the butler in his haste. His need to see his little sister safe and sound was the only issue his racing thoughts could focus on in the moment, and etiquette was the furthest thing from his mind as he bounded up the stairs two at a time. Arriving on the first-floor landing, he swung his head about, inspecting the doors available.

Where is she?

Determining that the drawing room would likely overlook the street, he rushed over to the far door with no concern about waiting for the heavy steps of the butler on the stairs behind him. Aidan grabbed the handle, throwing the door open to look inside. Across from him, Lily and her husband sat on a settee, his tiny sister pale and shaking with the new baron's arm around her waist.

"Lily!"

She looked up at him as Aidan strode in. He knew he must be a sight, his face flushed with the exertion he had expended to reach her.

"Aidan? How did you get here so quickly?"

Even from afar, he noted the redness around her neck. The blackguard must have held her by her throat. Aidan wished to throw his head back and howl in distress. Lily could have been killed because of his perfidy.

It is my fault!

"Ran here … as soon as we heard the news … Left our parents … to take the carriage … Terrifying … to hear you had been attacked. I …" Aidan raked his hands through his damp hair before crossing the room to drop on a knee by her side. Taking her hands up in his, and shaking his head as he sought words, he exhaled sharply. "This is my fault! If I had taken care of you that night, instead of abandoning you to carouse with my friends..."

Lily frowned, reaching out to pull on his lapels before lifting her arms to hug him. "It is not, Aidan. I am well. Gracious! You must have run like the wind to arrive here so quickly."

"I should never have left you alone."

"But you did, and now I am married. Life goes on."

Aidan groaned, his chest tight with the burden of culpability. "Until it does not."

"I am safe. See, you are speaking with me at this very moment. The entire matter is settled."

Aidan pulled away. His sister was so small that even lowered to one knee, they were practically eye level. From this close, he could see the marks of abuse on her throat. If the offending footman had not been killed, he would spring to his feet to beat the man to death himself. How could anyone be so craven as to attack a lovely young girl like his sister?

"Is it over? Was the footman the one who committed the murder?"

Brendan Ridley, the new Baron of Filminster now that his father had been killed, cleared his throat. "No, I am afraid not. He claims he was paid to conceal the identity of the killer. At least we know now that it was nobody in the household."

Aidan jumped to his feet. "How do we know it is true?"

Lily's husband must have felt uncomfortable with Aidan towering over them. He rose up, walking into the cleared space in the middle of the room. Filminster finally replied. "I suppose we shall search his things to find evidence of the payoff."

Aidan's nostrils flared. "If it is true, then there is still a killer out there. Someone who might harm my sister!"

"We will keep our guards to patrol the house—"

"What?"

Filminster glanced over at Lily, who had straightened up with a look of dismay. "They do not need to shadow you. Simply take care of our home until we know we are safe. In addition to that, we will have a new housekeeper and maids at the end of the week, so Ridley House will be properly staffed, along with a new lady's maid. It will be far more difficult for any attempt at intrusion once there is a full staff on duty."

Lily turned her gaze to Aidan, who was only mildly mollified by her husband's assertions.

"See that you do, Filminster. My sister is irreplaceable."

CHAPTER 1

"The aim of the wise is not to secure pleasure, but to avoid pain."

Aristotle

* * *

AUGUST 3, 1821

*A*idan had not slept for the past two nights. Lily's encounter with the footman had been a rude awakening in regard to his own behavior. The thought of harm befalling his sister was more than he could bear, which was why he was sitting in Filminster's study for the third time in as many days.

"I need your help."

Filminster's declaration punctuated the tension in the room.

Aidan straightened in his seat, eager to help resolve the danger Lily faced in any way he could. The feeling of helplessness was unbearable, so any action would be an improvement to his state of mind.

Across from him sprawled the fool, Lord Julius Trafford, in his ridiculous attire, while Aidan's brother-in-law, Filminster, stood at the window with his hands clasped behind his back.

"What has happened? Is Lily safe?" Aidan had been drowning in guilt since he had abandoned his sister—all that had unfurled from that one decision still had Aidan reeling in the aftermath.

"I have discovered the letter that my ... father ... wrote. I now know what led to his murder on the night of the coronation."

Lord Trafford picked at his lapel of purple silk, the gold and emerald signet ring on his pinky flashing brightly, before purring in a supercilious tone. "Your father ... or your uncle?"

The baron turned from the window to scowl at his clownish friend. "You know of that?"

Trafford merely arched a brown eyebrow in response. Aidan experienced a surge of indignation at being left in the dark, leaning forward. "What is Trafford talking about?"

Filminster sighed. "I suppose the gossip has been circulating, so I might as well speak the truth ... The late baron was my uncle who married my mother to save the family from shame. My true father, his older brother, died weeks before the wedding."

Aidan pulled a face at this unsavory disclosure. "Faugh!"

His brother-in-law chuckled dryly. "Just so."

"May I read the letter?" Trafford had straightened from his lazing position. His indolent air had evaporated, and Aidan glimpsed for a moment what it was that Filminster appreciated about his arse of a friend.

Filminster pulled a folded page from inside his coat,

walking over and handing it to Trafford to read. Aidan watched intently, noting that the other honorary lord, heir to the Earl of Stirling, grew solemn. Trafford whistled through his teeth, looking up to shake his head in disbelief, his affectation of wheat curls bouncing over his cropped brown hair. "This provides a serious motive for murder. This is both wealth and power at stake."

Aidan held out his hand expectantly, Trafford handing the letter to him without comment. It was covered in splotches of ink which obscured some of the words as if a censor had taken a quill to it, but what he read made his blood run cold.

> Sir Robert Peel
>
> London, July 19, 1821
>
> Sir,
>
> It has come - - my attention that the true heir to Lord - - - - - - - - has not been acknowledged.
>
> I was speaking with his lordship before the coronation, and he informed me of his recent bout of ill health. He spoke fondly of his youngest brother, informing - - of his strength, intelligence, and wit at great length. There was no mention of his lordship's middle brother, Peter, who you may be aware died near twenty years - - -.
>
> Peter and I attended Oxford together, - - - his death was tragic - - - unexp- - - - -. I have thought of him often over the years, which is why I feel the need to pass this information - - - - - -u.
>
> Before departing England, Peter married a wom- - of Catholic descent. She convert- - - - - - - - - were married - - - - - Church of England, before leaving our shores. I maintained correspondence with him until his death. He had written just months before his death to inform me of the birth of his son.

I cannot say for certain where the boy and his mother are - - - - - all these years, but he would be the true heir and I implore you to look into th- - matter. - - - - - - - - - - is the true heir to the title of - - - - - and his father's legacy cannot be ignored.

I understand the trials of being a second son, and I cann- - allow this matter to stand. Whether - - - - terrible injustice is a mistake due to ignorance of the child Peter sired, or a deliberate obfuscation of the facts, I must speak on my friend's behalf. His son is the true heir and must be found immediately. I will locate our shared correspondence when I return to Somerset and have them forwarded to - - - - - - - - - - -

J. Ridley, Baron of Filminster

Aidan absorbed what he had just read before slowly exhaling, the implications setting in. "Lily is in serious danger if the killer believes his secret might be contained within the walls of Ridley House."

Trafford snorted. "And the culprit would be correct, considering the letter you are holding."

"There is insufficient information to reveal his identity!" Aidan's protest was met with a twist of Trafford's lips.

"There is enough. An elderly lord, suffering from a recent bout of ill health, with a younger brother named Peter who died some twenty years ago, and an even younger brother set to inherit his title. Who has likely killed the baron to conceal the knowledge of the true heir in order to secure his inheritance? It drastically reduces the number of suspects."

"Precisely," Filminster responded. "Lily and I spent last evening and this morning comparing a recent copy of Debrett's to a copy from thirty years ago to compile a list of peers. The runner, Briggs, is investigating what happened to each of the Peters to learn the circumstances of their deaths.

Thus far, we have a list of six heirs who might fit the description, which is why I need your help."

Aidan was brought back to the declaration that started this conversation. Filminster needed his assistance to secure Lily's safety. "What do you need?"

Filminster cleared his throat, twisting the toe of his boot on the bright Aubusson rug adorning his study floor while his dark chestnut curls fell forward over his face. "It is much to ask..."

Trafford smirked. "That has not stopped you before."

"This is different, Julius. My bride is in danger." Filminster inhaled deeply before continuing. "If anything happened to Lily, I would never forgive myself."

Nor would I.

Aidan could simply not imagine how he would ever recover from putting Lily at risk. If harm befell her, his guilt would consume him and there would be nothing in his dark future to console his soul. This was a matter of life and death.

With that realization, Aidan reached a decision. It was time to stop resisting this new relationship with his sister's husband. They needed to band together for Lily. His sweet, young sister deserved their cooperation and protection. Rising to his feet, he interrupted the tête-à-tête between Filminster and Trafford.

"Whatever you need, I will do it."

Filminster's brandy eyes flickered to Aidan, and he nodded. "Thank you ... Aidan."

Trafford heaved a heavy sigh. "I am in. What is next?"

Returning to the window, Filminster leaned against the sill. "I need your help to investigate these six men. Lily and I are still considered scandalous for our supposed tryst on the night of the coronation. Although the scandal is abating now that we have wed, it is difficult to be discreet when all eyes are upon us. You two gentlemen, as single young bucks around Town, will be welcomed into the homes of polite society with high hopes you might make a match with their daughters or nieces. That access will allow you to search for information that might shed light on their involvement."

Aidan rubbed a hand over his face. In the normal course of things, he would never agree to such unethical behavior. Gaining access under false pretenses was not the behavior of a man of character.

But this is for Lily.

He accepted the truth of it. A man of character would take steps to correct his mistakes, regardless of what he might be required to do. It was a matter of restoring his honor, and if he needed to dirty his hands for the greater good, then so be it.

"Where is the list?"

* * *

FREDERICK SMYTHE WAS the most irritating of men, Gwen decided, resisting the urge to clench her fists.

"We cannot afford it, Papa! I am five and twenty! On the shelf! A spinster! Pray tell, what is the point of spending money on yet another ball when none of the young men wish to dance with me?"

Her father's lips curled into his customary grin, the one that dissolved the resistance of family and friends. Gwen steeled herself not to be affected by his charm. "It is not the time to give up, Gwendolyn. It is only a matter of time before you meet a gentleman who appreciates your wit and grace."

Gwen could not help herself—she snorted. "Grace?" Twisting her face, she sang the refrain from her youth. *"Gwen, Gwen, the Spotted Giraffe!"*

Her father's grin faded. "I curse myself to this day for sending you to that school. Those harpies destroyed your confidence, but I see a great beauty when I gaze upon you, Gwendolyn. Your mother stole my very heart from my chest the moment I beheld her. And once she quoted Homer to me in Ancient Greek …" Her father raised a hand to his chest, his eyes gazing into the past with an expression of adoration and awe. He cleared his throat, returning to the present. "I shall never forget a moment of our time together."

Gwen felt tears prickling. Lifting a hand, she dabbed at her eyes, giving a discreet sniff. "Mama was majestic."

"As are you, daughter."

She shook her head, rejecting the notion that she was the beauty that her mother had been. "I am a ginger!"

"A Titian red."

"And spotted!"

"Delightfully freckled."

"Mama was an elegant auburn, Papa. I am a gangly, spotted ginger!"

Her father shook his head in denial. "You are glorious and your mother would agree."

Gwen fell silent, biting her lower lip. She wished her mother were here with them now to settle their argument. "Mama did not like to waste money."

"You are not a waste of money. The right man will recognize your worth and value. We will join forces with another family and grow our resources for your future and for Gareth."

Gwen smiled at the mention of her younger brother. Having him home for the summer had revealed how quickly he was growing up, and it had been a poignant moment to wave him goodbye when he had returned to Eton to continue his studies. "Gareth's grasp of Latin and Greek is impressive. Mama would be delighted."

"As you will be one day when you have children of your own."

Longing rose in Gwen's chest, which she squashed down ruthlessly. If the past few years had taught her anything, it was that no man would ever wed her. Nay, she was to be a spinster. Her only hope of progeny was to adopt a foundling to dote on. A child to whom she could pass on the love of learning as her mother had done with her and Gareth.

Since recent events had brought the knowledge of the tentative nature of life, and the need to pursue one's dreams while one had the opportunity to do so, Gwen had evaluated what was important to her. She planned to seek a foundling to adopt once her father admitted defeat—his plans for her grand union were just dreams. Frederick Smythe was tilting at windmills if he thought an honorable gentleman would ever take notice of Gwen, Gwen, the Spotted Giraffe.

The few men who had displayed interest were not to be considered. It was not Mr. Spalding's thinning hair or receding chin that ruled him out, but the many times he misattributed Socrates that had ensured she would never marry him. The thought of being irritated by his lack of intelligence for the rest of her days was too much to bear.

Mr. Rutledge had been pleasant, if a bit on the older side, but he conversed exclusively about fox hunting, which Gwen abhorred, and hounds, which was acceptable but monotonous.

Gwen wanted what her parents had shared, a meeting of the minds and hearts. If hearts were out of the question, she minimally required an intelligent husband to father her children, or she would be better without.

"No wedding, no children."

Her tone was sharp. Frederick Smythe was a dreamer, and she could not allow herself to be tempted into taking up a lance to joust the sails of a wind machine, convincing herself that there be giants.

Her father turned a sympathetic blue gaze to her, no taller

than Gwen herself, who stood at five feet nine inches. "You are lovely, Gwendolyn. The right man will appreciate you and provide you with the security you deserve while you will provide him with a worthy and challenging partnership."

Gwen looked down at the toes of her slippers peeking out from under her gown, her shoulders heaving with a heartfelt sigh. She wanted to believe her father, she really did. But hard-won experience proved he was deluded about her and her shortcomings. Mama had been a great beauty, and an excellent scholar. Gwen had inherited one of those traits, and it was not one that could be viewed in the reflection of a looking glass.

"Papa, we cannot waste money on such extravagances."

Her father strolled over to his desk, a man dapper for his years. He was filled with a youthful energy, a reflection of his strong interests. The sharp cut of his charcoal coat and trousers, along with his pristine white linen, spoke to his fastidious nature, but he had an easy manner which made him well-liked by most people. He managed their finances well, but as the third son of a baron, they were not a wealthy family and could not afford the lavish ball he held each year in her honor even as the men of the *ton* continued to ignore her presence.

This brought to mind the women who tittered behind their fans, giggling at her unfashionable appearance.

Gwen sighed, wondering how to explain to her idealistic father that she was a poor investment. How her mother had managed to be a graceful beauty despite her scarlet locks remained a mystery to her only daughter.

Mama was unique. Special.

And Gwen was merely an oddity.

A fact that Frederick Smythe refused to accept.

"Please, Papa. The money can be used for Oxford when Gareth is ready. It has been seven years, and I am still a wallflower. What could possibly happen this year that would be different from any other year?"

Her father cocked his head, his lips quirking into his characteristic grin. "This year you could encounter the right man. The one who recognizes the perfection of my only daughter and falls at her feet, defeated by her magnificence."

Gwen burst into laughter despite her resolve to steel herself against her father's whimsies. She finally found the breath to respond.

"You are incorrigible, Papa."

Blue eyes twinkled in the afternoon light. *"Nullum magnum ingenium sine mixtura dementiae fuit* ... There is no great genius without a touch of madness."

Gwen shook her head. "Aristotle will not sweeten my temper, old man."

"Ah, but we both know that is a lie."

She bit her lip to prevent a smile, unable to argue with her father's claim. It appeared there would be no dissuading him. The ball would proceed as stated over breakfast, and her visit to his study had not achieved a damned thing.

CHAPTER 2

"The ideal man bears the accidents of life with dignity and grace, making the best of circumstances."

Aristotle

* * *

AUGUST 13, 1821

The past ten days in Trafford's company had been excruciating. Together, they had attended several social events, to Aidan's chagrin, the pursuit of information notwithstanding. Trafford was not the kind of companion he wished to be associated with, but they had been seen in public together the length and breadth of Mayfair, while Aidan had been forced to put up with Trafford's antics.

Currently, Aidan stood by the corner, observing the home of Mr. Frederick Smythe amid the loud clatter of carriage wheels.

The night sky was adorned with silvery clouds and a large full moon, but his vantage point on the street blocked the view of the magical evening unfolding above.

"How do you plan to get in without an invitation?"

Trafford waved his hand in dismissal, contemplating the arriving guests with a focused gaze. Aidan growled in irritation, wishing for any other conspirator than this dandified fool. Nevertheless, he stepped back to give the other man the space he had requested.

This is for Lily.

The reminder helped quell his resentment of playing batman to the oaf whom Filminster had paired him with. He had attempted to question Lily about Trafford's involvement, but she had cheerfully chattered about the new books she had ordered for their library, as if she had not faced death and injury less than a fortnight earlier.

"If Brendan trusts Trafford, then so do I" was the only response she had provided. Which must have meant she did not know the fop all that well.

Aidan cracked his knuckles, pacing behind Trafford while he awaited the oaf's direction.

Suddenly, Trafford broke the silence. "I see my great-aunt, Gertrude, with her husband." With that, he took off toward the Smythe home, his gold silk tails flapping in his wake. Aidan watched hesitantly before reluctantly following his now-constant companion. Trafford weaved through the line of carriages in the rounded drive, skipping up to an elderly couple who were descending from the carriage in front.

"Aunty!"

A wizened old lady with stooped shoulders in blue silk squinted up at her nephew before clapping her hands in excitement. "Julius, my boy!"

Trafford leaned down, and a trembling hand was extended from beneath an embroidered shawl. She pinched his cheek between arthritic fingers, beaming with pleasure. Behind her was the husband, an equally ancient man in old-fashioned breeches, white stockings, and buckled shoes, which did little to disguise the march of time in that his legs were spindly from insufficient use.

"What are you doing here, boy?"

Aidan suppressed the urge to roll his eyes. Trafford was anything but a boy. The man clearly had dallied with numerous women of the *ton*, attired as a coxcomb with far too much allowance to waste on clothing. Only a nearsighted great-aunt could affectionately view him as a boy.

"I was just walking by with my friend." Trafford gestured in Aidan's direction, who gritted his teeth. They were on a small but elegant estate near the Thames—private property—which belied the notion that they happened to just be passing by. "Are you attending an event?"

"It is the Smythe ball. Frederick has a daughter he has been attempting to marry off for years. She is a dear girl, but the boys do not like her, I am afraid."

"That is a pity. I was hoping to catch up, but if you are otherwise occupied …" Trafford trailed off with deliberation, baiting his great-aunt.

"Come with us, Julius! Frederick will be delighted to have such strapping young men in attendance."

Trafford fell into place, joining arms with his relation and assisting her up the stairs into the lit entrance hall. Aidan puffed out a breath and followed them in reluctantly with the frail husband, fighting the impulse to hold out his own arm to help the aristocrat who doddered up the steps at a snail's pace.

Soon they stood in the long receiving line, Trafford chattering with his great-aunt while the husband stared sightlessly about as if lost in the recesses of his elderly mind.

From his considerable height, Aidan could see over the heads of most of the nobles. Up ahead, his attention was caught by a statuesque redhead greeting guests next to the host, a tidy man in his fifties similar in height.

The young woman was breathtaking. Worthy of adorning the Elgin Marbles that Parliament had acquired for the British Museum in recent years, salvaged from the Acropolis in Athens. A veritable Greek goddess with Titian red hair, an elegant Grecian nose, and creamy skin. But it was the delightful spray of freckles across her glowing skin that disappeared under the edge of her bodice that made his thoughts turn to lascivious activities.

Aidan had always had a fondness for scarlet tresses, but he had never seen a woman of such magnificence before. Her small, high breasts were artfully draped in the current fashion inspired by the sculptures of the ancient world, her tall figure and slim hips beautifully suited to the flowing ivory silk that made him think of a divine carving come to life to converse with the mere mortals.

The thought of peeling the fabric from her warm skin sent a rush of heat through his veins, a sensation that he was unaccustomed to, but this woman was unique, a daughter of polite society without comparison.

Was this the so-called ape-leader destined for spinsterhood? Were the men of London afflicted with blindness?

Rubbing a hand over his shaven chin, Aidan's spirits suddenly lifted at the realization that when he reached the end of the receiving line, he would meet the glowing deity gracing this earthly gathering with her presence.

"It is time to go."

Aidan slowly comprehended that the statement was

directed at him. Trafford was peering at him with a questioning look, clearly wondering what had Aidan so riveted but bobbing his head toward a side hall leading away from the receiving line. Disappointment made Aidan's spirits plummet once more, the recollection of Lily's situation a painful reminder that an introduction to the beauty at the end of the hall was not in the cards for this evening. For just a brief moment, he had been distracted from his recent troubles, but it was not to be. With a lingering sense of disappointment, he departed with Trafford from the hall of chattering guests.

Soon they stood together in a dimly lit library in silence.

"Do you have any notion how ridiculous you look in this —" Aidan threw his hand out at Trafford's gold coat.

"Now, now, Little Breeches. There is no need to tell Banbury stories ... I am unduly handsome in my brocade, which we both well know."

Aidan snorted in disgust. It was a farce to be engaged in this investigation with the clownish Trafford, but he had no choice. Filminster's other relations and close friends, the Earl of Saunton and the Duke of Halmesbury, had both departed for their country estates, which meant Trafford was the only other man Lily's husband trusted to assist in securing her safety.

Considering Aidan had only recently returned from his Grand Tour, he was hardly in a position to present trusted associates for Filminster to consider for inclusion in their plot to reveal a murderer.

"Did a certain young woman capture your eye out in the hall? You seemed rather bemused."

Aidan looked away, unwilling to discuss the magic of laying eyes on whom he assumed was the young Miss Smythe. He could hardly obtain an introduction to a debutante when he planned to uncover her father's involvement in a murder.

"Is *Aunty* not surprised at our departure? I thought you were to catch up?" His sneer was a thinly veiled shift of subject. Trafford grinned, his lean face lighting up in amusement at Aidan's obvious ploy.

"*Aunty* will quite forget she saw me tonight by the time she reaches the head of the line. She and Uncle are quite easily distracted these days, and I saw an opportunity to proceed with our plans."

It was a relief the other man did not pursue the subject of Miss Smythe. Aidan was still rather taken aback at his visceral reaction, and would like to consider what it meant when he had a moment of privacy. That would be much later tonight once he had completed this dastardly errand. This was not a time for musings, but for action!

"What is the plan?"

"I think I shall wander about and gather information while you search Smythe's office."

Aidan wanted to argue. Sneaking through a gentleman's private places was not his idea of an excellent or honorable pastime, but he could not deny that Trafford was better at soliciting information. Not least because the idiot seemed to know almost the entire *ton* and their servants, with the exception of marriageable misses. Aidan hated being disingenuous and violating peoples' trust by searching their homes, but …

This is for Lily! To keep her safe.

His father would have definite opinions about what Aidan had been doing these past two weeks, which was why Lord Moreland had not been informed of their informal enquiry into six heirs. To date, they had managed to rule out only one of the men on the list. The gentleman in question had been holed up in the country with his family after a serious fall, so could not have been the murderous visitor on the night of the coronation.

There were six men to investigate, but Smythe was the man at the top of their list. He was the heir to a baron, which made him a promising suspect because the murdered Baron of Filminster had been seated with other barons the day of his murder.

There were whispers of Smythe selling off assets in the clubs, and Filminster had pointed out that a suspect with some sort of financial difficulty could certainly be driven to a passionate act such as murder if the late baron had threatened his future inheritance.

"I will meet you in the ballroom when I am done."

Trafford nodded. "Have fun, Little Breeches. You might learn interesting things when you search through a man's private belongings."

Aidan frowned, unsure what Trafford was alluding to, but before he could respond, he was left alone, the ostentatious golden tails of the other man's coat the last thing one could see from the dim interior of the room.

Sighing heavily, Aidan walked over to the door to peek his head out and look about. Where would Smythe's private study be?

* * *

GWEN'S CHEEKS were hurting from the smile fixed on her face. She had stood by her father's side and welcomed every single guest into their home. Most of the men had barely acknowledged her, preferring her father's company. This was not surprising because her father possessed considerable charm, along with an irreverent wit which his companions enjoyed.

The women had been dismissive, smirking behind their

fans, except for a few older biddies who had sympathetically asked if anyone was courting her yet.

The latter was worse, in her opinion. Protracted conversations about her lack of success, while she attempted to shift the subject, had made the muscles in her face strain from the enforced platitudes and cheerful expressions under the onslaught of judgment.

How she wished she could be more ordinary. Her general appearance caught the attention of others, and exposed her to pity and ridicule, or disinterest. Gwen had once dreamed of making a match, despite her physical shortcomings, but it had only taken a Season or two to realize this was not to be. How she had wished her mother had still been here to offer her guidance, but by the time she was a young lady entering society, they had already lost their extraordinary light and Gwen had had to fend for herself. Soon she had learned how to shield herself from judgment so that she no longer paid any attention.

It still hurts.

Gwen skirted the ballroom and admitted the truth. After all these years, she remained disappointed that she had never found her match. Her parents had been deeply in love, and when her mother had become ill, her father had vowed to take care of Gwen and Gareth. They had spent their final time together in the privacy of their home, focusing all their attentions on enjoying Mama's last days together, and she had left this earth after securing a promise from each of them to attend each other.

Papa, Gwen, and Gareth had taken pains to remain a close family. It was their way of honoring Mama's wishes. Gareth wrote to them every week from Eton, her and Papa reading his letters together, and Gwen writing their mutual responses and news. Her mother would be pleased with their efforts.

If only Gwen could have made a match, she could have babes of her own who would continue their family legacy, but it was not to be. If her mother were here to speak with, Gwen would ask for her advice as a woman navigating the *ton*, but after seven unsuccessful Seasons, it was clear that she would never marry.

It would be easier to not think about the disappointment of unfulfilled yearnings if her father would stop dragging her onto the marriage market each year. He refused to accept that Gwen was undesirable to the men of the *beau monde*.

Gwen watched the dancers twirling on the floor, a flurry of colorful skirts and the dark hues of the men, and reflected on the irony that she barely danced at her own balls. A few of her father's friends would politely fill in her dance card, but she would be fortunate to fill even half of her dances.

Sighing, she looked down at the card tied to her wrist. She had three free dances, which in her estimation was sufficient time to take some air on the terrace, thus removing herself from prying eyes.

Decision made, Gwen began to weave her way through the guests chattering on the perimeter of the floor, heading toward the French doors on the other end.

"Miss Smythe!"

Gwen wished to ignore the call and keep moving to the doors, but her innate sense of honesty would not allow it. She paused and turned, finding Lady Gertrude Hays peering up at her. The old lady was a cheerful woman who was well-meaning but garrulous. Her heart sank.

"Are you enjoying your evening, Lady Hays?"

The woman bobbed her head, her hair as white as snow and gathered in a coiffure twenty years out of date. A blue plume hung at an alarming angle from a hideous turban, nearly catching her in the creases of her eye. Gwen smiled, gently reaching out to straighten the feather before Lady Hays put her eye out.

"My great-nephew is here. I would like to introduce him to you, if I may." She peered around the ballroom, her eyes so clouded with age that she squinted to see. After a few moments, she turned back to Gwen. "I am afraid I cannot see him. Have you met him? Lord Julius Trafford? He is a dear boy."

Gwen shook her head. Lord Trafford's reputation preceded him, though. Why on earth would he be attending their ball, she wondered in surprise. Perhaps there was a guest who had captured his attentions. "I have not had the pleasure, my lady."

"I shall locate him."

With great relief, Gwen watched Lady Hays walk away. This was her chance to make her escape. Grabbing hold of her ivory skirts to raise them off the floor, Gwen strode toward the terrace doors despite the inappropriate speed. The other guests were occupied, and they did not appreciate her as it was. Why worry what they might think of her racing through the room, if they paid her any mind at all?

Stepping around their guests, she finally reached the other end of the ballroom. Anticipating a respite from her duties, she reached out her hand to grasp the handle and, sweeping the door open, she exited the room and swung the door closed behind her.

Several guests were milling outside, leaning against the stone balustrade that overlooked the garden. Gwen moved away, walking around the corner and gasping in astonishment when she beheld a full moon. Puffy clouds were lit with its silver light while the star-studded heavens gazed down from their lofty heights. It was a beautiful night, and her bruised ego was forgotten as she took in the magic of the nocturnal tapestry.

It was an occasion of such romance, it took her breath away, and she wished that she had a young gentleman at her side to share the view with.

Gwen sighed, the loveliness of the moment melancholy with her unfulfilled desires. Every young woman should be able to share an evening like this with a lover at least once, she reflected. Alas, it was not to be.

CHAPTER 3

*"Love is born into every human being; it calls back the halves of
our original nature together;
it tries to make one out of two and heal the wound of human
nature. Each of us, then, is a matching half of a human whole ...
and each of us is always seeking the half that matches him."*

Plato

"Plato is dear to me, but dearer still is truth."

Aristotle

* * *

Aidan was fortunate in discovering Frederick Smythe's study at the end of the hall that Trafford had led him down, just two doors from the library. The room was in darkness when he entered it, but after fumbling around in the dark for several minutes, he managed to light a candle by the cabinet positioned near the door.

Holding the candle carefully, Aidan made his way over to the desk near the fireplace. He sat in the desk chair, grimacing in irritation at the height. Smythe was several inches shorter than he, making for an awkward placement of his long legs.

Opening the drawers on the right, Aidan pulled out a stack of pages into the lit space on the surface. Flipping through, he whistled quietly to himself in the shadows of the room.

He was holding bills of sale. Paintings, *objets d'art*, even a piece of land located north of London. Thousands of pounds, even tens of thousands. All within the past six months.

Rumors of Smythe's financial troubles had not been overstated. Why would a man need to liquidate so much? Had the heir fallen into debilitating gambling habits? Was he facing bankruptcy for some reason?

Excitement unfurled in Aidan's gut. The sheaf in his hand pointed to a tangible motive. Smythe appeared to be desperate for funds, which meant he could very well have been desperate to silence Filminster's uncle by thwacking him to death.

If they could uncover evidence of Smythe's violent act, and have him arrested, Lily would be safe and this terrible time would be over.

Aidan pulled an inkstand closer, picking up a quill and searching for a blank leaf of paper. Methodically, he made notes, writing down the details from the bills. The purchaser, the amount and the item sold of each, and any addresses mentioned. The runner, Briggs, could use the list to track down more information.

Finding the pounce, Aidan sprinkled it on to dry the ink. Blowing it off, he carefully folded the list and put it away in the inside pocket of his coat. His lurking had proved successful, and perhaps they had found their man. It would be a relief to end these furtive activities, which were a constant source of disquiet. He was not made to engage in such deceit, the ethics of the matter raising perpetual questions to dwell on.

Aidan carefully returned the bills to the drawer, then placed the inkstand and quill where he had found them and used a handkerchief to wipe away evidence of his presence from the surface of the desk. He rose, pushing in the seat where he had found it before making his way back to the cabinet to return the candle and its holder. Leaning down, he blew the flickering flame out.

Walking over to the door, he paused. The sound of voices in the hall outside made his heart pick up speed. Looking about in the light of the full moon, his eyes slowly adjusted to notice that the windows across the room were French doors leading to a terrace. The voices grew louder, and Aidan realized he needed to move quickly.

Loping across the room, he fumbled to open the doors. He flickered his eyes back and forth to ensure that no one was about to witness his departure from the study.

About thirty feet down the terrace stood a woman, framed by the light of the full moon and enthralled by the view. Aidan drew in a deep breath and prayed the door was well lubricated. If it squeaked, she would be alerted to his presence and know he had exited Smythe's study, which would ruin his mission.

He slowly opened the door and mentally praised the servants for their diligence when it failed to make even the slightest of sounds. Stepping through onto the terrace, he quietly drew the door shut behind him and made his way to the stone balustrade as if he had been viewing the gardens.

He placed his hands on the stone, which was still warm from the afternoon sun, gazing up at the silvery moon above and humbled by the majesty of the night sky.

Glancing to his right, he realized the woman must be Miss Smythe. The young woman from the receiving line was so taken by the evening firmament, she had failed to notice his arrival. The moon lit her in profile, revealing the curve of her chin along with the perfection of her elegant nose. Without thinking, he spoke the words that entered his heart in the sheer perfection of the moment.

"Who can know heaven except by its gifts?"

Miss Smythe jumped slightly, startled at his voice disrupting the silence of the night. After a moment, without turning to see who had interrupted her observation of the heavens, she responded in the most surprising manner.

"And who can find out God, unless the man who is himself an emanation from God?"

Aidan blinked, almost stepping back in his amazement. "You have read *Astronomica?*"

"Marcus Manilius was one of the greatest poets of Ancient Rome."

Her voice was melodic and confident, and Aidan realized he was beholding a scholar of the Classics with a deep appreciation for the works.

The breath caught in his lungs, and the words of Plato sprung unsummoned into his mind. Was Miss Smythe his other half?

The folded list in his breast pocket mocked his romantic optimism. Did he truly believe that the heavens would reveal the other half of his soul to be the child of the man responsible for the attack on his sister two weeks earlier?

Yet, how else did one explain this synchronization, this attraction he was feeling for the young lady? He had traveled the realm and the Continent and never encountered such feminine perfection as a divinity who quoted the great minds of the ancient world. How was such a woman unwed? Undesired by the bucks of the *ton*? Was she surrounded by deaf and blind imbeciles?

If only ...

His feet had a mind of their own, leading him to stand at her side to view the haunting grandeur of the night together. His duplicitous behavior was temporarily forgotten, all thoughts wiped from his mind other than to behold her with the awe of a mere mortal in the presence of sacred womanhood.

* * *

GWEN WAS NOT ACCUSTOMED to tall, handsome gentlemen seeking her out, but the stranger on the terrace now stood a mere foot away. Perhaps the dramatic evening landscape had drawn him in. Certainly, he was not aware that he was flirting with Gwen, Gwen the Spotted Giraffe.

Seconds earlier, she had wished she could enjoy a magical moment such as this with a suitable gentleman, and it would appear the deities had answered her fervent wish to experience the romance of a lover by her side. He had materialized as if wished into being by her very thoughts. Silent after their odd exchange about *Astronomica*.

Letting out a shaky breath, she accepted it for what it was. An aberration brought on by the pale light. Clearly the man had no idea he was standing next to a spotted ginger. He most likely thought she was a svelte brunette, with flawless skin that had never been touched by the sun's rays. Whatever his reasons, she was going to accept this opportunity to behold the beauty of the night and pretend she had a beau to share it with.

The fear of ruining the moment had her squeezing the stone beneath her fingers, as she clung to the fantasy that an eligible man wished to share the view with her. She was terrified she would ruin the moment and it would end before she had gathered every sense, every second, that she could before returning to the solitude of her real life.

Not only was he physically impressive, from what she could see from the corner of her eye, but he had perfectly translated the Latin poem and attributed it to the rightful source. He was a true scholar to engage in such a discussion, and for just a fleeting second, Gwen dared to believe that this was the man who her father had promised would appear. Gwen released her cynicism to allow the magic of possibilities to enter her heart.

It is to savor the moment, she told herself. But despite her pragmatic nature, deep in her soul she felt that something unexpected was unfolding.

From the corner of her eye, she saw that his hand had come to rest next to hers. It was the tiniest fraction of an inch away, so close she could feel the heat emanating from his glove to soak into her skin. If she had the courage to move, she could touch him, but she was too afraid it would end their interlude before it had begun. She willed her hand to remain in place.

It was without surprise when she felt his large hand extend to cover hers, and she accepted that she was dreaming this entire encounter. That soon she would awake to find out she had dozed off on the terrace and imagined this entire circumstance but, in the meanwhile, she would bury herself in the dream. If only every slumber included such wonderful happenings.

The man gently tugged at her hand, turning to pull her into his arms ever so slowly as if to give her the opportunity to protest, and Gwen was amazed at the realism of this apparition. She could feel the strength of his arms wrapping around her waist and shoulders, smell the leather of his boots and his freshly laundered linen, as he pulled her against his hard body. Tilting her chin, she watched him lower his head and accepted the press of his lips against hers, sighing in pleasure when she was enveloped in masculinity.

His lips were firm, hesitating before she felt them part and the flicker of his tongue. Her mouth fell open in invitation, well aware of this type of kissing due to her reading of their extensive library. Obviously, this was fantasy from the depths of her sleepy mind, so she imagined what she had read. They kissed deeply, his satin tongue tangling with hers to light the flames of desire, sweeping through her body to engulf her lower belly.

Gwen pressed her thighs together to quell the throbbing sensation springing to life, and kissed the stranger back with all the passion she had banked within her soul while she had waited, and then wearied of the search for the right man, as her father liked to refer to him.

Her arms stole up to circle the stranger's neck, and she heard him growl in the back of his throat with approval as he drew her closer to his muscled body. Her imagination was far more developed than she had previously realized, she thought to herself, as her bosom flattened against his hard chest. She wished she might sleep forever if she could hold on to this fairytale that a veritable Adonis had appeared out of her deepest desires to ravish her in the moonlight.

Moaning, she pressed closer, reveling in pressing her belly against the hardness that revealed his desire for her, and understanding what it was to be wanted by a man for the first time in her many years.

He was tall and muscular, a god stepped out of an Italian painting to wreak havoc on her senses, and he made her feel captivating as his lips trailed across her cheek to breathe deeply of her hair near her sensitive temple.

"Citrus ..." he whispered, before finding her earlobe and suckling it between his warm lips. Gwen gasped as delicious sensation shot out in waves, her head rolling back to give him better access as she delighted in the overwhelming pleasure.

She reached her hands up to curl her fingers into his dark hair, while his hands ran up and down her back, leaving a trail of fire in their wake. Panting hard, she felt his hands gradually slide down to cup her buttocks, his lips returning to hers while a growl emitted from deep within his chest. She shivered with the delight of the moment, his hips pressing against hers, and she wanted to grab his coat and rip it from his shoulders so she might—

Behind them, the sound of a door opening onto the terrace made her and the stranger freeze in each other's arms. Gwen panted, no longer with passion but with fear that curled through her organs as they parted slightly to stare at one another. The man slowly shut his eyes for a moment in a pained manner. When he reopened them, he turned his head to look over her shoulder.

Gwen prayed that he would find no one there, but she saw his eyes focus and knew without a doubt that they had been caught.

Her reputation was ruined.

With her unique height, even if the guest did not see her features, they would know who she was. That she had been caught in the arms of a man, and had sullied the only asset she possessed as a young woman of the *ton*—her pristine conduct.

He released her, placing himself between her and their newly arrived company. Gwen took the opportunity to straighten her gown and raise a hand to check her hair. The gentleman would bear little aftermath, but she ... she was about to bear the bitter consequences of losing her mind under a full moon.

She could only whisper a prayer that when she turned to

face her consequences, she would find her father rather than any of their guests. If it was anyone else, she was utterly ruined and would have to retreat from the public eye.

* * *

AIDAN WAS STILL drunk with desire for Miss Smythe, but he was sobering up quickly when he took in a crowd of guests who had spilled around the corner of the terrace and were now agog, staring at him as if he had sprouted a second head.

At the back, Trafford stood with wide eyes, before casting his anxious gaze down to run a hand through his wheat curls. A moment later, he threw out his hands as if to say there was nothing he could do.

Several matrons stood with their husbands, none of whom Aidan recognized, but apparently they recognized him.

"It's Moreland's heir!" The impasse was broken when an older woman with graying blonde hair practically shrieked.

"Is that Miss Smythe?" asked the gentleman she was holding by the arm.

Trafford cleared his throat. "I am sure it is not what we think. Lord Abbott is a nobleman of the highest order."

Aidan stared at his accomplice, thinking about the list in his breast pocket. Soon they might reveal Frederick Smythe as a murderer, and this revelation of womanhood, the only woman who had ever made him lose his head, would not just be publicly ruined by his actions tonight but would be even further humiliated by her father's arrest in the near future.

The thought of the lovely and intelligent Miss Smythe being destroyed within their rather cruel community made his blood run cold—a fact that could only be embraced as the last remnants of his passion subsided, to his relief. He could only hope the dark had hidden the evidence of his ardor when he shielded Miss Smythe with his body upon realizing they had acquired an audience.

Miss Smythe deserved better. He had instigated their kiss, and he had no choice as a gentleman but to act with honor. It was his duty to protect her, not just this night but all her future days when events unfolded as he thought they might.

Staring at Trafford, he slowly considered his options and found that the obvious solution was not one he unduly objected to. It seemed fitting somehow, despite the complications it would introduce.

Drawing a deep breath, Aidan prepared his announcement, certain it was the right thing to do. Trafford stared back at him, an expression of horror crossing his features as he comprehended what Aidan was about to do. He shook his head, putting a hand up to stay Aidan from his decision—

"I just offered for Miss Smythe's hand in marriage ... and she accepted."

CHAPTER 4

"The gods too are fond of a joke."

Aristotle

* * *

Gwen had still not peeked around Lord Abbott to see their audience, which was clearly not her father, but multiple guests. Any notions of discretion were out of the question, she supposed.

More importantly, her kiss with a stranger had been with the heir to Viscount Moreland, according to the multiple witnesses of her ruin.

"I just offered for Miss Smythe's hand in marriage … and she accepted."

After he made his announcement, in a mellifluous voice that stroked her interest to rise once more, she did not comprehend the words for several seconds.

Then it hit her.

The stranger knew who she was.

And he had just announced their betrothal.

The shock at her unrestrained behavior with a strange man, followed by the discovery that her moonlight lover was an honorable and highly eligible member of the *ton*, was too much to absorb.

She could not possibly hold him to his declaration, but she also could not believe that her father had been correct that a man such as him did, indeed, exist.

"You are to wed *Miss Smythe?*"

Gwen recognized the voice of Lady Astley, a sour grandmother of polite society who was quick with her scathing criticisms. Crouching slightly behind Lord Abbott's back, she pulled a face at the harridan's tone of disbelief. Gwen might be entering spinsterhood, but there was no need to be so blatantly incredulous.

"I am."

"Miss *Gwendolyn Smythe?*"

Again, Lady Astley was clearly baffled. Gwen forced back her irritation at the implied insult.

There was a pause, then a firm and low response from Lord Abbott. "I was overcome by Miss Smythe's beauty and wit. Her acceptance of my offer is a great honor that I will cherish for all my future days." He sounded irate, defensive even. Of her?

Gwen bit her lip. Hidden behind him, she soaked in the wonder of what he had just said. If only it were true. Sadly, Lord Abbott had simply been caught at the wrong time with the wrong woman. When he saw her clearly in the light and discovered she was a gangly spotted ginger, he would be deeply disappointed and understandably wish to retract his offer.

And she would allow him to do so because she could not possibly hold him to blame for her own ill-advised behavior. She had wanted him to kiss her. Had actively participated.

He could hardly be held responsible, and change the course of his entire future to include her, when they did not even know each other.

But he knows my name. Perhaps he knows me somehow?

It did not signify. She was on the shelf as it was. This scandalous encounter hardly ruined her non-existent prospects of courtship.

Squaring her shoulders, Gwen resolved to be honorable, too.

"Lord Abbott failed to understand me."

Her statement would be bolder if she confronted their observers. Stepping from behind Lord Abbott, she pretended to stare them down, but truly she simply focused on the French doors right behind them because she had not the courage to meet anyone's eyes.

"He made his offer, but I turned him down."

Lady Astley wasted no time with her astonished response. "*You* turned down the heir of Viscount Moreland?"

One could practically hear the exclamation mark at the end of the question. Truly, did the old peeress have nothing better to do than cast aspersions about Gwen's appearance and general worthiness as a mate?

"I did," she replied firmly.

From the corner of her eye, Gwen could see Lord Abbott cock his head and tense his square jaw at her statement, which had negated his attempt to defend her reputation. "I confess Miss Smythe had her reservations regarding my offer, and I was attempting to persuade her to change her mind."

Gwen nearly burst into hysterical giggles. To his credit, Lord Abbott was doing his best to raise her in status, inferring that he was the one who was inferior to her. What he did not understand was how little Gwen had to lose. She could not force a marriage onto a man, no matter his mutual culpability in her ruin. One should marry for true partnership, not because of what the *beau monde* might think or say on the subject.

While fear still coiled and uncoiled deep within her belly, she was a woman of strong character and she would never forgive herself if she forced a wedding on a man just to avoid social discomfort. Lord Abbott should have free will in whom he married, and she would take her punishment for falling into his arms like a besotted girl.

"I thank Lord Abbott for his offer, and for his attempt to protect my reputation, but I stand by my refusal."

The gathering broke into heated debate, and Gwen was sure she overheard someone exclaim that she was a stupid girl. Probably Lady Astley, a bitter old biddy who had never liked her.

Nevertheless, her principles were more important than what other people would say about her, and she would not steal a man's future just to benefit her reputation.

Her immediate future would be difficult, but after a while the scandal would die down. She had to live with herself for many years to come, so what she thought about herself must take precedence over the small-minded fault-finding of people who did not truly care about her one way or the other.

Next to her, Lord Abbott soughed under his breath before interrupting the storm of controversy in his deep voice. "It appears we cannot reach an agreement, so I believe that Miss Smythe and I should discuss this with Mr. Smythe."

Lord Astley's head immediately bobbed up. Waving a bony hand to shush his wife and the others standing with them, he spoke with the thin voice of an aged man. "Agreed, young man. I think we should step inside to find Frederick so you can debate this private matter without an audience."

Gwen could not refute this conclusion. It suited her fine to end this public display. "I will be in the study."

She quickly walked away from the growing crowd to enter her father's study from the terrace so she could wait for Lord Abbott and her father alone. Entering the ballroom to face a large audience after being caught in a passionate embrace was an impossibility, even for a strong woman of character.

Walking about the study, she lit the lamps before taking a seat on the sofa across from the desk, frowning slightly in surprise when she noticed that her father had tidied his desk, the inkstand and quill perfectly positioned together, the drawers fully shut, and the surface wiped clean of pounce.

Her father was fastidious with his clothing but notoriously clumsy with his work space, a quirk which caused him endless aggravation when he trapped the fine sand of the pounce in the intricate buttons of his sleeve cuffs, especially those grains blackened with ink.

Perhaps a servant had come in and cleaned up early? Strange that they had the time, considering all the preparations for the ball tonight.

The vagaries of her thoughts led her to realize she was quite anxious. She hoped her father would arrive soon and perhaps could direct her on what she must do now that she had ruined her reputation in society. Gwen had not comprehended how daunting it was to be in this position, her stomach in knots, and the terrifying thought of joining the guests made her palms damp with the mere prospect of it.

What have I done?

Allowing a stranger to touch her and kiss her in the most intimate of ways. Was she so starved for attention that her morals, her very boundaries of convention, had been tossed aside for pleasure?

She frowned to herself. Somehow, that did not seem right.

There had been something magical about the moment on the terrace. Something she had never felt before. A moment of perfect synchronization that had led her to accept and trust the man at her side. As if fate itself had taken a hand. Despite the fear she was feeling, she suspected that the event itself would be cherished by her for many years to come.

It was with some relief that she heard footsteps out in the hall and realized that she was about to be joined in the study. The riot of thoughts colliding in her head was too uncomfortable. Hopefully, her father could provide guidance on how to proceed. A firm path forward out of the muddle she had brought on their household.

The footsteps came to a halt, and the door opened. Gwen stiffened, leaning forward on the settee as she tried to prepare her words to explain to her father what had happened.

In walked a tall gentleman with broad shoulders and a square jaw. The stranger from the terrace!

Gwen grimaced when she beheld him in the light. He had rich brown hair and chocolate brown eyes, and he was ... utterly beautiful. So far above her in appearance that for a second, she thought she must be wrong about his identity. Why would such a young and handsome gentleman have approached her? A man from a wealthy and distinguished family? It was unfathomable.

He sought her out, hesitating, before crossing the room to take a seat at her side. Gwen remained in her rigid position on the edge of the settee, astonished to be near such a man and even more astonished that, even after laying eyes on her, he had chosen to sit next to her.

Looking back to the door, she discovered her father entering the room.

And her heart fell.

Her father was beaming with unrestrained delight, and Gwen knew exactly what he was thinking. He was ecstatic about the turn of events, so she could not expect support from him to turn Lord Abbott down.

Nay, Papa was clearly convinced she had finally found her match. The right man.

* * *

AIDAN WAS STILL REELING from the turmoil that had transpired outside these very doors. He had never acted in such a foolish manner. From a young age, his father had instilled in him the importance of respect and dignity. Being caught by numerous witnesses under the evening sky with his hands on the buttocks of a gently bred lady was incomprehensible. Later this evening he would have to inform the viscount of his roguish behavior, which was rather galling.

Truly, he had never done anything this appalling.

What about leaving Lily alone on the night of the coronation?

He shut his eyes briefly at the recollection of why he was in the Smythe home tonight. Apparently, galling behavior was becoming a pattern for him.

Nevertheless, he could not deny the frisson of excitement to be seated with the goddess alighted from his deepest desires. She was the very essence of a Renaissance masterpiece. The *Birth of Venus* perhaps, with her long, red hair framing her slim face.

He blinked at the thought of her disrobed and bared before him in the manner that Sandro Botticelli had painted, Aidan's heart picking up speed despite the presence of her father in the room. Just how far did that spray of freckles descend on her slender form?

When he first entered the room and she had turned those soulful eyes to find him, he had discovered that they were a deep blue like her father's. Her skin glowed in the dim lights of the study, and Aidan was compelled to sit next to her, still in awe that such a woman existed with the sharp mind of a scholar.

Now, seated beside her and distracted by the fragrance of citrus teasing his senses, Aidan sincerely hoped that she was not involved with her father's dark pursuits. Protecting his sister and the baron from future violence must be a priority, and it was a necessary evil to delve into what her father was involved with. He could help her in the aftermath once the truth was revealed, but only if he successfully forged an alliance with her tonight.

Frederick Smythe was evidently cheerful about the turn of events, closing the door and crossing the room to take a seat at his desk. Aidan noted that Smythe noticed nothing amiss from Aidan's earlier visit to his private sanctuary, which was a small mercy with what was about to unfold.

"So, when is the wedding?" Mr. Smythe was grinning as he clapped his hands together to peer at the two of them with twinkling blue eyes.

Next to him, Gwendolyn groaned.

"Papa, this is not a time for jesting! We have a serious situation at hand."

Smythe's grin broadened. "Levity in the face of trials is what makes life bearable, young one."

Aidan was amused, despite himself. Smythe had an infectious smile and a lighthearted mannerism which made him instantly likable. Which meant Aidan needed to be cautious about being drawn in by the man who probably murdered the baron.

It was a chilling thought, a brutal reminder that the servant who had attacked Lily two weeks earlier had been someone she had not suspected in the least. A signal that it was time to steer this conversation.

"I have explained to Mr. Smythe what happened on the terrace, and I have informed him of my intention to wed you."

Aidan watched her from the corner of his eye to observe her reaction. He was feeling a little shy now that they were in a lit room and conversing. She was even more breathtaking than he had imagined from afar, and he was having trouble reconciling the idea that he had recently had his tongue in her soft mouth. He growled softly in the back of his throat as a rush of heat accompanied the recollection.

Gwendolyn turned her head as if she had heard him, her forehead puckering.

* * *

LORD ABBOTT HAD EMITTED a low growl after his declaration, and Gwen was perturbed by the evidence of his reluctance. When he had taken a seat by her side, she had briefly entertained the notion that he truly was attracted to her, but the guttural accompaniment to his words revealed he was not as willing as she might have hoped.

Resolve was a welcome friend. Marrying Lord Abbott might be convenient, even desirable from her point of view, but it would be wrong. Forcing a man to wed her would be a despicable failing in character. Her father had sufficient means for Gwen to disappear from society, possibly pursue her academic interests in the country. Lord Abbott need not sacrifice his future to tie himself to her.

"And I have informed Lord Abbott that I appreciate his offer, but it is not necessary."

Her father's grin fell off his face like a distended fruit from an overloaded tree. "Not necessary?"

Gwen gave a firm nod. She had hoped that her father would understand her concerns, but his jovial attitude had made it clear that he thought his dreams of making a great alliance to secure her future were at hand. She was going to have to convince both men that it was a terrible idea, which would require fortitude and dedication.

"I have no wish to put Lord Abbott in that predicament. I am certain he has far better marriage prospects than myself, and I do not wish to tie the gentleman down for something we are both responsible for."

Next to her, Lord Abbott shifted, flexing his shoulders as if he were suffering from tension. "I assure your daughter that she is the very best of marriage prospects, and it would not be a hardship at all to announce our betrothal."

"And I wish to assure Lord Abbott that I am more than capable of taking care of myself. I free him to find a more suitable partner."

"I am perfectly capable of selecting a wife, and I believe that Miss Smythe should have a greater appreciation of her worth as a prospect for such."

Across from them, her father shifted his gaze back and forth between the two of them. He cocked his head with a perplexed expression, and Gwen realized that they were sparring while addressing their words at her father.

"Could one of you explain to me what exactly unfolded on the terrace?" Her father had a trace of steel in his tone, and Gwen bit her lip. It took much to raise his ire, and she had learned to pay it mind when he showed signs of growing irate.

"I thought Lord Abbott had informed you of what transpired?"

Lord Abbott shifted once more, his taut thigh making contact with her briefly through the thin silk of the gown when he dragged a hand through that lustrous hair. Good grief, he was the best-looking man she had ever sat this close to. Which was why she had been addressing her father, rather than him, directly. He was far too daunting to face.

"I simply laid out the broad strokes."

"Well, now I wish to hear the specifics." Papa's rejoinder was immediate and tense, his face having settled into suspicious lines.

Lord Abbott coughed into his hand. "I encountered ... your daughter on the terrace and was overtaken by the beauty of her in the moonlight. The words of Manilius sprang forth, and I was taken aback when Miss Smythe responded. Which is when I ... um ..." He coughed once more.

Gwen watched her father's face suddenly break into his customary grin, his head bobbing in confident rejoicing. "You witnessed the perfection of my only daughter and fell at her feet, defeated by her magnificence."

It was not a question, and Gwen was mortified. The words Papa had spoken a fortnight earlier had been said once more, hanging like smoke from a cannon after it had fired. Her instinct was to raise her hand and swat the words away as if clearing the air, but it was too late.

Next to her, Lord Abbott tilted his head in thought and then, to her alarm, a corresponding grin broke across his face as the two men gazed at each other with newfound *camaraderie*. "Quite so."

Papa turned his piercing gaze to her. "And then what happened?"

Gwen nervously bounced her legs, averting her eyes. "Lord Abbott approached me ... and then we ... um ... embraced."

"Embraced?"

"Well ... yes ... we ... uh ..." Gwen flung her arms about

wildly to demonstrate before deciding there was no helping it. She should just finish it without prolonging the agony.

"Kissed! We kissed! And then the guests walked out and found me, his lips pressed to mine and his hands upon my buttocks!"

Her father burst out laughing.

Lord Abbott had turned a deep red while she was speaking, Gwen herself blushing fiercely, but to her dismay, the gentleman at her side had burst into corresponding laughter.

What she truly did not need was for them to form a genuine bonhomie while she attempted to dissuade them from pursuing a wedding. She made a sound of disgust as the two men chuckled freely, unable to suppress a shiver of delight at the sound of Lord Abbott's husky merriment.

Egad, he is an enticing specimen of manhood!

She still had brief flashes of believing this might all be an elaborate dream. It was the only explanation why a man such as him would be arguing to marry her with such ferocity, while insisting she was the true catch.

Gwen, Gwen the Spotted Giraffe was arguing to *not* marry a very eligible gentleman. What would the girls she had attended school with have to say to that? It was incomprehensible.

To make matters worse, it was a certainty that out in the ballroom, the guests were freely discussing what had happened and waiting expectantly for an announcement to be made.

Gwen dropped her head into her hands, fiddling with her hair as she tried to catch a flicker of sanity anyplace she could find it. Her mind was unraveling with all the conflicting issues raging within.

At her side, Lord Abbott abruptly fell silent, and she suspected he had noticed her despair.

"Mr. Smythe, would you allow me to speak with your

daughter alone? We ... have much to settle between the two of us."

Her father responded in a cheery tone, his chair scraping to indicate he had come to his feet, but Gwen was obsessed with the rug beneath her slippers, so she continued to stare at the colorful pattern in the hopes it would cause her swirling thoughts to subside into their familiar structure.

"I shall be on the terrace."

Papa's light footsteps proclaimed his departure from the room, the French doors closing with a slight click that was almost inaudible.

"Gwendolyn—"

"Gwen. Only Papa addresses me as Gwendolyn."

There was a pause. "Gwen," he finally breathed. "It is lovely. A lovely name for a lovely woman."

Gwen scowled at the rug. "There is no need to flatter now that you have seen me in the light. I am well aware of my appearance."

A large hand appeared and gently took hold of hers. She allowed him to pull it down onto the settee, but resolutely held her head with the other while attempting to burn a hole in the woven floor covering with her stare.

"I saw you in the entry hall from the receiving line. I knew who you were when I met you on the terrace."

Gwen froze before dropping her hand to look at him. He gazed back at her, a mix of sympathy and admiration in his eyes. She fidgeted, unsure what to do with such attention.

"Truly?"

"You put me in mind of a Botticelli masterpiece." Lord Abbott reached out a hand to tuck the errant tresses back into her coiffure, which made Gwen realize she must look a fright after mussing up her hair.

She wanted to believe him. What woman would not want

to believe such adoring words? If it were just the smallest bit true...

"You have seen Botticelli first hand?"

He nodded. "I could take you to Italy. A Grand Tour, if you desire it."

Gwen sucked in a breath, her eyes widening at the possibility of viewing great art. "I do not wish to force you into a union. The kiss was just as much my fault as it was yours."

Lord Abbott's eyes raked over her face. "There is no force. I ... find I ... I find that I wish ..." He halted, rubbing a hand over his face as he searched for the words he wished to say to her. Gwen was fascinated by this, acknowledging the gentleman was just as compromised by this disaster as she was. What would he say when he finally found those words ... She found she waited with bated breath.

"Before this night I had no desire to marry, but now that we are here together, I wish to do the right thing and I find that there are no reservations creeping in the corners of my mind. This is what I wish to do. It would be an honor to make you my wife."

Lord Abbott's gaze found hers with the final statement, and Gwen saw nothing but sincerity in the depths of his rich brown eyes. Compelled to speak, she parted her lips to pronounce the lines that cleared all other thoughts from her mind, leaving only one bright hope for the future.

"If I could write the beauty of your eyes, And in fresh numbers number all your graces—"

His gaze did not falter, even for a second. He responded, his deep voice confident.

"—The age to come would say 'This poet lies; Such heavenly touches ne'er touched earthly faces.'"

Gwen shook her head, fascinated by his voice. By him.

She imagined marrying this man, learning who he was, being bedded by him. She imagined babes with chocolate thatches of fine hair and bright brown eyes, and books, and poetry, and warming fires on Christmas Eve. She imagined moonlight and kisses, soft touches and sighs, strong hands and delighted shivers.

Gwen remembered the unwavering love between her father and mother, the joy of Gareth's arrival in the world, her own hopes she had locked deep in the recesses of her heart, and she knew she wanted to say yes.

"Are you certain?"

Lord Abbott's lips quirked into a crooked smile. "I am."

Gwen's thoughts raced as she considered her options.

Societal ruin, or taking a chance with this man.

She had not personally met his father, Lord Moreland, but knew him by reputation. The Abbotts were known to be a strong family. Loyal. Philanthropic. Conservative with their vast wealth. Lord Abbott's name had not been linked with any scandal, to her knowledge.

She had not heard of any debauched activities, nor scandals other than recent whispers of a sister who had made a love match under what appeared to be rushed circumstances.

"I like to read."

"So do I."

"You do not mind if I maintain my studies?"

He grinned. "I encourage it. We shall debate the merits of the various philosophers and argue who made the best points."

"It will be a real marriage? Not merely an arrangement for the sake of propriety?"

Lord Abbott's gaze fell to her lips, which she licked nervously. A suggestive smile spread across his face before he purred. "It will be a real marriage. Of that you can be certain."

Gwen flushed, glancing away only to find herself then inadvertently staring at the broad chest that she had crushed her breasts against. The chest she had wished to uncover and touch with restless fingers earlier on the terrace. She watched in a distant state of horror as her hand reached up, as if possessed by a will of its own, to run down the slope of the wool coat that encased his hard muscled planes. Beneath her fingertips, his heart was beating at a rapid pace to match her own.

She recalled vaguely that she was to maintain her fortitude and persuade her father and Lord Abbott to abandon this path, but at heart she was still a little girl who dreamed of sharing love and a family with the right man.

Of curling into the strong arms of a lover and speaking about future hopes and past adversities.

Of imagining new paths and exploring her possibilities as her mother had done before.

Exhaling a deep breath, she gave her final answer.

"Then we shall see where this path might lead."

She hoped it was the right decision, recalling his growl of reluctance at the start and wondering what could possibly provide motive for such a man to pursue her.

Even as Lord Abbott's face lit up, and he leaned in to buss her on the lips, Gwen frowned. She did not recall him on the guest list for the ball. How had he come to be here this evening?

CHAPTER 5

"Quality is not an act, it is a habit."

Aristotle

* * *

AUGUST 14, 1821

Gwen opened one eye to find that morning had long since arrived. A thought, not fully materialized, tickled the back of her mind, but she could not quite catch it. Something about the ball.

Turning over, she settled down to fall back to sleep. She was far too exhausted to rise yet. The ball had been long, as they always were, and she needed to recover—

Her eyelids flew open as the vague, niggling thought erupted into memories of the night before.

"Stuff!"

Across the room, there was a movement and Octavia

Hanning, her lady's maid, came running into view as if she had been waiting for signs of Gwen's awakening.

"Is it true?"

Fluttering her eyes, Gwen attempted to clear the cobwebs and catch up to her flying thoughts. "Is what true?"

"You're betrothed? To Lord Moreland's heir?"

Gwen groaned, pulling the coverlet over her head to bury her face in her pillow. Last night had not been a dream, she surmised.

"Well? Are you to wed?" Octavia was relentless, clearly far too secure in her role as Gwen's confidante these past seven years, so there were no boundaries to be observed between them. The thin servant of about forty years of age was hopefully pragmatic, sometimes crotchety, frequently crass in the privacy of Gwen's bedroom, and she knew not where the class lines lay, but Gwen did not care because Octavia was always loyal and a close friend after so many years together.

"If Lord Moreland does not raise an objection and forbid the match, then I suppose I am to wed."

"You allowed a gentleman to lay his hands upon you?"

Gwen groaned once more, burrowing farther into her pillow.

"And he kissed you? On the lips?"

"Go away!" Gwen recalled that she had champagne the night before, after her father had announced the betrothal and called for their guests to celebrate into the early hours.

Champagne! That must be why her head felt so dull this morning.

"I'm so impressed!"

Gwen frowned into her downy cushion, then slowly raised her head to scowl at Octavia. "Impressed?"

"You landed your gentleman by compromising him!"

Gwen tilted her head, her scowl altering into disbelief. "I did not compromise him! He laid his hands on me!"

Octavia shook her head, which was just a wee too big for her reed-thin body, not listening to a word Gwen was uttering. "I knew you could do it. I told everyone belowstairs that Gwendolyn Smythe is not destined to be on the shelf. Our mistress will take action to make sure it dinnit happen. The right man will notice her and she'll get married, I told 'em."

Gwen pulled a face. There it was again—the right man. Had everyone in her household been waiting for the arrival of the right man?

"That is sentimental claptrap! What is a right man?"

Octavia turned bulbous blue eyes to regard her in amazement, quirking her head as if to exclaim. "The man who realizes that you're an original, of course. Lord Abbott is the one! Why else would he've followed you onto the terrace if not to pursue you?"

Gwen stared at Octavia, thunderstruck by what the maid had just voiced. Had Lord Abbott followed her onto the terrace? Gwen had been around the corner from the ballroom, in the deserted section outside her father's study. How had he discovered her there unless he had followed her?

She shook her head. "That does not make sense! Why would Lord Abbott follow me?"

Octavia straightened up, her fists coming to rest on her waist, to scold Gwen from her towering position. The lady's maid was a short woman, but she towered over reclining Gwen in an intimidating manner. "Because you're a beautiful young woman. An original. He recognized your worth."

Gwen pulled the coverlet back over her head. "That is ridiculous."

"No, it's not! Those girls at school were repugnant little arses. You should not heed the mockery of silly little children."

"Not children. Married ladies of the *ton* who are fond of reminding me of my shortcomings at every turn."

Octavia snorted. "More like married tarts of the *ton*! And who're they to know? Their husbands keep mistresses on the side while they pretend all's well. The footmen told me of the goings-on in the little drawing room down the hall."

"So, Lord Abbott will marry me and discard me to seek his pleasure elsewhere."

"Nay, this is different! Lord Abbott was so besotted, he trapped himself in marriage to taste your lips. This will be a love match!"

Gwen moaned in despair. "Sodding hell! That is what people will say. They will say this is a love match before they bray like hyenas at Gwen, Gwen the Spotted Giraffe marrying a future viscount."

Silence fell. After several long moments, Gwen lowered the coverlet to find Octavia stewing. "I wish you'd stop paying heed to those women. They're not experts on what a gentleman might be seeking. They're only experts on what their mothers tell 'em because they've no minds of their own."

Gwen twisted her lips in denial. "They are experts. On how to get married."

"You're getting married!"

"Because of the scandal! Because Lord Abbott feels compelled to be a gentleman. If not for that, I would merely be a scandalous spinster!"

"You're not a spinster. You're a young woman of worth and your mama would be proud of you!"

Gwen's jaw set into mutinous lines. "She would not be proud of me trapping a man in marriage!"

Octavia sighed, pushing Gwen's hip so she would make space before taking a seat on the bed beside her. "Mrs. Smythe would understand that in a single magical moment, the right man found you and then fate happened."

Gwen fell silent once more, saddened to think of her absent mama.

Octavia Hanning had been taking care of the Smythe women for many years. She was practically part of the family. Gwen's friend throughout the past lonely years. Being an intelligent woman with scholarly pursuits made Gwen unattractive both to men and women of her class, but Octavia had always been at her side to encourage her.

"I know not what happened. One moment I was wishing that I had a suitor with whom to share the glorious view of the heavens, and next thing Lord Abbott was at my side. Before I knew it, we had embraced and half the ballroom stumbled upon us."

Octavia nodded. "I think Lord Abbott is a good man."

"Why do you say that?"

"There is no gossip about him. He finished at Oxford, then went on his Grand Tour. Since he returned, he has caroused with his friends, but he has not visited any widows or courtesans, nor danced with any young ladies."

The widespread web of the belowstairs gossip was often a source of amazement to Gwen. Octavia knew things about noble families that Gwen had yet to even meet.

"What of his family?"

"Lord and Lady Moreland have a pristine reputation. There're no paramours for either of them, and they're committed to each other, by all reports."

How would Lord Moreland feel about his heir being required to marry her, Gwen pondered.

"And the sister? The one who was recently in the scandal sheets?"

Octavia grunted. "We're all rather confused about that. The Abbott servants do not like to gossip about their household. Miss Abbott claimed she was with Lord Filminster the night of the coronation, when it became clear he was to be arrested. There's no word of inappropriate behavior from any household she's visited, or even much contact with Lord Filminster, so I cannit say how they had the opportunity to …" Octavia bobbed her hands in a lewd gesture to indicate the coming together of two lovers. "They wed within a few days, and the servants of Ridley House will not speak on anything happening there."

Gwen reflected on this. The servants were either scared to speak, or they were intensely loyal to the Baron of Filminster and his new wife.

It was strange to think she would marry into a family she had never even met. Lord Abbott himself was a stranger. A handsome stranger with firm lips and passionate eyes, who accurately quoted great poetry, but a stranger nevertheless.

"Do you know why Lord Abbott was at the ball?"

Octavia shook her head, causing little tendrils of her mousy brown hair to escape the knot at her nape. "The footmen are amazed. Dennis said he thought that perhaps he saw Lord Abbott and another gentleman enter with Lord and Lady Hays, but it's all so unexpected. There's no news of Lord Abbott seeking a wife, so no one knows why he would have attended the ball."

"Not only that, the ball is not even in the Season. Many families have already left for the country since the coronation. I do not know why the Morelands or Lord Abbott were still in London. Papa scheduled it now in a bid to save coin on the event."

Octavia clapped her hands together. "What does it matter? You're finally to wed. You'll be a beautiful bride and join a great and powerful family. Then you'll have babes and one of those babes will be the future Viscount Moreland!"

Gwen thought of a little boy with chocolate brown hair and bright eyes as she had done the night before, and a wave of yearning threaded through her veins to settle in the region of her heart. This might be a strange beginning to a marriage, but, if nothing else, her desire for children of her own would be fulfilled. Little ones she could teach the wonders of the ancient world to.

And Lord Abbott had promised a real marriage. And fidelity was a family trait, from what Octavia had revealed.

It was rather overwhelming to contemplate her sudden change in circumstances. The only issue that nagged at the edges of her consciousness was to mull over why Lord Abbott had been at the ball.

Why had he been on the terrace?

And, why in heaven had he kissed her when no eligible man before him had displayed any desire to do the same?

There was no denying that Lord Abbott was an enigma.

"He is coming to negotiate marriage contracts today."

Octavia grinned, revealing a crooked smile. "It's a wonderful day. Your mama would be overjoyed that you finally found a handsome gentleman of your own."

Gwen thought about what her mama would say if she were here. She would have been impressed with Lord Abbott's knowledge of Manilius and Shakespeare, but she would have had questions about his presence at the Smythe ball.

Questions that Gwen should ask, but of whom?

Would Lord Abbott tell her the truth about his presence, and his appearance at her side under the pale light of the celestial bodies above, if she were to pose them to him?

She might be betrothed, but she knew not her distinguished groom.

It seemed unbearably rude to question him about his attendance at the ball after the monumental steps he was taking to protect her reputation in polite society.

What was she to do—blatantly accuse him of illicitly entering their home as if he were unwelcome? He was certainly higher in stature than the Smythes, so it seemed wrong to inadvertently imply some sort of wrongdoing.

Gwen wished there was a way to get to the bottom of it. To understand why he had been at the ball, and what had made him say those romantic things in the study when he had persuaded her to proceed with the nuptials.

Octavia chose that moment to interrupt her musings with a blissful sigh. "Just think, I'm to attend a future viscountess!"

Gwen huffed in laughter, her friend's naked ambition pushing all concerns from her mind as she buried her head into Octavia's bony shoulder and thought about what it would be like to have access to the huge libraries of the Moreland estates. Lord Abbott had even promised a trip to Italy if she desired.

* * *

"WHAT HAVE YOU DONE?"

His mother's wail was earsplitting. To be fair, Lady Moreland had been asked once again to contend with a family scandal. Just the month before, Lily had been compromised by providing an alibi to his brother-in-law; now Aidan had compromised a young lady in his bid to protect Lily. It was a bad time for Christiana Abbott.

Hugh Abbott quickly rose to sit by his wife, placing a comforting arm about her. "Calm yourself, Christiana. It will all work out."

"What has happened to our children? Did I fail to raise them correctly? Two scandals in a month!" His mother dropped her face into her hands and openly wept.

Aidan winced. Perhaps he should have spoken to his father first, instead of surprising both of them simultaneously.

"I apologize, Mother. I have taken steps to make the matter right."

His mother raised her head, her chocolate brown eyes wet with tears, to howl in response. "How?"

Aidan stared back at her, speechless and unwilling to upset her further.

His father glanced over at him and sighed, evidently guessing what the rest of Aidan's news was to be. "Aidan has done the right thing. The honorable thing."

Lady Moreland swung her head to peer at her husband in confusion, who narrowed his eyes in thought before elucidating what Aidan was about to inform them of. "If all goes well, Aidan will provide another heir to the Moreland title in the near future."

Aidan blinked. Had his father just swung the prior night's events into good news?

His mother's face gradually cleared up as she contemplated her husband's words. "Aidan is to wed?"

Lord Moreland nodded, reaching up with his handkerchief to gently dab his wife's eyes dry, wiping away the salty evidence of her distress. "And then he will have babes. Sons and daughters. Our grandchildren."

Thoughts flitted across Lady Moreland's face as she digested this notion. "I should have the servants visit the attics to bring me Aidan's and Lily's baby things."

Lord Moreland nodded. "An inventory should be taken immediately."

She rose with an expression of interest. "I shall see to it right away."

Lord Moreland and Aidan watched her sweep out of the room in a swirl of skirts before turning to stare at each other. "Your mother has suffered great anguish. First Lily was compromised, then some of our acquaintances snubbed your mother and canceled invitations. Then Lily was almost ..." Lord Moreland waved his hands in the air.

"I am so sorry for what has happened. I should have spoken to you alone before involving Mother."

Lord Moreland sighed, leaning back to stretch his long legs out and gaze at Aidan. "And what exactly has happened? What were you doing at the Smythe ball? I was not aware you wished to find a bride."

Aidan broke eye contact. "I was ... searching ..." he mumbled.

He heard his father inhale deeply before posing the inevitable question. "Searching for what?"

"Evidence that Mr. Smythe might be the man who killed Lord Filminster last month." Aidan continued to stare at his polished riding boots, not missing the barely audible groan emitted by his father.

"Is that a genuine possibility?"

"It is."

His father cursed, causing Aidan to flinch in surprise. "I do not know him well, but Smythe is a charming fellow with many friends. His older brother is quite fond of him, from what I hear."

Aidan thought of the letter he had read from the late Baron of Filminster, which had stated that precise detail. His certainty that Smythe was their man, the one who had bludgeoned the baron to death on the night of the coronation, was growing.

"Miss Smythe is innocent of any wrongdoing. Considering my actions, it is now my duty to protect her. Now ... and in the future."

Lord Moreland slowly shook his head. "And perhaps you can illuminate for me how you came to compromise a young lady of the *ton*. Your mother is correct—it is not how we raised you. The concept of right and wrong ..." He growled his disappointment.

"I ... lost my head." Aidan raised his gaze defiantly.

Lord Moreland cocked his head in question. Aidan knew his father and he were close in form and facial features, although Aidan possessed his mother's rich coloring. His thoughts flittered to the notion of a son who looked like them, but with Gwen's rich red hair and intense blue eyes.

"You do not usually involve yourself with women?" Lord Moreland's statement brought Aidan back to their conversation.

"I do not usually meet women like Gwen."

His father contemplated him before finally responding. "This young woman has made an impression, then?"

Aidan immediately bobbed his head in assent. "She is Venus, with the mind of a scholar."

"And how exactly did you compromise her? Details would be nice, considering high society is going to be whispering about this all across London this morning."

"I ... we ... I was embracing her"—Aidan stopped, recalling how Gwen had finally spat out the details in a similar circumstance—"I had my hands upon her *derriere* and we were kissing ... passionately."

It was mortifying. He was an errant lad who had been caught stealing cake from the pantry rather than an educated, traveled gentleman of five and twenty.

Lord Moreland rubbed his large hands over his face, mumbling another curse under his breath before speaking. "That is rather damning. Not to mention out of character?"

The last was a question, and Aidan squirmed in his seat while attempting to find the words to explain his roguish actions. "I was overcome. She was ravishing in the moonlight, and when I quoted Manilius, she responded in kind."

His father pressed his lips together. "She sounds unique."

Gwen was unique. An original. And soon she would be his. The thought of bedding her was never far from his thoughts since their encounter on the terrace. "She is."

"And her father might have murdered a peer to protect his inheritance?"

Aidan groaned. "I know. What have I done?"

"I am not entirely certain. The only sure thing is that we have a marriage contract to negotiate. It would be fortuitous if you could refrain from finding evidence of Smythe's guilt until after the wedding."

His father's announcement had Aidan mildly confused, raising an eyebrow in question.

Lord Moreland waved a hand as if his statement was self-explanatory. "I would prefer to break further bad news to your mother in small, digestible pieces. First the wedding. Then the news of an arrest. Not together, if you please. She still needs some time to recover from Lily's attack."

Aidan thought this over before finally replying. "I can refrain from investigating Mr. Smythe until after the wedding."

Lord Moreland nodded. "Which will be soon, considering the scandalous aspect of this arrangement."

"You are in agreement with my offer?"

"The young lady's situation with her father does not signify. You must behave as a man of quality. Your decision to embrace an innocent gentlewoman sealed your fate, so we will bear the consequences together."

Aidan thought about how his father had always been a bastion of honor. How he had accepted Lily's decision to follow her conscience, and now accepted Aidan's decision to wed Gwen, and he appreciated that he possessed his father's support under such circumstances.

"I am ... sorry ... for bringing this on the Abbott name."

"You have always behaved in an exemplary manner, so I

must assume that there is something special about this young lady or you would not have behaved as you did. I confess I am intrigued to meet Miss Smythe myself, now that she has turned your head so thoroughly."

Thinking about his betrothed made Aidan smile. Despite the trying circumstances, he had yet to regret that he had done his duty as an heir and found his bride. His glowing divinity of womanhood. "She is bewitching."

Lord Moreland raked a hand through the thick head of hair that Aidan had inherited from him, not listening to Aidan's admiration as he attempted to prepare for the coming days. "Perhaps after the wedding I shall take your mother to our country estate. If Smythe is arrested, it would be better that we are not ensconced in London when the news breaks. Perhaps you could join us there to remove Gwen from the initial disturbance, if matters progress as you suspect."

Aidan grunted, recollecting the full scope of his troubles. It was unfortunate that Mr. Smythe was rather likable. Investigating his future father-in-law with the intent of proving him guilty of murder would be far easier if Smythe were a cold, cruel man. Especially if Gwen needed to be rescued from a dire family situation.

Instead, Aidan's actions could lead to breaking her heart, and he would have to help piece her back together in the wake of a second, and unrelenting, scandal that could not be so easily repaired by offering her marriage. The one consolation was that the Moreland title would provide some defense against the onslaught that would follow.

"Smythe informed me that he would be available this afternoon to negotiate the marriage contracts. I was hopeful you and I could meet with him?"

Lord Moreland nodded. "I will cancel my appointments. It is imperative we get ahead of the scandal."

Aidan rolled his shoulders to relieve the tension in his neck. It was less than a month since his father had dropped everything to make arrangements for Lily's marriage to Filminster. He felt terrible to put his parent in this position again. Who would have thought both he and Lily would wed under a cloud of controversy?

* * *

NOTHING ENRAGED Gwen more than witnessing the mistreatment of others. Which was why she banged on the window, alerting the coachman that she wished to stop. Octavia, sitting on the bench opposite her, groaned loudly as the carriage drew to a halt.

"Please don't involve yourself!"

She glanced at her lady's maid, who sat next to the pile of books Gwen had just purchased. "I cannot do that."

"London is filled with sad stories. You can't shoulder the burdens of the world."

"But I can do something about this one."

The footman opened the door, lowering the steps so Gwen could disembark. She quickly climbed down, with Octavia mumbling rebukes as she followed Gwen out onto the street. "This is a bad part of town. We shouldn't be stopping here."

"We have both a footman and a coachman to defend us if needed. Gird your loins and stir your stumps!"

A heavy sough was the only answer, as Gwen strode back up the street.

A hulking halfpenny showman in a tan overcoat and a battered, old three-pointed hat was operating his mechanical exhibition of puppets, squeaking in a ludicrously high voice as the role of Punch, she supposed, who must be moving across the tiny stage hidden from view.

"Sir, do you make it a habit to mistreat weak creatures?"

The showman looked up, his broad face scowling at her interruption. A mother stood with three children, two of which stood upon a bench and had their faces pressed to the little viewing holes to watch the show within the mechanical contrivance of the traveling tinker.

Behind his dull buckled shoes, tied to a piece of string at the opening of an alleyway, a small white and brown mongrel cowered in the shadows.

"Wha' ye want?" grumbled the showman.

The two children looked up from their viewing holes to see what the interruption to their show was about.

"Your dog. I saw what you did." Gwen firmed her jaw in what she hoped was a menacing manner.

The tinker scowled again, narrowing his bloodshot eyes. "An' wha' do ye think ye saw?"

"You kicked him. Hard. In the ribs. See?" Gwen pointed at the shivering mongrel, who was hunched over as if wounded. The mother of the three children gasped, bending to peer around the wooden show cabinet.

The woman rose back up with a look of outrage. "Mister, is that true?"

"Wha' of it?" The defensive posturing of the scruffy reprobate did not unsettle Gwen at all. At least, not too much. She moved closer to narrow her eyes at him. He topped her by a few inches, but she refused to be intimidated.

"The dog is defenseless. There was no cause to kick him so."

"The cur wa' annoying me."

The mother gasped again. "Come. We are leaving, boys."

The two lads standing on the bench groaned. "Mama, we want to finish the show!"

"We will find another amusement elsewhere. Come along."

The older daughter followed as their mother grabbed hold of her boys' hands and led them away. The girl looked back as they walked away, peeking at Gwen in something akin to awe. "Cor! You be brave, miss. That man is huge!"

Gwen smiled in acknowledgment before returning her attention to the showman.

He had moved closer, towering over her in a menacing fashion. "Now, lookie here! See wha' ye done? That be me audience. Ye done lost me money."

A stockinged calf swept at the mongrel, which had come forward during the disturbance to sniff at Gwen's slippers. The dog whimpered, backing up to avoid the club-like appendage. Gwen noted that the little thing was gaunt. Clearly, the brute was not feeding his animal enough.

Gwen stared down at the dog who suffered at the feet of the bully who had him tied to a dirty string, and she could not walk away. Having confronted the man, and subsequently losing him business, Gwen knew precisely who would bear the brunt of his frustrations. She may have made matters worse for the poor mongrel.

Octavia shifted from foot to foot by her side. "Don't you do it, Gwendolyn Smythe. Don't you do it!" she muttered just loud enough for Gwen to hear.

The showman leaned closer, his fetid breath causing Gwen to bend away in disgust. "Wha's that?"

Gwen raised her head to stare him in the eye. "She asked how much for the pup?"

"Tarnation!" Octavia sounded peeved, probably contemplating the fact that the dog would be the cause of untold troubles once Gwen took him home.

But the mongrel, which must have had the blood of North Country Beagle coursing through its thready veins, was staring up at her with big brown eyes and floppy chestnut ears. All she could think of was how the filthy little animal needed her help.

The showman straightened up in surprise. "Me dog?"

"Aye, how much for the dog?"

He shook his head, his hair lank over his collar. "The dog is a pest, inna 'e? No good to ye."

"How much?" Gwen stared at him, unwavering in her resolve to remove the little pest as far from the tinker as she could take him.

He grunted, shrugging. "A shilling."

Gwen fumbled through her reticule, feeling about her coins until her fingers measured out one the size of a shilling. She yanked it out and presented it triumphantly.

The halfpenny showman took it from her with large, blunt fingers. His long, grimy fingernails made her nauseous at the sight, but she released the shilling and took the string from his opposite hand.

He shook his head in a dazed amazement. "The dog a cur, ain't 'e?"

Gwen raised herself to her full height, squaring her shoulders. "But now, sir, he is my cur."

With that, she turned and led the dog away. Octavia groaned, catching up to her side and mumbling beneath her breath the entire length of their walk.

When they reached the carriage, Gwen leaned down to pick the dog up and place it inside, wondering if her gloves would survive the contact with so much filth.

"Faugh! He reeks something fierce." Octavia's exclamation barely registered as Gwen fought back the impulse to gag, almost dizzy from the pungency of such a little animal. "He's a right skunk!"

"She. She is a right skunk. And a good wash will do her wonders." Gwen had checked when she had picked the animal up, an action that she was sure had cost her a favorite pair of gloves. Surely such a depth of odor could not simply be washed away?

Octavia mumbled as she followed Gwen back into the interior of the carriage, quickly cranking the windows open to let in fresh air. "It better wash away or that beast will be living in the stables."

Gwen looked down into the big brown eyes staring at her from the shadow of the bench. "She will be fine."

Octavia settled in next to the pile of books, shaking her head in perplexment. "I will never understand why you are so quick to defend others, but not yourself, Gwendolyn Smythe."

Gwen stared back at the dog, whose snout was quivering with interest, sniffing the air of the carriage. How it did not gag on its own smell was a mystery. "I do not know. It is easier when it is not me."

"You've a fire in your belly, girl. You need to use it against your adversaries, or you'll never claim your rightful place in society."

Sighing, Gwen leaned back into the puffy squabs to catch a breath of fresh air from the open window before the impulse to cast up her accounts could best her. The little hound's stench had a life and will of its own which permeated the entire carriage with its power. "I do not need the approval of others. I will find my own way."

Octavia shook her large head again, her bulbous eyes sympathetic in the dim light. "We all need connections. You must allow your new betrothed a chance to bring you happiness and status within that high society. You deserve it more than anyone I know."

Gwen nodded, but she did not know what she was agreeing to. Mostly it was just a signal she had heard what Octavia had to say. It still seemed an impossibility that she was to marry a man like Lord Abbott.

When she had learned this morning that Lord Abbott, his father, and their solicitor would be meeting with Papa in his study, Gwen had hurriedly made plans to depart their home for the day.

She was not ready to meet Viscount Moreland after being caught with his heir and forcing a marriage. For her cowardice, she had acquired a malodorous little dog to care for, and had only postponed the inevitable meeting with Lord Abbott's presumably disappointed parents.

CHAPTER 6

"We make war that we may live in peace."

Aristotle

* * *

AUGUST 15, 1821

Aidan entered the club and made his way through a bank of tables and chairs to join Filminster and Trafford in the farthest corner. Several gentlemen stopped mid-conversation to follow him with their eyes. Whispers dogged his heels as he reached the other side in relief, noting that the location had been chosen by his fellow conspirators because it was too far for anyone to overhear their discussion.

Dropping into a plump armchair, Aidan breathed deeply. Being the subject of gossip was a new experience for him. Thus far, he had always stayed out of trouble, following his conscience to live an honorable life. He hoped Gwen was not suffering too sharply as a result of their tryst two nights earlier.

Across from him, Trafford scowled before leaning forward to thrust a news sheet across the table between them. Aidan glanced down, reading about the chaos he had created when he was found with Gwen's lithe body pressed against his, the impression of her soft breasts against his chest still heating his blood at the briefest recollection of it. He liked that she was taller than most women. It had been easy to lean down and claim her lips with his.

"Have you lost your mind, Little Breeches?"

Trafford's idle air was not in evidence this morning. Filminster held out a hand to quieten him.

"It appears that matters have gotten out of hand." His brother-in-law was eyeing Aidan with curiosity. "Or did you find something that cleared Smythe of the murder before ..." Filminster raised his brows suggestively.

"Before you stuck your tongue down his daughter's throat in a marvelous display of discretion and judgment, Little Breeches?" Trafford's ire was obvious, the lines of his body suggesting he was holding down a fine temper.

"Why are you angry?" Aidan was genuinely curious to see the other heir so outraged.

"This one and his wife are in danger"—Trafford gestured at Filminster—"and you were meant to be tactful about investigating the man. Now you have drawn unwarranted attention not only to yourself, but to me. Aunty Gertrude sent a note to my father yesterday to inform him that I was at the ball, and that my companion has ruined an innocent. The whole family is in an uproar over it."

Filminster coughed into his fist. "To be fair, Trafford, you did complain that you were bored."

Trafford scowled. "I create my own entertainment. Involving Father is not entertaining."

Aidan's brother-in-law hid a smile, clearly teasing his friend, which Aidan supposed was a good sign. Life was returning to normal at Ridley House if they could just make certain that the killer was apprehended. It was the only path to secure Lily's future safety.

"I think Smythe might be our man." Aidan pulled out the list he had written on the night of the ball, placing it on the table in front of Filminster. The other man raked a hand through his dark curls, staring down at the page before picking it up to unfold it.

"It is a list of assets that Smythe has sold. All within the past two months if you check the dates. He appears to have some sort of financial trouble, which would certainly provide motive for protecting his inheritance."

Filminster ran a finger down the list, turning the page. He whistled, looking up at Trafford. "This is a small fortune. Smythe must be spending a lot of blunt to need this."

Trafford frowned, pulling the list to read it himself. "I have been busy looking into our other suspects, but I have heard no mention of gambling or mistresses in regards to Smythe. No rumors that would explain why he needs funds."

Filminster leaned forward, viewing the list again. "Could he be involved in a land purchase? That might explain the need for funds?"

Aidan considered this. "There was no mention during our negotiations yesterday. Miss Smythe's dowry does not amount to much, so my father made generous concessions in the interests of expediency. I shall have to raise the subject with Smythe the next time we meet to learn if there are any legitimate reasons for him to be liquidating in this manner."

Filminster nodded. "Your sister is astonished at the news.

She tells me it is quite unlike you to be caught in such a dishonorable manner."

Aidan straightened up, feeling defensive. "Gwen is ... special."

"So special that you are willing to risk marrying into a family that you are investigating for murder?"

Aidan dropped his gaze to stare at the grain of the table. He could not explain what had happened in the moonlight. He just knew his desire to take care of the young woman, to protect his beauty from the cruelty of the *beau monde*, and to ensure she did not fall into neglect or poverty, had become essential to him since they had been caught together.

"If Smythe is our man, Gwen will need protection. No matter what comes, she is innocent and does not deserve to face the world alone if her father is arrested."

Trafford interjected, which was a welcome respite, pointing to the list lying in front of them. "I am looking into the other men on the list, but there are no indications of a tangible motive such as this. This certainly signals that there is more to Smythe than meets the eye. He is selling off property, art, jewels. There is little doubt that he is hiding something here."

Aidan nodded. "I spoke with my father about it, and he thought it was a suspicious number of transactions. He noted it was either to cover crippling debts or to make a major purchase of some sort. Filminster, perhaps you can put out queries about such a purchase while Trafford continues to look into the other men on the list?"

"I have ruled out at least one of these men." Trafford pulled out a notebook, turning to a page where he had listed the suspects. Looking about to ensure no club employees were in earshot, he returned to the page. "Miller, along with his older brother who holds the title, was at a soirée until the early hours after the coronation. The servants witnessed them throughout and told me both brothers were too soused to walk, never mind leave the soirée. I confirmed the dinner was too far to walk to Ridley House, and they did not call for their carriage until after dawn. I think it is safe to scratch him from the list."

Filminster nodded. "My runner, Briggs, confirmed that Miller is wealthy in his own right, so there is no indication of a motive."

Trafford pulled out a pencil to scratch the name, leaving the names of four heirs. Aidan stared down at the names, but it was Smythe's name, first on the list, that held his attention.

"The more I think about the baron's letter, the more convinced I am that Smythe is the man we seek. His older brother is a baron, which means that your uncle sat with him or near him at the coronation, which was the primary opportunity for the baron to speak with anyone before his murder. He has some sort of financial mess, and my father tells me that his older brother who holds the title is exceptionally fond of him—just as the letter stated."

Filminster shook his head, his expression sympathetic. "God help you, if that is the case, Aidan. I cannot imagine having to break that kind of news to Lily. Your bride will be devastated if her father is tried and hanged—more so if her husband is the accuser. I do not envy the position you are in."

Aidan's reticence returned. "Lily must be protected, no matter how difficult it might be. And I will take care of Gwen if that comes to pass."

"I understand, but … I hope for your sake and that of your betrothed that we uncover another suspect."

"I concur. It is quite a pickle you have put yourself in, Little Breeches." Trafford had returned to his usual state of repose, his ire forgotten. "Your bride is going to hate you if you do this."

Aidan did not like this thought. He certainly did not want

to see Gwen with hate in her eyes or on her lips. What he wanted was her warm body against his, to take her mouth with his and feel her glorious responsiveness as she moaned in the back of her throat. He wanted to hear Manilius and Shakespeare spoken in her melodic voice, and argue about Aristotle's teachings in front of the fireplace. Love, intelligence, and honor for the rest of their days.

"I will work it out." He could hear the note of uncertainty, shutting his eyes to dig deep within his soul.

I have to work it out.

"I will work it out." This time, his tone was resolute. Firm.

Filminster glanced down, clearly uncomfortable about pressing the issue. He and Aidan were not close—they barely knew each other. They were united by the cause of defending Lily from the murderous fiend who had taken the late baron's life.

Even so, it was difficult to openly discuss their inner thoughts about how matters were unfolding when they were veritable strangers. Aidan regretted that he found himself without close friends in London after being on a Grand Tour for the past three years. He had no one with whom to freely discuss the quagmire he was sinking into.

Filminster rubbed his jaw, evidently trying to think of how to commiserate with his newly acquired relation. "Perhaps we will find another viable suspect. Maybe Smythe has a reasonable explanation for these funds he is procuring."

That would be the best possible outcome, but Aidan knew that Smythe was up to something, so he did not hold much hope that he would not find himself in the untenable situation of accusing Gwen's father. It was imperative Aidan wed her before the investigation progressed. Then he could take care of her and her younger brother, regardless of how muddled matters might become.

* * *

Gwen and Octavia entered the modiste rooms owned by Signora Ricci with a list in hand. Her father had instructed her to prepare for a wedding and a new rank. Once Lord Abbott and she took their vows, she would no longer be the mere niece of a baron. Nay, she would ascend to be the wife of a future viscount from a powerful and wealthy family.

Daunting as that was, Signora Ricci was Gwen's secret weapon. A talisman of self-assurance. It had been many years earlier when she had hunted through Mayfair to find a competent dressmaker who could make the best of her unduly tall form and slight … feminine qualities.

Gwen had needed to build her confidence in the aftermath of a particularly grueling ball—with too many nasty digs from her old schoolmates—and Signora Ricci was the artiste who lifted Gwen's spirits with her draping gowns and compliments.

With a thick Italian accent, the signora had waved away the silly remarks of foolish English debutantes to inform Gwen that she would be considered an ornate gem of great value on the Continent.

Gwen was not a fool. She understood the proprietress made coin by flattering her patrons, but it had been a boon to hear such compliments when she had really needed it, and the new gowns had been far more flattering than her previous dismal wardrobe.

Octavia took off ahead of her to flitter through bolts of fabric, smoothing silks and cottons with her hands while shaking her head in dismissal at others. The lady's maid had impeccable taste when it came to preparing Gwen for the public eye. She was also an entertaining chaperone for outings such as these.

Gwen stooped to peer at a display of gloves near the

front, when behind her she heard the door open and the attached bell ringing to announce the arrival of another patron. Glancing over her shoulder, her stomach tightened in dread when she saw who had arrived.

Millicent 'Milly' Jameson, now Lady Tuttle of West Essex.

And Gwen's least favorite nemesis from when they had attended school together nearly a decade before.

Milly paused, taking in the sight of Gwen with narrowed eyes and her customary sneer.

"Well, well. Gwen, Gwen…"

Milly did not finish the moniker, but it was left hanging in the air, spelled out in giant letters—*Gwen, Gwen, the Spotted Giraffe.*

Gwen straightened and, as usual, found herself without a defense against the unwarranted disdain that her peeresses insisted on perpetuating all these years. She stared at the other woman, finding no retort.

"Milly…" she finally croaked out.

"Is it true, Gwen-Gwen? Are you to join our ranks as a viscountess?"

Gwen swallowed, unsure of what to say. She was usually so good with words, but when she encountered one of the old guard from school, she simply fell apart at the memory of her two years of torment.

The other girls had hated her, and they had not allowed a day to pass without playing cruel jokes or taunting her with the horrible sobriquet aimed at the fact that she had a growth spurt and towered above the other students. Her father had not realized what was happening, dealing with the repercussions of her mother's death, until it had been too late. He had brought her home once he knew, but Gwen's confidence had been shattered by the animosity she had experienced.

The only time she was happy and confident was with her books and learning. Any contact with society inevitably led to encountering one of her old sorority, and she was ill-prepared to contend with Milly at the moment.

Octavia appeared out of nowhere to stand at her side, her attitude one of a mother hen. "That's correct. Miss Smythe is betrothed to Lord Abbott."

Milly did not acknowledge the servant, her eyes flickering over Gwen to find fault. The woman was high-society perfection. Slender, about six or seven inches shorter than Gwen, with a full bosom and perfect blonde curls. She had the refined nose and rosebud mouth. She had received several proposals in her first Season, and not held back about ensuring Gwen was aware, before making a match with a middle-aged viscount.

Milly arched her blonde eyebrows in a dismissive manner. "Lord Abbott is quite the catch, although I had not heard he was blind."

The implication was clear, as Milly's cold blue eyes raked over Gwen in disparagement. Gwen's disquiet grew, barely noticing the growl that her companion emitted by her side.

Ouch!

Gwen threw an angry glance at Octavia, who was smiling beatifically, not at all the expression of a woman who had just kicked her in the ankle. The lady's maid narrowed her eyes pointedly, tilting her head ever so slightly. Octavia was clearly of the belief that Gwen needed to be more aggressive.

Gwen cleared her throat to respond. "Lord Abbott and I are to wed." Another growl from Octavia indicated that she expected Gwen to stand up for herself. "He is ... quite taken with me."

Milly burst out laughing, the mocking tone reminding Gwen of school. Of being too tall. Of not fitting in. Of missing her mother, and wishing she could return home. Of not wanting to burden her father with her problems when they all had their mourning to deal with.

"Is he?"

Octavia squared her shoulders, rearing to say something to the spiteful peeress. And Gwen suddenly surged out of her head to watch the interaction from above, perceiving the entire situation from a different angle than she was accustomed to. She realized she felt ... emboldened.

Lord Abbott had said he knew who she was. He had tugged her into his arms for a passionate kiss and later compared her to Venus by Botticelli. He declared the soft words of great poets in the moonlight. A handsome young gentleman such as him had no reason to seek her out as he had—unless he had wanted to do so.

"He is."

It was stated with firm conviction. She had given him several opportunities to walk away, and he had remained at her side, persuading her to marry him.

Octavia shot her a look, surprised but delighted by Gwen's self-defense.

Milly blinked, clearly startled that Gwen had found her backbone. She forced a laugh. "Certainly, dear. An heir needs to ensure the continuation of the line."

Ha! So I am nothing more than a broodmare?

But Lord Abbott had not been seeking a wife. No rumors of his courting had been spoken of. He himself had stated that he had had no thoughts of marriage, but, despite this, he found himself willing to wed her.

"Certainly, that is his duty," affirmed Gwen, without any distress. What did Milly know of what had transpired between her and Lord Abbott?

The other woman narrowed her eyes, obviously intent on finding a chink in her armor. "Do not be alarmed when he grows bored and seeks the attention of other ... lovelier ... ladies of the *ton*. I, myself, was hailed as a diamond of the first water."

Milly smugly tucked a lock of blonde hair behind her ear. The inference being that Gwen's betrothed would find someone like her far more enticing than Gwen herself once they wed.

Octavia's head bobbed forward, her crooked teeth practically bared, but Gwen realized she did not need someone to stand up for her. Instead, she found her feet—it was time to fight back.

"I heard your *old* Lord Tuttle is continuing his line. His mistress in Cheapside is increasing, I believe?"

Milly drew back, almost hissing. Men of the peerage kept their mistresses, as Octavia had stated the day before, but no one acknowledged such.

"I am just thankful that my betrothed is young ... and besotted with me." Gwen reached up to lovingly finger her much-maligned ginger tresses, realizing she was rather excited to marry Lord Abbott. Their moment in the moonlight had been transcendent, and his comparison of her to the *Birth of Venus* had not been glib. She *was* tall and slender, and she certainly possessed the red hair of the subject of that masterpiece.

His ardor had not been feigned, if the recollection of a certain rigidness in the region of his falls were anything to go by.

She was not a broodmare courted on the marriage mart, but an object of passion for the gentleman.

"Which is why we will enjoy our travels to Italy together once we are married."

Lawks! She hoped she was not overstepping with her announcement.

It was just that for a moment she had found empowerment in owning her change in circumstances, and finally believing Lord Abbott's declaration of interest in her.

It was invigorating to believe in the possibility of love.

The kind of great adoration that her parents had shared. To dare to hope their moonlight passion might turn into a match for the ages, and that they would have babes to cherish who, in turn, would gaze upon their parents with awe.

Milly huffed. "We shall see."

It was a weak rejoinder, the other woman not having any other retort to give.

Gwen smiled. "We will."

Octavia shot her a look of approval, bouncing with excitement to finally see her mistress standing up for herself. Gwen made a slight face in response, thrilled to attack rather than retreat, but still startled to...

Lawks! I truly hope I did not overstep!

She did not want to make the mistake of becoming overconfident and then discover a fly in the ointment that invalidated her tentative bravado. But Lord Abbott struck her as an honorable gentleman, and Octavia had imparted only positive news regarding the Abbott family, so perhaps this was finally her time.

CHAPTER 7

"In all things of nature there is something of the marvelous."

Aristotle

* * *

AUGUST 17, 1821

Gwen stared at herself in the mirror, nervously fidgeting with the skirts of her gown while Buttercup whined at her feet. A groom had given the pup a good wash in the mews two days earlier, presenting Gwen with what appeared to be a new dog under all that grime.

Fortunately, Buttercup had proved to be a placid companion who liked to follow Gwen around the house and stare at her for endless hours with big brown eyes and a twitching snout.

"What if they do not like me?"

Octavia snorted, her thin fingers twisting Gwen's hair into an elegant coiffure. "What's not to like? You are a delight."

Gwen twisted her lips. "Not according to anyone I know."

"The girls from school are envious, and the boys empty-headed. Older members of the *ton* find you a delight."

Gwen shook her head. "You should have heard how incredulous Lady Astley was when they found us on the terrace."

"Lady Astley is well known to be an embittered old bat. She would've reacted that way to any young lady. If you could hear the stories her servants tell …" Octavia shook her head, causing mousy tendrils to escape from the nape of her neck. "She's a vile shrew."

Gwen bit her lip, rhythmically clasping her fingers and releasing them again and again.

"Stop that!" Octavia reached down to smack her on the back of her hand. "You'll ruin your gown before the dinner even begins."

Octavia's admonishment brought Gwen's attention back from the swirl of worries running through her head. Looking down, she realized she had been pulling on the delicate silk of her gown for several minutes, forming a small patch of wrinkles.

Wincing in alarm, Gwen smoothed the patch with a trembling hand. Meeting Lord and Lady Moreland for the first time had occupied her thoughts since the dinner had been scheduled.

I am to meet his parents!

Butterflies took flight once more in the region of her stomach, and Gwen felt a brief wave of nausea. What did they think of what had happened between her and Lord Abbott?

Aidan.

Gwen mouthed his name beneath her breath, still struggling to comprehend that she was to marry such an esteemed gentleman.

Reaching out, she picked up her copy of Debrett's *Peerage*, and opened it to the entry about Lord Moreland... again.

The Abbott family had a long and illustrious line of important ancestors, while her father was the third son of a minor baron. The only reason Papa was set to inherit was because her father's oldest brother had no issue, and his next brother in line had died twenty years earlier. And her mama had been the daughter of a lowly scholar, with no claim to high society, or even the gentry.

What could they possibly think of Aidan Abbott's offer of marriage to insignificant Gwendolyn Smythe?

Gwen, Gwen the Spotted Giraffe echoed in her ears once more, and the jolt of bravado she had acquired when confronting Milly at the modiste dissipated at the thought of meeting the parents.

What if they were incredulous as Lady Astley had been?

What if they deemed her unworthy?

What if they did not like her?

"Right, you're ready." Octavia stepped back. Gwen looked up to find she now had a fall of red curls framing her face, while the rest of her thick hair was gathered into an intricate design. She cocked her head and attempted to see herself as Aidan had described. Not Gwen, Gwen the Spotted Giraffe, but Venus as painted by Botticelli.

She squinted and tried the opposite tilt. Biting her lip, she tried once more, and for a fleeting second Gwen was able to perceive the similarities before the illusion collapsed once more and her stomach set flight at the thought that the Morelands would be arriving for dinner soon.

"They will hate me."

Octavia firmed her lips in disapproval. Grabbing Gwen

by the arm, she tugged her to a standing position. The maid came up to Gwen's chin, highlighting the disparity in height and making Gwen's stomach lurch with nerves.

With determination, Octavia marched her out of the room, closing Buttercup inside. Then down the hall and to the stairs. As they descended, the servant was forced to let her go, their gait wholly mismatched.

Gwen briefly considered running away to hide, but dismissed this as foolish. Eventually, she would be forced to meet her future in-laws and then their first impression would be that she had disappeared for their dinner.

Surely that would make matters worse?

Logic aside, it was still tempting!

Reaching the first level, Octavia followed her into the small drawing room, where Gwen stopped in the middle of the room to contemplate the silk wallpaper.

"Shall I bring you some tea while you wait?"

"That is not necessary. Papa will join me to await their arrival at any moment." Gwen began to pace the room, agitated.

"You'll wear a hole in the rug," declared Octavia, narrowing her gaze to Gwen's feet. Her too-large, unwomanly feet.

Gwen stopped, gnawing on her lower lip. "They must hate me! Their lauded heir forced to wed a spotted ginger! Think what their grandchildren will look like!"

Octavia drew herself to her full height, many inches shorter than Gwen. Her arms akimbo, the lady's maid wore an expression of rebuke.

"Gwendolyn Smythe, you're a treasure. The Morelands are lucky to invite you into their ranks!"

Gwen's mouth fell open, and she stared in horror at the woman who had stepped into the doorway behind Papa just as Octavia made her declaration. An elegant woman with chocolate brown hair and eyes just like Aidan's, her gown a rich collection of hues. Despite her youthful appearance, it was obvious by the slight sprinkling of gray whom Gwen was beholding.

Behind her, a tall gentleman with a square face and graying hair, who looked suspiciously like Lord Aidan Abbott, suppressed a smile.

Octavia must have caught a reflection in the opposite window, spinning around to clap a hand over her mouth when she made eye contact with Lady Moreland.

Dipping into a deep curtsy, Octavia stumbled slightly in her distress. "Milady!"

"And who might you be?"

"Mrs. Hanning, milady. I am lady's maid to Miss Smythe." Octavia's voice quavered.

Lady Moreland arched a chocolate eyebrow as she walked up to the servant to inspect her carefully. "Indeed. Is it customary to address your mistress by her first name?"

Octavia made a sound of distress, shaking Gwen from her surprise.

"Mrs. Hanning served my mother in my youth. We are ... rather close."

While she had responded, the room had filled. Her father, Lord Moreland, and Aidan Abbott were now all standing in the doorway, watching the confrontation between Lady Moreland and Octavia, who was quivering as she threw a glance back at Gwen. It was terrifying to draw the glare of condemnation on herself, but she did it to defend Octavia.

Lady Moreland's gaze moved to Gwen, who wished the floor would open and swallow her up. She squashed a grimace even as Octavia took the opportunity to abruptly depart the room, evidently too overcome to attempt further explanation.

"Miss Gwendolyn Smythe, I presume?"

Gwen bowed her head in affirmation, her stomach churning with anxiety. Lady Moreland came sweeping forward, taking hold of Gwen's upper arms in something akin to an embrace.

"Your lady's maid is not wrong, Gwendolyn. We are very fortunate to invite a young woman of such accomplishment into our family." Reaching up, Lady Moreland bussed her on the cheek.

Gwen's eyes widened in shock, flicking over to Lord Abbott—Aidan—in question. He smiled with a small shrug, apparently accustomed to his mother's inconsistencies.

"We will welcome your babes as if they are our own children."

Gwen blinked repeatedly. "Babes?"

"Our grandchildren. Have you thought about names yet? I can suggest a number of estimable family names from the Abbott line."

Her mouth dropped open in amazement—Gwen was sure she must be dreaming. Surely this was not how one met the parents of one's betrothed? It must surely be the night before the dinner, and she was still in a deep slumber?

Lord Moreland came forward, taking hold of Gwen's hand to bow as his wife stepped aside. "A pleasure, Gwendolyn. Lady Moreland is quite excited to welcome a new generation of Abbotts, but first I think we have a wedding to discuss, my dear."

The last was directed to Lady Moreland, who waved her hand in dismissal, as if such trivial details were not worthy of attention when grandchildren were under discussion. Gwen surreptitiously reached down to pinch herself on the leg. Just to be sure. It was a genuine possibility that she was dreaming this introduction.

Nothing changed, and Gwen wondered if she could have merely dreamed the pinch. Across the room, her father was beaming with his blue eyes twinkling. Apparently, the mention of future grandchildren had met with his approval. It seemed like an ill-conceived idea, considering the fact that Gwen was clearly losing her mind. She managed to drop into an awkward curtsy. "Thank you, Lord Moreland."

With some relief, she found herself facing her betrothed. His handsome face bore an expression of sympathy as he bowed in greeting. "Good evening, Gwen. You are ravishing tonight."

His gaze swept over her in appreciation, and for a moment, the stresses were forgotten as Gwen was struck by the memory of their moonlight interlude.

"Lord Abbott," she breathed out. It was strange to think that they were only meeting for the second time. She had grown closer to this man than any other in a matter of one night. They had shared a passionate embrace, and then the intimacy of a marriage offer, all in the course of one evening. Now she was meeting his parents, and the subject of grandchildren had been raised.

Just a week earlier, she had been convinced she was destined to remain on the shelf, and yet here she was, experiencing the clumsiness of meeting her future relations and discussing inappropriate and intimate subjects.

"I think it is acceptable to address me as Aidan?"

His lively brown eyes were dancing in the dim light of the oil lamps, daring her to reject his offer.

Aidan.

She had been mouthing the name to herself since she had found it in Debrett's.

Lady Gwendolyn Abbott.

That had been playing through her head, too. She liked the sound of it.

Lord and Lady Abbott.

Gwen realized she had been staring at her betrothed for

several seconds without responding. She was woolgathering while their parents watched on.

"Aidan," she said hastily, wrenching her hand back.

This was all too good to be true. She had a handsome, eligible heir contracted to marry her. His parents were accepting her without question, with a list of names for future issue. Her father was grinning like a cat who was preparing to pounce on a slow, overweight pigeon for his dinner.

Something was bound to go awry.

Although she had attended numerous social functions, Gwen felt entirely out of her depth, unsure what came next. Which was when God himself took pity on her—in the form of Jenson appearing in the doorway to make an announcement.

"Dinner is served."

Aidan held out his arm—his muscular, male arm—and Gwen peered down at it in momentary confusion before hesitantly taking hold of it to accompany him to the dining room.

Beneath her fingers, his arm flexed, and she wanted to sigh and stroke it in appreciation, but, fortunately, good breeding and the presence of his parents prevented her from such an offensive act.

* * *

AIDAN HAD BEEN STRUCK ONCE MORE by the beauty of his Venus, barely registering the bizarre interaction between his mother and Gwen's maid. Her hand on his arm was steering his thoughts to lascivious activities as they walked down the hall.

Which was when Aidan noticed the missing paintings. Every second or third spot where there should have been a portrait or whatnot, there was instead an unfaded rectangle of wallpaper, indicating that it had recently been covered by something.

It was further evidence of Smythe selling off his assets, but as Aidan swept his gaze over the length of the hall, it was obvious that the man had sold far more than the list Aidan had made. Smythe must have been liquidating his assets for far longer than the two-month stack.

Entering the dining room, Aidan was torn between spending time in Gwen's company and noticing that the shelving along one wall held very few *objets d'art*. Less than half of what one might expect in a wealthy home. He had hoped to enjoy the evening with his betrothed, celebrating their impending nuptials, but his thoughts swung to the dead baron and his sister's safety as he took in what was not there.

What should be there.

He had promised his father to hold off investigating Smythe until the wedding in a few days, but the mounting clues to the man's troubles made Aidan's skin crawl with the notion that Lily was still in danger. His little sister with a big mouth and a bigger heart, who deserved better than he, a lousy brother who had failed her.

As their parents took their seats, he and Gwen walked around to the other side of the table. He pulled her chair out for her before taking his place beside her, determined to set aside his thoughts until a more appropriate time.

Trafford and Filminster had pointed out how difficult his path forward would be, attempting to be a good husband to Gwen while defending Lily from a violent killer, and Aidan blew out his breath in a puff. Gwen must have heard him as her head bobbed in his direction, curious at this sign of distress.

Aidan smiled to reassure her. Reaching under the table, he clasped her hand, gently stroking his thumb over her fingers. To his delight, her hand curled into his, and for several seconds, they held hands while his parents chattered with Smythe.

Footmen brought in the courses, laying them out while his mother offered Smythe several names from the Abbott family tree. Smythe, in turn, offered some from their history.

Gwen was biting her lip as she picked up a spoon to begin eating.

"Chestnut?" he asked.

Gwen nodded. "It is Papa's favorite."

"And what is yours?"

"I do not much care for soup," she responded.

"What do you care for?"

"Fruit. Oranges, especially."

Aidan growled in the back of his throat, recalling how she had tasted of citrus when they had kissed. Heat shot through his veins, and he considered that soon they would be joined in matrimony ... which meant that soon they would be joined. He had never experienced such a visceral interest in bedding a woman, but the thought of Gwen's hair flowing free on the sheets as he lowered himself over her ... He would invite her for a walk on the terrace after dinner so he could sip on her lips once more.

Lowering his voice so their parents could not hear, Aidan asked, "Is that the scent I breathed?"

Gwen colored, a warm flush rising from the edge of her bodice to temporarily conceal her delightful freckles. "There is bergamot in my soap."

Aidan bent his head toward her, drawing her smell in to make his mouth water. "The moon shines bright. In such a night as this. When the sweet wind did gently kiss the trees and they did make no noise, in such a night ..."

His betrothed nearly choked on the soup she had just sipped, throwing him a glance of rebuke before flickering her eyes to ensure his parents had not heard his allusion to their fated kiss. "Shhh."

Aidan grinned. "Not for a moment, sweet Venus."

He was not accustomed to flirting with a woman, but she made him think of great poetry and ... other things. Soft curves, creamy skin, and bergamot-scented hair tangled around him. He shook his head to clear his thoughts, his imagination captured by musings of their approaching wedding night.

"We used to travel up north during the summer but, alas, this year I will remain in London." Frederick's warm baritone interrupted Aidan's musings of Gwen's intriguing form. There had been a bill of sale for a property in Yorkshire in the sheaf that Aidan had illicitly rifled through.

It was a rude reminder of why he had met the Smythes in the first place. Recollecting the conversation with Trafford and Filminster, Aidan realized this was his opportunity to find out if Smythe had a legitimate reason for his recent activities.

"Father and I were just discussing the purchase of new property to add to our portfolio. Do you have any suggestions, Mr. Smythe?" Aidan watched the other man carefully as he posed his question. It would be heaven-sent if the man admitted he was purchasing something, thus disproving that he was desperate for funds and canceling him as a suspect from their list.

Smythe hesitated, his eyebrows coming together for just a second before responding. "No, I am afraid not. It has been some time since I dealt with any land purchases."

Aidan's heart sank.

"Do you intend on any large investments in the near future?"

The question was jarring, causing his father to throw him a cautionary glance. Aidan kept a straight face, but he knew

Hugh Abbott was aware that he was attempting to gather information.

Frederick Smythe sobered for several seconds, while Aidan prayed he would admit to something—anything—that would provide an explanation for his bills of sale. Then Gwen's father smiled his customary grin. "What could I possibly purchase? A gentleman has no need of anything but property!"

"Indeed!" agreed Aidan's mother. "Owning land is the ultimate investment. There is no need of any other."

Smythe cocked his head, his gaze falling for a fraction of a second, enough for Aidan to know that something was wrong. Then he laughed and banged the table with his hand. "Land is the best investment."

Next to him, Gwen dropped her head to stare at her bowl of soup. And Aidan knew. He knew the gentleman had a secret, and that it was possible that Gwen knew what it was. Aidan could only hope her involvement was minimal.

Curses!

He had never even contemplated that Gwen might have had some involvement in Smythe's problems. It was one thing to plot Smythe's arrest, another to consider his betrothed might be engaged in nefarious activities. The very thought of it made his chest tight.

Lord Moreland chose that moment to shift the subject, flickering his eyes in warning at Aidan. "How is Lord Weston? I know him well from Lords, but I have not seen him since the coronation."

Smythe grimaced. "My brother is well, but he was called away. Our family home caught fire, you see. He was called away to attend to it."

Aidan's parents exclaimed their horror in unison.

"Was anybody hurt?"

"Did the building survive?"

"The staff are well. They managed to rescue the contents, but the west wing was destroyed."

Aidan's interest was piqued as the conversation turned to the disaster that had befallen the Smythe family. Could this be why Gwen's father needed funds?

But no, that did not make sense. The bills of sale demonstrated that Smythe had been selling off for a minimum of the past two months, and news of the fire must have reached his brother after the coronation if Aidan's own father had met him there.

Aidan felt the deep bite of disappointment that Smythe still did not have a bona fide reason that might remove him from their list of suspects for the killing of Lord Filminster. How much simpler his future would be if he could clear Smythe of the crime!

After dinner, they adjourned together to a small drawing room, and Aidan invited Gwen to the terrace with him. One of the privileges of being betrothed was the allowance of certain concessions, such as walking alone. Many couples took advantage of this in anticipation of their wedding vows. Aidan simply wanted to forget his worries over Smythe's guilt for even a few minutes. A reprieve from the burden of Lily being in danger to enjoy the company of a beautiful and intelligent woman. Not to mention, to discover the extent of Gwen's involvement in this intrigue.

Gwen nodded, standing to link her arm with his, and they departed through the French doors, leaving their parents to talk. Despite his desire for respite, Aidan asked the question burning in his mind as soon as they were alone.

"Why is it you are not leaving London this year?"

His companion firmed her chin, watching the last rays of sunset on the horizon as they both stood with their hands upon the stone banister. "My father found the need to sell the property." Her tone was defensive. "He did not wish to disclose it because land ownership is the mark of a true gentleman."

"Why?"

She shook her head. "He has a plan, but he has not discussed it with me. He merely informed me that it was necessary to sell."

A surge of relief hit Aidan. He was practically giddy at the news. Gwen had been honest about what she knew, and knew no more. Whatever Smythe was up to, likely crippling debts and the murder of a peer, she was not involved. And soon she would be under his protection, cushioned against any forthcoming scandal.

"Tell me something of yourself."

Gwen tilted her head in question, and Aidan hungrily took in the sight of her fiery red hair lit by the dying light. "Such as?"

"What do you do with your day?"

Her blue eyes found his, defiance reflected in their depths. "My mother was a scholar of the ancient world, like her father before her. I study in the library ... and I have published papers."

"Truly?"

"Yes, under a pseudonym, of course."

Aidan smiled. "Of course."

"As my mother did before me."

"I would love to read them."

"Truly?"

He nodded. "Truly."

"You do not mind that I ... engage in such inappropriate pursuits?"

"If it leads to reciting Manilius in the moonlight, I am all for it. Imagine what you will teach our children."

The sun had fully disappeared and night was falling

quickly. But her groan was audible. "Your mother is obsessed!"

He chuckled. "My father chose to make our ... situation ... palatable by commenting on the benefits of our union. My mother has been distressed lately, but the idea of grandchildren has quite lifted her spirits."

There was no response for several seconds before Gwen finally answered. "Then, I suppose I am happy to be of service in some small way."

Aidan turned toward her. "You are of great service, Venus."

With that, he gently drew her into his arms to lower his lips to hers. Breathing in her citrus scent, he sipped at her lips. When she sighed, it was all the invitation he needed to tangle his tongue with hers in a hungry, all-consuming kiss.

Gwen moaned as he cupped her head with one hand to deepen their union. Heat rose in a tidal wave to wash through his body and settle in the region of his groin. Repositioning her so she was caught against the banister, Aidan pressed closer to glory in her softness against him.

One hand found her right knee, where he tugged at the silk warmed by her skin until he was able to slip underneath to stroke the stocking-clad leg beneath. She was smooth and captivating, and he wished he could lift her in his arms to find her rooms and lay her down on the bed. He would release her hair and remove her gown ...

Lifting his head, he found that he was breathless. Overtaken in a manner he had never experienced before. No matter what ugliness the coming days brought, he could never regret finding this woman.

Gwen slowly opened her eyes to gaze up at him in the night, her lips swollen from their kisses and her breath escaping in pants to mirror his own.

Bringing his hand around to cup her chin, he stroked a

thumb over her creamy cheek. "From her fair and unpolluted flesh, May violets spring."

She stared back at him with awe as he did his best to stamp down his passions, and Aidan imagined being married to this wondrous creature for the rest of his days. He only hoped he could hold on to the admiration in her expression when events unfolded.

CHAPTER 8

"Youth is easily deceived because it is quick to hope."

Aristotle

* * *

AUGUST 18, 1821

Gwen awoke with a sense of guilt to find an unblinking Buttercup on the bed beside her, staring as if to criticize her for what she had done the previous night.

"Do not look at me that way."

Buttercup's slender snout twitched, and she whined in the back of her little throat, before rising to drop onto the floor and run out the door. Perhaps the dog needed the necessary, Gwen mused. She had certainly left in a hurry.

Gwen flopped over onto her back and thought about what she had done. Would it injure her father's pride if he knew she had disclosed the truth of the Yorkshire property to Aidan? He had asked her a direct question, and she was poor at obfuscation. Her inherent honesty had the confession leaving her lips without fully intending to do so, but Aidan was bound to discover the truth at some point.

Being a member of high society was frustrating. There were so many constraints on behavior. The property belonged to Papa. It was his to sell. Why that had to be an embarrassment was ridiculous, but after the sale of that estate, her father had only the small London estate where they lived. In the eyes of the *beau monde*, that barely made him a landowner.

And everyone knew that there was nothing more important, more lauded, than being a landowner.

She supposed it was fortuitous that she was to marry. If word that the property had been sold got out, she would have been even less desirable than before. Their connections were weak, their wealth limited, and now her father only owned the one property.

Gwen suspected why her father was selling off his assets, but he had been close-lipped about it, even to her.

"Do not concern yourself, Gwendolyn. I know what I am doing."

Gwen turned over, watching as Octavia opened the drapes to reveal the morning light. She hoped he did, but what could she do but trust him? For years, her father had insisted that the right man would come along, and somehow, he had been proved right.

"Word of your wedding is out," announced Octavia.

Gwen looked up at her lady's maid, whose head appeared to precariously balance on her shoulders from this angle. Sighing, Gwen pushed herself into a seated position to lean against the headboard.

"Apparently, it's a love match," Octavia continued.

Gwen huffed a laugh. "That is a bit rich. We only just met the night of the ..." She waved a hand, unwilling to state the details.

"I have it on good authority that Lady Astley is telling everyone that Lord Abbott is smitten with your red hair."

Gwen frowned, disconcerted. "Does he have a history of chasing women with red hair?"

Octavia shook her head. "He has no reputation in regard to women. Lord Abbott returned from his Grand Tour a couple of months ago, and until the ball, his name had not been linked with anyone."

Noticing that Gwen had raised an eyebrow at her, Octavia shrugged. "I checked again. No history of redheads. No history at all."

Gwen swallowed, staring down at her hands. "Do you think ... that he is genuinely enthralled with me?"

Octavia leaned down and gave her a hug. "I do."

"Would it be so! Imagine if we could be faithful partners and have many children together. Gareth would be an uncle, our family would grow, and Papa would have grandchildren. We have all been so lonely since Mama—" Gwen broke off, her throat thick with tears. "I could teach them—"

The maid straightened up. "Just like Mrs. Smythe did."

Gwen swiped the tears from her lashes, nodding. "Just so."

"It's well deserved, you hear! All these Seasons, I knew you were a catch. We were just waiting for the—"

"Right man." They said it together, before looking at each other and chuckling.

"Mr. Smythe said he would appear. The master said there'd be a gentleman who was overcome by your magnificence, and the perfection of your mind, and would fall at your feet ... and he was right."

"Papa is an eternal optimist."

Octavia grinned, baring her crooked teeth. "What's the alternative, Gwendolyn Smythe?"

Gwen pulled a face, trying to think. "To be an embittered old bat?"

A shout of laughter followed. "That's right! The alternative is to be Lady Astley."

"Who is now telling everyone that it is my red hair that attracted the gentleman to my side? Last year she was telling her acquaintances in private that my red hair was a curse, and the reason I would never wed."

"Huh! Not so private, from what I hear."

Gwen twisted her coverlet between her fingers, reluctant to admit the secret in her heart, but needing to state it aloud. "I ... like him, Octavia. I really do. I want this to work out. He is handsome and kind and clever, but I never dreamed of finding such a match."

A bony hand came out to tap her on the thigh. Gwen moved farther into the bed so that Octavia could sit on the mattress.

"Those girls at school muddled your head. You were always destined to make a great match with a wonderful man, but they convinced you that you are ugly. Do you know why they did it?"

Gwen shook her head, stricken by the thought it might be true.

"They envied you. You sailed through your lessons. No matter what you put your mind to, you do it well. Whether it be Ancient Greek, or needlework and music lessons. Your ability to learn intimidated them, and they banded together to make nothing of you. It was cruel and meaningless because you're a nice girl who would have helped them to succeed, too, if they'd only asked."

"But, Octavia, Mama was a revered beauty while I have been mocked for nearly ten years."

"And now a gentleman has seen what I see. A true original."

In her heart of hearts, Gwen wanted to believe in moonlight and magic. That a decent, intelligent gentleman had noticed her. That she did not have to choose between an inferior marriage or being a childless spinster.

Gwen heaved a deep sigh. "I have to make this work. This is my chance to build a family."

"That's the spirit, Gwendolyn Smythe!"

* * *

AIDAN STARED at the note in his hand with a feeling of hope and dread. The cryptic contents revealed not which emotion he should pursue.

There has been a development - Filminster

Damn his brother-in-law. Why could he not state what the development was? Something that vindicated Frederick Smythe, or something that implicated him? Or, was the development completely unrelated?

Stretching his neck from side to side, Aidan decided to finish his breakfast while the servants prepared his mount. He had not slept well, and eating would assist him with his flagging energy.

Gesturing to their head footman, Thomas, Aidan made his request before returning to his eggs and ham. There had been much interruption to his routine of late because of the investigations they were doing into the other suspects. Ensuring he ate while he had the opportunity seemed well-advised, and the note had not indicated urgency.

Soon, he departed from the Abbott townhouse and headed to Ridley House. The butler, Michaels, who had saved his sister's life from a desperate servant, answered the door. Aidan had thanked the man for his service the day of the attack, but the upper servant was known to have a cantankerous temperament, so Aidan had not been able to read the older man's reaction. This meant Aidan had been having some difficulty trying to decide how to behave toward the man since the incident earlier in August.

Members of the upper class were meant to mostly ignore the servants, but the Abbott family had developed a relationship with some of theirs over time—a natural consequence of being a rather personable family that appreciated their retainers. Out of politeness, Aidan did not presume that servants in other households would expect or welcome undue attention from guests.

But what if the servant in question has saved a valued sister?

"Michaels." Aidan settled for acknowledging the butler with a brief bow of the head. Michaels stared back at him, unblinking.

Aidan gritted his teeth. "Is Lord Filminster home?"

Michaels nodded curtly. Standing aside, he allowed Aidan entry into the hall. Shutting the door, he proceeded to lead the way to Filminster's study, his heavy tread smacking the floor as if a troop of soldiers were encamping.

Aidan followed behind, shaking his head at the enigmatic servant. Lily had mentioned that Michaels had been offered retirement in gratitude, but had chosen to remain on, so Aidan supposed he must enjoy his role in some manner that was unclear from his sullen demeanor. He found the man odd, but considering what Michaels had done for Lily, Aidan understood it was his lot to tolerate the awkwardness of their interactions for as long as Michaels saw fit to continue in his role.

Mayhap Michaels remaining in his post was fortuitous,

considering the killer was still on the loose and the butler had proved to be a man of action when it counted.

Being shown into Filminster's study, Aidan discovered Trafford was there, lounging in an armchair. He still thought the other heir was something of a pontificating fool with his elaborate coats, waistcoats, and collection of breeches, pantaloons, and trousers. However, it was certainly to the man's merit that he had been consistently contributing to their murder investigation. Aidan conceded that Trafford had demonstrated persistence and loyalty these past two weeks, which meant Aidan had to begrudgingly acknowledge that there were hidden depths to the clownish friend.

Taking a seat in a faded armchair, Aidan stretched out his legs and turned to his brother-in-law who was seated behind his mahogany desk.

"Well, Ridley, are you going to brief Little Breeches here or not?"

Aidan squashed his irritation at Trafford's languid demand. Despite his resolve to maintain his composure, he heard himself say, "It is Filminster, not Ridley."

Trafford narrowed his eyes and tilted his head toward Aidan. "Is he not Brendan Ridley, my old chum from around Town?"

Aidan snarled. "Is he not now the Baron of Filminster? Lord Filminster? Otherwise known to his peers as … *Filminster?*"

Trafford waved a hand in dismissal. "Tempers are short and patience is frayed. I will allow your comments to pass without further rebuke."

Soughing heavily, Aidan reflected it was not untrue that his patience was frayed.

He wished to end the risk to Lily's safety.

He also wished to find a killer other than Smythe for the sake of his future bride.

None of that took into account the restless night of dreaming of Gwen's body pressed against his, the hungry return of her kisses, and the almost inaudible moans she made from the back of her throat, firing his blood and jolting him from his sleep. Perhaps it had been a mistake to take her out on the terrace after dinner, but the truth was he had to do it. The compulsion to be close, to breathe in her citrus scent and to sip on her honeyed lips, had been too much to resist.

"I apologize. You have known Filminster for some years, so address him as you wish."

Trafford snickered. "I shall, Little Breeches."

Aidan curled his fingers into a fist. The ongoing taunt was not worthy of acknowledgment. Trafford might very well never cease using it if Aidan allowed him the knowledge that it was so very irritating. This was his own fault for engaging rather than allowing Filminster to respond to Trafford's prompt.

"Did something happen?" Aidan turned his attention back to his sister's husband, who had clearly not been paying a smidgen of attention to the tense confrontation.

Instead, he was staring down at the colorful rug on the floor with a bemused expression. Aidan knew that look. It was how he must appear when he had time alone with his thoughts. He knew the precise and incessant thought that ran through his head that caused that look.

How do I find the killer, and resolve this muddle, before Lily is hurt again?

Trafford cleared his throat pointedly, causing Filminster to blink and return to their conversation.

"What happened?" Aidan questioned, when he still said nothing.

"The runner, Briggs, has had a couple men in the street monitoring Ridley House, and he reported that someone is watching the house. At his advice, I had the guards reduce their visibility to find out what the watchers would do ... One of them broke into the library last evening but evaded the Johns when they attempted to capture him."

Aidan jumped to his feet. "How long has the house been under surveillance? Why was I not informed?"

Filminster made eye contact with him, his eyes dull in the morning light. "There was no reason to cause your undue concern."

A tide of fear on Lily's behalf washed over Aidan as he began to pace. Throwing his hands up, he barked his next question. "Why do you not simply take Lily to Somerset? Remove her from this danger?"

Filminster sighed. "Briggs advises me it is safer to remain here. Here, we have guards and servants to defend Ridley House. If we depart, we will be in carriages and exposed."

"But they are attempting to break in so they might search for the letter, not specifically for you or Lily!"

"If the killer who hired them believes we have found the letter, he might send a party after us. Out on the turnpikes, we would have little defense."

"But the evidence we need might be there! We could solve this."

"It is not that simple. My ... uncle ... kept copious records of everything. There are entire attics full of papers, journals, and accounts dating back decades. I can hardly endanger Lily's safety on a long journey through the country, exposed to attack. Separating is out of the question. And, even then, once we were to reach Filminster, I would have weeks or months of pawing through piles of documentation to find anything useful because I can only entrust such a sensitive task to myself and perhaps some of Briggs's men. Nay, the most expedient course is to flush the killer out with this investigation."

Aidan growled, returning to his pacing while he tried to think. "Then remove with Lily to my parents' home."

Trafford stood up, rolling his shoulders. "It will not help, Little Breeches. Here Filminster has guards, as well as Michaels and the staff. Your parents are taking many of their servants with them to the country after the wedding, from what I understand. It is better for Ridley and his wife to remain here."

"We need to solve this! Lily cannot remain in Ridley House forever!"

"Today is Saturday, which means you wed in a week. Lord and Lady Moreland will depart the following week, so you will be free to investigate Smythe and find out if there is a connection between his disposal of assets and the murder. Briggs has been looking into the sales, but it has not led to any new revelations."

"How? How will I find out anything? I collect my bride on Saturday morning and then we will live in my parents' home while our own home is being prepared."

Filminster interrupted their exchange. "Perhaps you can convince Smythe to host you in his home? Perhaps ... your parents' townhouse is in need of urgent repairs and you think it will be less upheaval for Miss Smythe and you to remain in Smythe's home until your new residence is ready?"

Aidan rubbed a hand over his face, considering the suggestion. His father had instructed that one of his London properties be prepared for Aidan and his bride, but it take a few weeks yet.

"It will be a strange request, but I suppose I could visit Smythe and put the request to him. I shall propose we marry in the Smythe home if I am to pretend repairs of such magnitude are required. It will not do for him to visit our home."

"That might be best." Filminster hesitated. "I know it is much to ask, but I would truly appreciate it. Smythe is the only suspect from our list who has any indications of questionable activities. He could be the one."

As his heart sank, Aidan raised a hand to knead at his chest. He was hoping that one of the other investigations into their list of four suspects would bear fruit. Anything rather than hurt his intended in the near future.

Filminster must have noted his distress. "We will keep investigating the other men, but if Smythe killed my uncle, he will have to pay the price."

"I know that. Lily's safety is at risk, so I do not need reminding that it is my duty to reveal him as the killer if he did do it."

"I regret that you are in this position ... Aidan." Filminster had moved closer, patting him on the shoulder even as he appeared uncomfortable. But Aidan appreciated the gesture.

Clearing his throat, he attempted to reciprocate. "Thank you ... Brendan."

Trafford chuckled, resuming his languid sprawl in the armchair. "It is heartwarming to witness family closeness."

Aidan shut his eyes in aggravation. Trust the fop to ruin the moment. "Sod off, Trafford."

Brendan laughed, his earlier bemusement forgotten, and Aidan caught a glimpse of the carefree fellow that his brother-in-law might be under less trying circumstances. "You are one of us now, Aidan. Only Trafford's nearest and dearest tell him to sod off."

Aidan shook his head. "If we reach the day that Trafford and I are friends, you should take me out back and put a musket ball through my head because it can only mean I have achieved a preposterous level of farce."

Trafford pulled a face. "Careful, Little Breeches. You might hurt my feelings."

"Do you have any?" Aidan shot back.

The clown shrugged. "Occasionally."

Aidan snorted in disgust, albeit with an iota of gratitude that the fool did make him forget his troubles for a moment here or there. He supposed the other heir might have some use under the right circumstances, such as when a man was doing his best to act with honor to the women in his life.

How on earth had he managed to find himself toiling to secure Lily's safety at the same time as protecting Gwen from scandal? Next week he would wed and this muddle would become ever more complicated.

CHAPTER 9

"Hope is a waking dream."

Aristotle

* * *

AUGUST 25, 1821

Buttercup, Octavia, and Gwen stood in the family hall watching footmen moving Aidan's trunks into the bedroom next to hers. Aidan's valet, a gaunt man with a fastidious sense of style and an effeminate voice, directed the servants.

It was all rather strange, but her father had informed her that they would be staying with him until their new residence was ready.

Gwen did not know of higher-ranking members of the *ton* moving into the homes of lower-ranking members for an extended length of time, but she supposed it made sense, what with Lord and Lady Moreland leaving London in a few days.

"What do you suppose is in Lord Abbott's trunks? There are so many." The footmen were showing some signs of strain as they filed past the door of Gwen's room to enter the next one.

Gwen drew a speculative breath before finally answering with an air of confidence. "Books. The extra trunks are his books."

Octavia frowned in question.

"He just returned from the Continent. He quotes Marcus Manilius and William Shakespeare with an accuracy and detail that imply a frequent interaction with his books."

A smile broke over Octavia's face. "He doesn't possess the form of a scholar." She held up her hands to indicate the width of his shoulders compared to his lean hips, finishing off with a slight cupping motion that provided evidence she had noticed—Gwen stopped breathing at the thought—his *derriere*.

"Octavia!" Gwen's remonstration was halfhearted. After several years of the servant's company, she was well aware that the woman was entirely incorrigible.

The lady's maid shrugged without remorse. "I know you've noticed, Gwendolyn Smythe."

Buttercup whined at their feet, a dangling tongue hanging out of her mouth as if to agree with Octavia's lewd assessment.

Gwen blushed, well aware that when she did so, it was a fiery red that spread quickly from her décolletage, up her neck and across her face. The roots of her hair were practically singed by the increase in heat. She said nothing, knowing Octavia could evaluate the answer without comment.

The servant shot her a sideways glance. "I thought so. Just think—tonight's your wedding night. You'll have the opportunity to behold ... first hand." Again the cupping motion, the implication crystal clear.

Gwen exhaled in a puff, the thought of Aidan entering her bedroom ensuring that the blush did not subside even a fraction. She certainly had thought about what it would be like to kiss in privacy, remove his coat and run her hands on that broad chest that felt so hard pressed against the mounds of her breasts.

"Did you ever find out why the wedding was delayed 'til now?" Octavia must have taken pity on the beleaguered Gwen, shifting the subject to less ... passionate ... subjects.

"It was to allow for his cousin to return from Somerset for the wedding. Lord Moreland was adamant that the scandal had sufficiently abated with news of the wedding to send for his niece and her family to attend. Apparently, she grew up with Aidan and his sister in their household."

Octavia tilted her head, obviously perplexed. Then her eyes widened in alarm. "Do you mean the Countess of Saunton?"

"I think that was it. Lady Sophia Balfour."

Her lady's maid emitted a choking sound. "Lord Saunton's accompanying her?"

Gwen nodded, turning from the hall to peer at Octavia in surprise. "Yes, what of it?"

"Do you know who Lord Saunton is?"

"No, not really."

"His father was Lord Satan, the infamous defiler of servants. I heard that the younger Lord Saunton followed in his footsteps until he unexpectedly wed a girl he barely knew. Last year, he acknowledged that he had sired a bastard with a maid. The boy's now living with them."

This news seemed out of character from what Octavia

had told her of the Abbott family. "Why would a prestigious family allow such a match?" she wondered out loud before an alarming thought struck. "Do we need to warn the women belowstairs to be careful?"

Octavia raised a hand to nibble on a thumbnail, her tension etched in the lines of her wide face. Dropping her hand, the servant straightened up. "I've not heard anything recently, but I'll inform the housekeeper. Cook will know if there is any risk involved in serving him."

"Perhaps the maids should remain out of sight until he departs. The footmen could take over their duties on the main level."

The lady's maid nodded, darting off in a manner that reminded Gwen of the starlings that visited the Smythe gardens. As she raced down the hall, Octavia's gray skirts fluttered behind her like their palpitating wings while her head bobbed in the same agitated manner. Her distress was palpable, and Gwen pouted a lip in contemplation.

Buttercup watched the lady's maid depart, slightly baring her teeth as if to remark on the dire danger women could find themselves in. Gwen could not blame Buttercup for her sentiments, considering the circumstances of their meeting.

Nevertheless, Gwen could not help but be intrigued. What would it be like to meet such an infamous rogue? It was hardly the kind of gentleman whom her father would invite within their circle, but if the servants were safe, Gwen thought it was all rather exciting to meet such a person and observe his character for herself.

Lady Sophia Balfour allowed his bastard to live in her household! Had the noblewoman been required to do so by her husband? Was she humiliated by the situation?

The link to the Abbott family was certainly unexpected, given everything that Octavia had told her about them.

Turning back into her room, she carefully nudged Buttercup back inside, giving her a quick scratch before shutting the door to go stand in front of the mirror.

Signora Ricci had made her a gown of azure for the nuptials this morning, and the fine blue silk clung to her slight curves. Gwen had ordered it, thinking of how Aidan had compared her to the *Birth of Venus*, thinking that the soft blue was reminiscent of a hazy morning by the sea. Gwen had been more adventurous about offsetting the red of her hair against the hue, hoping that Aidan had been sincere in his admiration of her ginger tresses.

Nerves fluttered in the region of her stomach, and Gwen considered if she should descend to meet the arriving guests with her father on her own, or await the return of Octavia to accompany her. Then she recollected the last interaction her lady's maid had had with Lady Moreland and winced.

She had a sneaking suspicion that Octavia, having been rather intimidated by Aidan's mother, might use this opportunity to remain out of sight.

Alone it is.

Squaring her shoulders, she summoned her confidence, assuring herself she had assessed Aidan's preferences correctly.

She had, despite her cynicism, developed a number of hopes about this unexpected match. Her father's optimism had infected her, and Gwen prayed she would not regret opening up her mind to the possibilities of a grand future with an intelligent and handsome gentleman at her side. After so many miserable years circulating the edges of the *beau monde*, Gwen crossed her fingers that all would be well with her and Aidan.

Preparing to depart her room, she turned to Buttercup and said, "Sorry, girl. This is not the time to follow me."

The little dog whined in protest, wiggling her bottom against the floor, but remained seated near the mirror as if she planned to wait for Gwen's return.

Gwen shut the door and made her way downstairs, then entered into the small drawing room, where she had met Aidan's parents, and discovered that their guests had arrived. Aidan quickly stepped forward, bowing before offering her his arm. He was sartorial perfection, wearing a coat of navy wool that fit over his broad shoulders.

"You are ravishing this morning, Miss Smythe." Aidan's deep voice sent a thrill of pleasure chasing through her veins. Gwen accepted his arm and took in the group, which was larger than she had expected.

By the window stood a very large gentleman, many inches over six feet. He had the appearance of a marauder from the shores of Norway, with his blond hair and gray eyes. Gwen thought she might recognize him from the social events she had attended, but she did not think he had been introduced. By his side stood an elegant young woman with a pile of dark chestnut curls. Aidan led her toward the couple, which suggested that the imposing gentleman was the highest-ranking peer present.

Coming to a halt, Aidan introduced him with deference. "Miss Smythe, I present to you His Grace, the Duke of Halmesbury."

Gwen's eyebrows shot up. She had indeed recognized him. The duke bowed before speaking in a deep baritone. "The pleasure is mine, Miss Smythe. Felicitations on your wedding."

She curtsied, mumbling a reply while surreptitiously glancing around to see who else she would be meeting this morning. Her father was at the fireplace, bouncing on his toes with his grin in place. Clearly, he was ecstatic at the new connections Aidan was bringing to their lowly family.

Aidan turned to the lady next to the duke. "Your Grace, I present Miss Smythe."

Gwen realized that this must be the duke's wife. She quickly curtsied. The duchess was taller than the average woman, just two or three inches shorter than Gwen herself. Her Grace also had a rounded belly, obviously increasing, and her brandy eyes reflected warmth when she smiled in greeting. "Miss Smythe, welcome to the family."

"F-family?" Gwen shot a questioning look at her betrothed, but it was the duchess who responded.

"My brother, Lord Filminster, is married to Abbott's sister. His Grace insisted we return to London when we were informed of the nuptials."

"Oh." It was not an adequate reply, but Gwen was thinking she was going to have words with Octavia later this morning. Why had her confidante not informed her of the connection to Halmesbury, one of the most lauded peers in the realm? It seemed such news would be notable.

Aidan proceeded to introduce her to Lord and Lady Saunton. Despite Octavia's *on dit* about Lord Saunton's proclivities, Gwen found him to be pleasant and quite amusing. The emerald-eyed lord was seemingly obsessed with his wife, who was an attractive and thoughtful young woman with reddish-blonde hair. The countess did not appear beleaguered by a roguish husband. She seemed calm and confident, her arm linked with the earl's the entire time they spoke.

Gwen was startled when Lady Saunton's skirts seemed to take on a life of their own, before a small boy erupted from behind her. He was a miniature of Lord Saunton with matching eyes and sable hair.

"Hallo."

Not quite understanding, she responded, "How do you do?"

"Are you Cousin Aidan's new wife?"

Lady Saunton chuckled. "They have not yet wed, Ethan."

His sweet little face fell in disappointment. "Does she play chess, Mama?"

"I do not know. Perhaps you should ask her."

Ethan's little face grew pensive, peering at Gwen with a touch of shyness. "Do you play chess?" he finally asked.

"I do."

"After you marry, will you play with me?"

"We will have to enjoy the wedding breakfast first."

"And then we can play?"

Gwen grinned at the lad's persistence. "Then we can play."

"Good."

Ethan disappeared back behind the countess's skirts, the tails of his green coat the last she saw of him. Gwen was bemused that Lady Saunton and the boy, who must be the illegitimate child Octavia had mentioned, seemed as close as any mother and child. There were no signs of domestic strife between the trio.

Next, Gwen greeted their local vicar, a cheery and cherubic man with long white side-whiskers and a bald pate.

"I appreciate your presence this morning, vicar."

"Not at all, Miss Smythe. Lord Moreland made a generous donation to our parish to secure my presence. Our church is quite grateful."

Next, Lord Filminster was introduced. He had the same dark chestnut locks and brandy eyes as the duchess, the family resemblance obvious. Lord Filminster bowed and smiled politely, but he was not as effusive as the other guests, observing her with an air of reserve.

Aidan continued his introductions, increasingly less formal as he moved through the guests. "And this is my sister, Lady Filminster."

A petite young woman with the chocolate brown hair and eyes of Gwen's betrothed stepped forward, grabbing Gwen by the hands. "Please call me Lily! We are to be sisters, are we not? I do love weddings so! They make one think of the future and possibilities and babes. Here we are with another scandalous match, just a month after my own ruin! What a strange turn of events."

Gwen blinked several times, rather taken aback by the torrent of words.

"Aidan tells me that you love to read. I have been enjoying books on French military strategy. What is your favorite reading?"

Realizing she was staring, Gwen hesitantly opened her mouth while she tried to follow the many paths the young baroness had begun. "I favor the Ancient Greeks. Aristotle. Homer."

Her betrothed emitted a purr of pleasure, glancing at her in appreciation.

Lily nodded. "That is quite beyond my language skills. Aidan and Sophia are far more studious than me. I have to use a dictionary to study in French, but it must be fascinating."

The baroness glanced over at her father in a strange manner, her countenance serious when she turned back to face Gwen. "Welcome to the family. Whatever the future brings, I am thrilled to have you as a sister."

Then the young woman gave her a clumsy embrace before stepping away. Gwen felt practically winded by the exchange. Aidan's sister might be no larger than a schoolgirl, but she certainly had infinite zest. Her personality was much larger than her physical stature.

Finally, Aidan walked Gwen over to greet his parents, where Gwen was surprised to find that they had been joined by an elderly servant. The old woman was dressed as a maid, with wispy white hair in a halo around her head and a mobcap practically falling off. Lady Moreland greeted Gwen, then turned to fix the servant's cap.

Aidan brought Gwen to a halt in front of the servant without comment. Lady Moreland leaned over and shrieked into the old woman's ear, causing Gwen to flinch in surprise. "THIS IS MASTER AIDAN'S BRIDE!"

The servant blinked filmy eyes, slowly focusing on Gwen and smiling with a clumsy curtsy.

"This is my father's nursemaid. Nancy helped raise us and has acted as Lily's companion until recently. My parents thought she would enjoy attending this morning."

Gwen experienced a surge of affinity for the Abbott family in that moment. Apparently, the Smythes and the Abbotts had something in common. They both appreciated their close family retainers.

Lady Moreland must have read her thoughts. "Where is that odd lady's maid of yours? Does she not wish to attend your vows?"

Gwen realized that she and Octavia must have misread Lady Moreland's reaction when they had first met. She beamed. "I shall ring for her."

"Yes, my dear. We should not make the vicar wait too long. I am sure he has work to attend to."

Octavia was summoned, and Gwen looked about in surprised awe. So many important new relations, and they were all so welcoming and pleasant. Lord Filminster seemed reserved, but that could simply be his personality. Perhaps this was all going to turn out to be better than she had hoped for. Aidan had been throwing her glances of admiration, his eyes lingering on her lips as if he, too, were thinking of their first night together.

Despite her misgivings that something was bound to go

wrong, Gwen found herself daring to believe in her father's vision of the future. Perhaps this would become the love match she had once dreamed of.

* * *

WHILE THEY TOOK THEIR VOWS, Aidan felt both bliss and remorse. It had been quite a surprise when he had learned that the duke and duchess had returned, along with his cousin, Sophia, and her husband, the Earl of Saunton.

The linked families had all met yesterday, except for his own parents. Lord Moreland did not want to involve Lady Moreland in the discussion. Aidan agreed that there was no reason to distress his mother when they did not yet know the truth about the baron's murder.

It had soon become clear that their arrival was not merely to celebrate the wedding. It was a show of support for his bride in the event that Smythe was accused of murdering Brendan's father. Apparently, his brother-in-law had apprised them of the murder investigation.

The duchess had commiserated over the complexity of the situation, pointing out that she understood the troubles that a father could bring on his daughter. Aidan had not known that she had had a troubled relationship with the late baron, but he was aware that Brendan Ridley and the late baron had been estranged because the news sheets had reported on it.

There had been a lengthy discussion with all parties present at Ridley House, where the murder had taken place a month before. A rather grisly and sobering reminder of why Aidan was in this strange position.

Nevertheless, as he gazed down at Gwen in her soft blue dress, he could not bring himself to regret this wedding. He could only be thankful that Trafford was not in attendance to remind him of his shortcomings and future troubles if Smythe turned out to be the culprit.

Today was a complicated union of interests, but at this moment, Aidan was mostly anxious about what would happen this evening when he joined his bride in her bed. In the home of a potential murderer.

Frederick Smythe was clearly exuberant about the connections who visited his home this morning, grinning and rubbing his hands together in greedy, childlike joy. Aidan supposed any man would be overjoyed to scale the ladder of high society so abruptly, but there was an element of naked ambition to his behavior that was repellant.

Unfortunately, despite Aidan watching Smythe closely during the introductions, Smythe had displayed no telling reaction to meeting Lily and Filminster, which Aidan had hoped he might, given the circumstances.

"Wilt thou have this woman to thy wedded wife, to live together after God's ordinance in the holy estate of Matrimony? Wilt thou love her, comfort her, honor, and keep her, in sickness and in health; and, forsaking all other, keep thee only unto her, so long as ye both shall live?" intoned the vicar.

On the one hand, Aidan wished they could resolve the murder in order to ensure Lily's safety. On the other hand, it was with a sense of dread that he considered informing Gwen of such terrible news. It was obvious she was close to her father. He imagined if he found out that his own father had murdered a man—such a revelation would be utterly devastating. All he could do was resolve to remain at her side and be a good husband and partner, no matter what might come to light.

"I will," Aidan stated, his voice firm and confident.

And then, he could no longer think about the future because it had quietly arrived and his thoughts returned to their wedding night.

"Wilt thou have this man to thy wedded husband, to live together after God's ordinance in the holy estate of Matrimony? Wilt thou obey him, and serve him, love, honor, and keep him, in sickness and in health; and, forsaking all other, keep thee only unto him, so long as ye both shall live?"

He watched Gwen, who hesitated before responding in a shy voice, "I will."

Aidan was captivated by her radiance in the morning light shining through the great fan-arched windows and prayed that Trafford would uncover a different suspect.

He wanted his bride to experience a long and happy life, but as his eyes flickered over to Frederick Smythe, he could not help thinking that his new father-in-law craved these new connections to Aidan's family. It certainly lent credence to their suspicions that Gwen's father might become desperate at the idea that the late baron would prevent him from receiving his title and the accompanying inheritance.

The vicar laboriously completed the service. When it was over, Gwen looked up at Aidan, her blue eyes aglow. He smiled down at her. "We are wed."

She swallowed hard, licking her lips. "We are wed."

Aidan's thoughts once again turned to their wedding night, both anticipation and a creeping anxiety rolling through his gut.

They linked arms and led the wedding party from the drawing room for the wedding breakfast.

* * *

GWEN PICKED AT HER BREAKFAST, scarcely able to believe that she was finally married. Tonight her groom would come to her bedroom and they would begin their quest for children, a thought that sent a shiver of delight down her spine.

Aidan was resplendent. Tall, confident, and youthful as he debated with his sister on his other side.

You barely know him.

The whisper of her consciousness was an unwelcome disquiet.

I will learn about him.

The argumentative voice struck back without pause.

You do not know what kind of husband he will be. What if he is cruel?

Gwen shut her eyes for a brief second, attempting to squash the angst washing over her. She was simply nervous about her wedding night. Aidan had proved to be a thoughtful suitor, and if he had hidden intentions, he would not move into her father's home where her father could observe any untoward behavior. His family were all upstanding members of society—with perhaps the exception of Lord Saunton, but even he seemed a pleasant fellow.

"Are you done eating?" A childish voice interrupted her thoughts. Gwen looked up to find little Ethan gazing at her with large, hopeful eyes a little way down the table.

Lady Saunton smiled at Gwen in apology. "Hush, Ethan. Allow Lady Abbott to finish her meal in peace. She will not forget her promise to play."

"Why do I call him Cousin Aidan, but I must call her Lady Abbott?" Ethan pointed a diminutive finger at Gwen and her groom.

"It is up to Lady Abbott to decide how she wishes to be addressed. We only just met her this morning."

Gwen laughed. The lad was lively and charming—not at all what she was expecting when Octavia had told her of the Sauntons' situation. "Cousin Gwen would be acceptable to me."

Ethan beamed. "Are you finished eating yet, Cousin Gwen?"

She looked down at her plate and determined that her appetite was nowhere to be found. "Shall we play in the library?"

Ethan clapped his hands in excitement. "Yes!"

He scrambled out of his chair, running around the table to wait for Gwen.

Aidan leaned over to speak in a low voice near her ear. "You are part of the family now. Ethan will expect a game in all future encounters."

His words chased down her neck, a blaze of pleasure that swept through her body at his deep velvet voice. Gwen nodded in acknowledgment. "I do not mind."

Once she had risen, she took hold of Ethan's tiny hand and they walked together to the library. Gwen contemplated what it would be like to have a tyke of her own to take care of, and then realized in mild disbelief that it had become a genuine possibility.

Huzzah! I am married!

Several hours later, their party of guests began to depart. Gwen and Aidan stood with her father in the hall bidding them goodbye. His sister and her husband were the last to leave, Lily chattering in a nervous manner before once again embracing Gwen awkwardly.

Once the door closed, the three of them stood in silence until her father announced he would be in his study and left the two of them alone.

Gwen watched Aidan in a state of pensive anticipation. Would he kiss her now that they were alone?

Aidan blew out a breath, before turning to smile at her. He seemed ... nervous?

"I ... have a meeting at my club ... and I shall return later."

Disappointment washed over Gwen. He seemed reluctant

to be with her. The way he had stated his appointment sounded disingenuous, as if he sought a reason to leave.

Was he unhappy about their marriage born from scandal, after all? He had seemed committed to their union, even keen. Now he appeared desperate to get away.

"Um ... I shall ensure the servants have unpacked your things and ... await your return, then."

Aidan nodded, not quite making eye contact before he bowed in a manner that Gwen found rather formal, considering that they had just wed, before racing out the front door.

How was he going to reach his club without transport? Was he to catch a hackney?

Gwen held her arms at her sides and shook out her hands in agitation, feeling decidedly nervous and hoping that her groom was not regretting their vows. It was far too late to change course now.

* * *

AIDAN HAD WALKED SEVERAL MILES, attempting to clear his thoughts. It had not worked. He could not stop thinking about this evening and what was expected of him. The mechanics of it were not a mystery, but that did nothing to dispel his turmoil.

Sitting alone at a back table in his club, he stared down at the drink he had ordered, while other gentlemen imbibed in deep discussion and fine French brandy. Like the rest of the Abbotts, Aidan did not drink spirits in respect to his cousin, Sophia, but he occasionally ordered a brandy to placate the servers who would hover in apprehension at leaving him unserved.

Aidan briefly considered downing the brandy. Perhaps it

would help him fulfill his duties? Not that it should be an undue chore. He had imagined bedding Gwen numerous times since their encounter on the terrace that first night.

It was not a matter of want. It was a matter of how. Gwen was an innocent maiden who deserved something better than a clumsy fumbling.

"Little Breeches."

Aidan grunted in irritation. How he managed to choose the one club where he would encounter the aggravating Trafford... Looking up, he tensed his jaw and forced a stiff smile.

Trafford was dressed in a bronze jacquard coat over an ebony waistcoat. More ridiculous attire. Whatever the Earl of Stirling provided as an allowance, it was far too much if Trafford's expensive and foppish clothes were anything to judge by.

The other heir dropped into a chair across from him, sweeping a hand through the artful tangle of wheat curls at the crown of his head. Aidan rolled his eyes. There was nothing more affected than Trafford's two-toned hair. His valet obviously bleached the top, while the back and sides were a contrasting brown.

"I thought you wed today."

"I did."

"Then why are you here?"

Aidan rolled his shoulders, forcing himself back into the chair in a feigned pose of relaxation. "No reason."

"Is the whole ..." Trafford waved his hand in the air.

"No." The muddle with Gwen's father, and the fact that with Gwen's future secured, he would now continue his investigation into Smythe, was a constant burden upon his conscience. Today, however, that was the least of his concerns.

"Are you well, Little Breeches?"

Aidan snorted. Trafford was both sympathetic and insulting in the same breath.

"What are you doing here?"

The other heir broke eye contact, staring down at his lap. "I ... cannot be at home right now. There are ... issues."

Aidan cocked his head. Trafford was clearly uncomfortable. "Are you staying at the club?"

A nod was the only response. Aidan did not welcome the feeling of empathy that developed slowly, like a fire being lit in the hearth. Apparently, they both had problems they were not discussing.

Trafford shook his head as if to discard his thoughts before leaning on the table. "But what of you, Little Breeches? You appear melancholy and your bride awaits."

Aidan cleared his throat, dropping his gaze to the floor. "I think you know, considering your charming little sobriquet for me."

This pronouncement was followed by silence. A hand entered into his peripheral vision to grab his drink, which was pulled away. The sound of swallowing followed before Trafford finally spoke. "It is true, then?"

Aidan nodded, a flush of embarrassment heating his skin.

"You have never ... lain with a woman?"

He gave another reluctant nod.

Trafford sighed. "I suspected this was the case. There was no mention of women from anyone. There was even speculation that you ... Well, never mind that. I have seen how you look at Miss Sm—Lady Abbott—so it is painfully clear that you prefer women. Why have you never ...?"

By Jupiter, this is an uncomfortable subject!

Aidan had been away from England for so long that he had no close friends to speak with about it. The fact that he now discussed it with Trafford of all people was a waking nightmare, but somehow, considering the other man's vast experience, there was something mildly comforting about finally admitting the truth of it. "I believe that such an activity should be shared by two people who care for each other. I never met a woman I wished to commit to ... until Gwen."

Trafford was quiet for several seconds before huffing out a laugh. "A man with standards. I am calling for another drink so I may toast that which Diogenes only dreamed of—I have found an honest man."

Aidan groaned. "I am deceiving my bride, so not as honest as I would wish to be."

"That aside, I think it is endearing, Little Breeches. You come from an upstanding family and you have morals. There is nothing to be ashamed of."

"I am not ashamed. Unless"—Aidan leaned forward, his hands curling into fists—"you decide to share this conversation, in which case I will beat you within an inch of your life."

Trafford's lips quirked into a smile. "This conversation is our secret. I am just profoundly impressed with my ability to gather gossip. When I first asked around about you, the thought had crossed my mind, but I dismissed it as implausible. Turns out I am quite the investigator."

"Fantastic! Find a murderer other than Smythe, then. It would save Gwen a lot of pain if we find someone else with a motive."

"I am working on it. Ridley is rather dear to me, old chap."

Aidan rolled his shoulders once more. "I suppose I should go home and ..." He made a vague gesture that approximated the task at hand.

"There is a book in my rooms that might assist you."

Trafford jumped to his feet and swiftly left the area. Within a few minutes, he returned, retaking his seat and placing a leather-bound book on the table. Aidan picked it up and frowned in confusion.

"I am quite the scholar, Trafford, but even I do not read Sanskrit."

Trafford shook his head as if Aidan were an imbecile. Leaning over, he opened the book and began to flip through the pages. "There are illustrations, Little Breeches."

Aidan drew the book closer and scanned the images Trafford had revealed, growing hot under the collar when he realized what he was looking at. The figures were engaged in lewd and explicit activities.

"Is this legal?"

"The activities are, for the most part. The book itself—probably not."

"I know the mechanics of the deed. I do not need these." He pushed the book toward Trafford.

Trafford snickered and slid it back. "There are many different ways to accomplish the task. Trust me, and pay attention to the illustrations."

Aidan took the book and quickly pocketed it. He would hire a hackney and explore the images in privacy.

"Now, I shall impart some of my wisdom on the subject." Trafford's drawl was smug.

"Please do not."

"You want to know what I know, Little Breeches. Gwendolyn Abbott will be a very happy woman if you listen up."

Aidan groaned and considered his options—return home with a hazy idea of what was involved; return to the Abbott townhouse to question his father; or remain here and endure Trafford's explanations.

"Bloody hell, just make it painless."

Trafford tsked. "Do you want painless, or effective?"

Aidan dropped his head into his hands, mortified to receive lessons on carnal relations from the pompous coxcomb he could barely tolerate. "Effective, I suppose."

Trafford needed no further encouragement, launching into a detailed explanation of the female anatomy.

CHAPTER 10

"Love is composed of a single soul inhabiting two bodies."

Aristotle

* * *

Gwen was not sure what to do. It would appear her new husband had abandoned her, having left hours earlier. It was time to prepare for dinner, but she had envisioned that they would retire to her room earlier. In her azure gown.

Should she change for dinner, or keep her wedding gown on?

They were frivolous thoughts in lieu of the panic building in the pit of her stomach since Aidan had left so hurriedly. Gwen was growing more certain that he regretted their marriage, which was all the more painful to consider now that she had met all his relations.

She had enjoyed her afternoon with little Ethan and the adults. Usually, she spent time with the older people in society, the young women being rather spiteful toward her while the disinterest of the younger gentlemen had led to few conversations over the years.

Keeping company with intelligent men and women of an age with her, Gwen had become hopeful for the future. It seemed a whole new world was opening up. She anticipated future engagements with his extended family while she and Aidan started a new chapter of their own.

Gwen closed her wardrobe. She had been staring into it for several minutes and still not reached a decision.

"He hates being married to me."

"Nonsense!" Octavia retorted quickly, but there was a note of hesitation in her tone. "He ... just had ... something ... important to do ... someone important to see."

Buttercup whined in agreement, sitting at Octavia's heels and her brown eyes contemplating Gwen with interest.

"On our wedding day?"

Octavia turned away, clearly at a loss. The dog remained seated, her gaze never leaving Gwen, who shifted around the room restlessly to pick up items and then place them back where she found them. Buttercup watched on, her little head cocked to one side, but she made no remarks about the agitated behavior of her new mistress.

"Should I change for dinner?"

"Perhaps I should bring up a tray?"

Gwen nodded. Her father had already stated he would not be available for dinner, so she would be eating alone at the dining table, while she worried about Aidan's continued absence, if she went downstairs. An unappealing prospect.

Octavia left, and Gwen went to sit at the window. Picking up her copy of *The Odyssey*, she attempted to focus on Homer's epic poem before tossing the book back on the side table. Buttercup followed her to settle heavily upon her slippered feet as if to remark that Gwen needed to calm herself.

Have I made a mistake?

It was disheartening to think such thoughts within hours of their vows. It would have been nice if it had taken several days for the first doubts to set in.

Gwen drummed her fingers on the plump stuffing of her favorite armchair. Sitting here provided a view of the garden, with the Thames twinkling beyond the lawn. It might be her father's only remaining property, but it was a beauty, an oasis within London that she would miss when she and Aidan moved to their new home.

The indigo wingback seat had once belonged to her mother, and she planned to take it with her because of the comfort it brought her to remember the times they had spent together.

Mama would tell me to buck up and take action.

But how? She did not even know where Aidan was. And noblewomen did not run about Town, left to their own devices.

Although ...

She was married. That meant she had more freedoms like that horrible Milly. Perhaps it was time to storm some clubs and find her missing groom?

Gwen gently slipped her feet from under the resting Buttercup and stood up, resolved to take some sort of action. For years she had retreated into her library, away from the unwarranted aggression that had begun in school, but this was her chance to have a babe of her own. To build a life.

She strode toward the door, resolute that she would wait no longer. Aidan needed to do his duty and then he could have all the regrets he desired once she was increasing.

Whipping open the door, she let out a shriek when she found Aidan facing her on the other side. He stood with no boots or stockings, merely his buckskin breeches, a shirt, and his coat. Even his waistcoat was missing. The tanned column of his throat exposed, and his large naked feet upon the floor, were shocking to behold.

Clapping a hand over her hammering heart, Gwen clung to the door.

"Where have you been?" The cry was out before she could sort out her thoughts at his sudden appearance.

"Thinking about you."

Her brows drew together. It was tempting to believe his words, but that did not make sense, did it?

"What does that mean—that you were thinking of me?"

Aidan drew a deep breath. "I was considering the honor of joining you in your bed."

The very air in her lungs froze as his eyes dropped to her lips with a sweep of deep brown lashes. He lowered his voice, speaking in a deep and pleasurable tone like a fine wine sweetened with a drop of honey. "O Helena, goddess, nymph, perfect, divine! To what, my love, shall I compare thine eyne? Thy lips, those kissing cherries, tempting grow!"

A low growl emitted from the region of her ankles. Both she and Aidan looked down, startled.

"You have a dog," he said in a surprised tone.

"Buttercup. I rescued her from a halfpenny showman last week after I saw him kick her in the ribs."

He arched an eyebrow in response, staring down at the bristling canine at her feet. "She has thoughts about me entering your room."

It was true. Buttercup had her teeth bared and was growling from the back of her throat.

"I think she wishes to protect you."

Gwen smiled at Buttercup's antics, musing that animals were much simpler than humans. "I am afraid you have to leave now, girl." Gwen leaned over to take hold of Buttercup and gently sweep the dog out into the hall. When she looked up, Aidan's eyes were back on her.

Gwen's breath quickened to huffing pants as her blood heated in response to the naked desire on Aidan's face. His recital of *A Midsummer Night's Dream* had been intoxicating, and she had never dreamed of hearing such exquisite words directed toward her.

Gwen licked her lips, noticing how his gaze followed the movement and he, too, became flushed and his breathing frayed. A muscled arm wrapped around her waist, pulling her against his long, hard body before he drove them into her room.

Reaching behind him, Aidan groped around for the edge of the door, his gaze never leaving her face as he shut it firmly behind him and his lips descended. Gwen's lids fell shut as she tilted her chin up to meet his kiss.

When their mouths made contact, it was as electric as rubbing silk over a glass rod, their lips fusing together as if finally finding their purpose. To join, to become one, to … rip each other's clothes from their bodies.

Even as their tongues tangled together, Gwen distantly realized that there were no longer any barriers. Their previous kisses had been muted compared to the fire that was now blazing between them, with the knowledge that they were finally alone and there was no longer any reason to hold back their passions.

Growling caused them to raise their heads and look about. Buttercup had apparently re-entered the room before the door had been shut. A silly oversight to not have closed it right away, Gwen supposed.

Aidan huffed impatiently, turning to open the door. Gwen quickly dropped down and pushed the bristling Buttercup out the door, holding the dog with a firm hand while Aidan carefully closed it once more, until only a small gap remained. She pulled her hand back in, which was followed by a decisive click.

A short, rough bark sounded from the other side, followed by scampering paws to announce the little dog's departure from the family hall.

Gwen stood up, quickly returning to passion as her hands came up to fumble with Aidan's lapels. Desperate to finally place her hands upon his broad chest with only thin linen to defend him from her exploration, she tugged at his wool coat.

"Citrus," he mumbled, before sliding his lips across her cheek. Reaching the side of her face, he drew on her earlobe to suckle. Sensation burst in every direction as Gwen's head dropped back, and she moaned in agonized pleasure as his tongue gently circled and his teeth nipped.

"Faith!" she cried out, bucking against him when he slid his lips down her neck to lick at the throbbing pulse at the base of her throat.

Gwen yanked at his obstinate coat, which immediately got stuck over his arms. Aidan gave a husky laugh, shaking the garment off so it fell to the floor. Reaching up, she spread her trembling hands across the chest that had invaded her dreams since their moonlight interlude.

Aidan's lips came back up to meet hers, his hand cupping the back of her head as he leaned in to sip deeply. He was a ravenous beast, exploring her mouth thoroughly while his free hand swept down her body to cup a buttock. He pulled her firmly against his body, revealing the rigid length in the region of his falls pressing against her mound. Heat rose in flames from her core to engulf her belly, and she pressed ever closer.

Gwen vaguely registered a keening sound, like a wild animal in distress, before realizing it was her! She was moaning like a wounded beast, but even as the thought entered her head, it was gone. Wiped away by Aidan, reaching down to hoist her into his strong arms without the slightest sign of strain. Their lips never parted as he strode across the room to deposit her on the bed and climb in beside her, leaning over so that their mouths remained consumed in the manner of starving men presented with a feast.

When Aidan finally lifted his head to gaze down at her with chocolate brown eyes glazed with passion, his face revealed his raw ardor and Gwen was brought back to the magic of their first meeting on the terrace. When reality had departed and the dream of two people, perfectly matched, awed by the beauty of the night, had discovered momentous synchronism. As if the very words of Aristotle had echoed down the ages to materialize in the form of a single soul inhabiting two bodies.

She and Aidan, somehow one within the grand infinite universe. The very gods had swung the hands of fate to bring them together as they were meant to be.

Aidan pulled away before taking hold of the hem of his shirt to yank it off and throw it aside. Gwen watched in fascination, lifting a hand to trace over the strong musculature of his chest and brush through the crisp curling of hair dusting his bronzed skin. Her gaze came back to meet his, and she marveled at how beautiful and empowered her new husband made her feel with his admiring glances and the sweet poetry that he recited so well.

"You are so utterly beautiful, Gwen Abbott," he breathed, groaning as her hand brushed ever lower to follow the trail of hair arrowing down to his buckskins. Closing his eyes in exquisite agony, he reached up to take the errant hand in his own.

When he reopened his lids, his blazing brown irises found her, and Gwen quite lost the will to draw air into her lungs.

"It is my turn, sweetheart."

His head lowered to trail kisses down her neck to the top

of her bodice, his tongue lapping at her exposed skin. His arms came round her, and she felt him fumbling with the buttons. Curling her arms around his neck, she rose up to assist him, and soon he was tugging the gown off. Gwen lifted her hips, brushing against him as he pulled the gown down over her legs and sent it sliding to the floor. Bearing back to lean on his haunches, kneeling beside her, Aidan swept burning eyes over her before extending a hand to run it over her stays.

"It will be easier to undress me if I am on top," she whispered hoarsely.

Aidan shut his eyes, licking his lips. "Yes," he said, taking hold of her and making her yelp in surprise when he suddenly rolled, pulling her along with him until their positions were reversed.

It was decadent and delicious. Her body layered over his so she could feel every indent and curve of his muscles, his thighs, and ... the evidence of his interest. Biting her lip, Gwen lowered her knees on either side of his powerful thighs to straddle him before slowly rising up. Her intimate muscles clenched as her melting core made contact with his erection through his breeches. He watched her from his new position, his hands running over her flared hips and up to cup her breasts through the stays.

Aidan swallowed, riveted, as Gwen reached behind her to loosen the tapes. She looked down to see what had caught his attention so and realized her breasts were pushed forward and up. Feeling like Venus rising from the waves, she slowly peeled the stays from her bosom, turning her torso to flick them to the floor.

Her groom groaned loudly, his eyes focused on the jutting points of her nipples now visible through the linen of her shift. Gwen briefly toyed with shyness before reaching a decision to revel in her power as a desirable woman. His rigid length between her legs, his falls scraping against her pulsing center, brooked no argument regarding his interest. Aidan wanted her.

Her!

Gwen, Gwen the Spotted Giraffe had an intelligent and handsome gentleman splayed out beneath her with lust in his eyes.

Aidan's hands came back down on her hips, languidly sliding up over her belly to come to a rest again below her unbound breasts. They stared at each other for several heart-pounding seconds.

"Take down your hair, Venus."

Gwen raised her shaking hands, pulling out her pins and throwing them toward the floor. Aidan watched as she unfurled her locks, draping them over both shoulders while never breaking eye contact.

He sighed deeply, then finally shifted up to caress her rounded breasts with his hot palms. Aidan kneaded gently, his eyes remaining fixed on hers with flags of color across his cheeks and a heaving chest, before brushing his thumbs over the turgid tips.

Gwen threw her head back, and she exhaled in a guttural moan, overcome by the revelations of making love. Beneath her, Aidan rocked his hips, brushing against her slickened pearl at the apex of her slit which cascaded overwhelming waves of pleasure in chaotic abandon.

* * *

BEING FORCED to listen to lessons on carnal relations from Trafford had been torturous. The conversation, on one hand, made him exceptionally ill at ease. On the other hand, the thought of sharing the experiences Trafford had described with Gwen—to be in her bed over her, underneath her, or behind her—was the most alluring notion he could conceive of.

Feeling her lithe form bucking in his lap, observing her arousal as he gently stroked her hardened nipples, Aidan could not be sure he could complete this task successfully. He was raging heat and fractured breathing, harder than he had ever been, and desperate to join with the incredible woman who seemed to be unaware that she was riding him in her excitement.

If he had any hope of bringing her to completion before him, he had to change their positions quickly. Aidan dropped his hands to grab hold of her thin shift, sitting up so he could peel it off her body. Soon Gwen was naked before his eyes, and he greedily took in the sight of her tawny nipples, turning his head to take one into his mouth. Gwen bucked even harder, rubbing against him in a manner that almost made him spend. Grabbing one of her hips, he stilled her motion as he swirled the areola and flicked the nipple once more. Gwen surged forward, pushing her breast against him while tugging on his head.

Aidan realized he could not restrain himself in this position any longer, despite the precaution he had taken before entering Gwen's room. An embarrassing preliminary activity to secure his stamina for the coming exertions that had involved intimate thoughts of his bride naked in his bed. Reality far exceeded his imagination.

His arm banded around her waist, and he gently lowered her back, turning to lick the other pleading nipple as he pulled back onto his knees and lowered her down onto the counterpane.

Once he had her on her back, the fire in his loins banked just a little. Enough to trail down her belly until his mouth was hovering over her mound. He caressed a shaved cheek over the silky red curls that shielded her from his gaze, breathing in the scent of her salty sweetness before extending his tongue to sweep over her slit and find the nub that controlled her pleasure.

A loud wail ensued, and Aidan chuckled and winced simultaneously. If Smythe or his servants entered the family hall, they would quickly depart when they overheard the loud antics in Gwen's bedroom.

Doing his best not to hear Trafford's voice instructing him as he carried out the suggested methods, Aidan swirled his tongue over Gwen's swollen pearl, flicking and sweeping rhythmically while she keened and moaned, her legs open in invitation as he invaded her most private region with determined lapping.

Her breathing grew more and more labored, her hips moving urgently on the bed until, finally, she wailed loudly once more and stiffened with her hips thrust up toward his questing mouth.

Like the tide gently receding from the shore, she relaxed, falling back onto the bed as her panting slowed. Aidan pulled away, stumbling onto the floor to work the buttons of his buckskins. On the bed, Gwen turned her head and languidly opened her eyes to watch him. Her eyes focused on the straining against his falls, curiosity in her expression.

Aidan finally got the breeches undone, pushing them and his small clothes over his hips to reveal his hardened cock. Gwen's eyes widened, and she began to reach out a hand, but Aidan drew back in mild alarm. He needed to finish this, and if she touched him ...

He stepped out of the pool of garments, returning to lower himself over her flushed body and quickly overcome at the softness of her creamy skin against him. The golden freckles he had dreamed about spread in every direction, and he wished he had the patience to trace every one with his mouth, but his need to join with her was all he could think about.

"This might hurt, sweetheart."

Her eyes were a vivid blue when she nodded. "I know."

Aidan took his length in hand, carefully guiding himself to her honeyed entrance, slick with arousal from his ministrations, and he found himself headily proud of his achievement. That he had brought her mindless, keening pleasure. However he completed this, he had succeeded in bringing his Venus to the peaks of pleasure.

Gwen was a passionate woman, highly responsive to his prior kisses and to his inexperienced efforts, which was profoundly gratifying. Trafford had assured him that bringing her to her peak before completing the deed would ease what was to follow, and Aidan hoped he was right because he hated the thought of causing her pain.

Pushing forward, he invaded her quivering channel as Gwen gasped and shut her eyes tightly, seating himself all the way inside her before coming to a complete stop.

Lands! Stopping was the hardest thing he had ever done! Feeling her wrapped tightly around him, at once soft and tight, hot and wet, he wanted to thrust decisively and find his pleasure. He had never experienced such a euphoria, finally making love to a woman but being forced to remain still.

Aidan was a hot-blooded male. He had always been interested in females, but he had never been able to bring himself to take advantage of any of the women he had encountered in the past. It should mean something, and women were vulnerable within their society. The idea of paying coin had been abhorrent, the concept of keeping a mistress despicable. He could not father bastard children with a woman he claimed to have affection for, as did many men of their set. And if he cared for a woman, he could not, of course, take advantage of her or ruin her. The only honorable option had been to wait until he found a true mate, and then wed her. Something which had been far from his mind until the night he had laid eyes on Gwen.

When meeting her later on the terrace and discovering that her ravishing exterior was nothing to the sharp intellect beneath, Aidan had been utterly captivated. He knew he had found the woman he wanted to marry and bed, even as circumstances forced their union along.

Beneath him—around him—Gwen relaxed, and Aidan needed no further encouragement. He gently withdrew and thrust forward, wanting to throw his head back and howl at the wonder of making love to the magnificent woman who had agreed to be his wife. The urge to thrust wildly had to be beaten back with an iron will.

Beneath him, Gwen moaned as she gyrated her hips and her eyes flickered open. "I need you" was all she said before her eyes closed once more.

Aidan groaned and thrust, and when she did not complain but moaned in unison, it was all the invitation Aidan needed. He surged in and out, harder than he had ever been, rushing to the peak of intense ecstasy. Gwen moaned again, raking her fingernails over his back and gyrating her hips urgently against him as they both sought their final pleasure.

So it was that Gwen wailed once more, just as Aidan hit his peak and spent inside her in a flood of heat, holding himself above her as he discovered the purest ecstasy. When the ability to process thought returned, he rolled over, so that Gwen lay draped over him and they both sought their breath.

As his pulse returned to normal, Aidan contemplated the hell that he was in. He had married the most engrossing woman he had ever encountered, but there was a distinct possibility that he would soon break the very worst of news to her and shatter her world.

It was imperative that he forge a strong connection with her so he might assist her with her future troubles when the time came to do so.

* * *

AFTER AIDAN HAD FOUND the washbasin and cleaned both of them, Gwen rested in the crook of his arm with her head against his chest. She listened in amazed satisfaction at the beat of his heart, while her husband toyed with locks of her hair.

It was the only time they made love that night, Aidan insisting they needed to be restrained for her first time.

Eventually he rose to find a dinner tray waiting outside the door, and Gwen had watched him walk across the room with an unfamiliar sense of proprietorship, observing his muscular buttocks as he made his way.

They were married! For the rest of her days, she would have this man.

When Aidan rejoined her in bed, feeding her bits of fruit from the tray, he quoted random bits of poetry. Lines about admiration and beauty from an array of great writers, and Gwen listened in avid awe.

Aidan was clever, admiring, and complimentary. She had never received such attentions from a gentleman before, and several times through the pursuant hours, she wanted to pinch herself to ensure it was not all a lovely dream. But the idea of waking up to her old life was too painful to consider, so she never attempted the pinch.

Gwen wanted this with Aidan. She wanted to be the center of his world and hear his adoring words spoken in his deep voice. To forge a partnership, to share their darkest secrets, and to provide mutual solace in their future troubles. To touch him and kiss him as they did several times, and to fall asleep in his arms.

As sleep stole over her like the arrival of the night once the sun has set, Gwen moved closer to him, wrapping an arm around his naked waist and mumbling the words that had been circling her mind since she had found him at her door.

"I love you," she said as she fell into a deep sleep.

CHAPTER 11

"The law is reason, free from passion."

Aristotle

* * *

AUGUST 26, 1821

With the arrival of dawn, Aidan opened his eyes. Gwen was still curled in his arms, and he wished he could remain here and pretend that there was no wrong in the world. That Lily was safe, that the baron had not been murdered, and that Smythe was not probably the killer.

But if not for those intrinsic truths, he would never have met Gwen. A thought that made his heart skip a beat in his chest. Raising a hand, he gently brushed her hair from her face and thought about how happy he was to have met her.

So be it. If this was his challenge, he would deal with it.

Somehow he would hold on to Gwen and find the killer, even if it was Smythe.

He recalled the words she had mumbled against his skin as she had fallen asleep.

Pressing a kiss against her forehead, he whispered a vow. "I will endeavor to be worthy of your love. I promise this to you, Gwen Abbott."

Aidan gently rolled Gwen back onto her pillow, where she shifted around in her sleep before settling back down. Carefully he rose from the bed, dressing in his clothes that were divested across the floor. He did not fail to notice that there were two empty spaces on Gwen's wall where paintings once hung. Yet more sold-off valuables, he assumed.

Loping to the door, careful not to disturb his slumbering bride, Aidan cracked it open then slipped out into the hall where he found Buttercup waiting with bared teeth. Low growling informed him of his lack of welcome. Aidan swung the door wider, encouraging the animal to enter Gwen's room. "Go, Buttercup. Go find Gwen."

The dog did not need any further encouragement. She scampered in and took a leap to land on the side of the bed where Aidan had slept. Circling about for a moment, Buttercup collapsed down with her head tucked over one of her paws to stare at his sleeping bride.

Pulling the door closed, Aidan heard a creak behind him. Spinning around, he saw his father-in-law had come around the corner from the stairs.

"Mr. Smythe?"

Gwen's father looked up with a start, furtively stuffing a notebook into his pocket and his face spreading into his customary wide grin.

"Aidan, my boy. It is a fine morning, I tell you. I have already been up and taking in the splendor of the sunrise."

He kept his face composed, but Aidan noted that Smythe

had to be lying. He was wearing the same clothes from the day before. It would appear the man was only just coming to bed. There had been no mention of attending societal events after the wedding, so the only conclusion to reach was that Smythe was hiding where he had been all night.

It was a chilling reminder of why Aidan had orchestrated moving into the Smythe home. He was here to investigate this man up close, and now that he had taken care of his obligations with Gwen, it was time to return to his mission.

Aidan fought down a frisson of frustration when Smythe passed him to enter his own rooms down the hall. If only Aidan had not been obsessing over making love to Gwen, he might have been here to follow Smythe and find out what his father-in-law was up to, but instead he had wasted hours the day before walking through London, dillydallying at his clubs, and receiving instruction from Trafford on carnal relations.

He would have to be more attentive, Aidan resolved. If he was ever going to sort out this muddle with Lily and Filminster, he would need to discover what Smythe was doing.

Aidan strode off in disappointment, lamenting lost opportunities and his wonderful night with Gwen forgotten with the bitter reminder that a killer was on the loose and Lily was relying on him to investigate Smythe.

* * *

GWEN WOKE up and stretched out. Her wedding night had been far more than she had hoped for. Romantic poetry, making love, melting kisses, and soft caresses.

Turning over, she was disappointed to find she was all alone except for Buttercup. Aidan must have let her back into the room when he had left. The dog was asleep, with her long ears splayed out on the coverlet. Gwen smiled fondly.

Then she recalled her last words before sleep had overtaken her. She sat up in alarm, grabbing the sheet to cover her naked body.

Did I tell Aidan that I love him?

It could have been a dream. She had no clear recollection of making the decision to say it. It had just popped into her head. But perhaps she had simply drifted into slumber and it had been a figment of her imagination.

But had Aidan pulled her closer into his embrace?

Zounds! What a disaster if she had mumbled the words to him. It was too soon!

Gwen scrambled out of bed, ringing the bell to summon Octavia and racing around the room to wash up. She needed to locate her husband and then observe his reaction to her this morning.

Buttercup raised her head, drowsy eyes watching Gwen with a mild interest before lowering down to fall back to sleep.

Why? Why would I do that? We barely know each other!

If she had said it, Aidan would think she was a weak-minded fool. How could she possibly declare her love so soon into their marriage? They had only interacted ... Gwen counted out the number of times they had met.

If the moonlight bewitchment and the offer of marriage were two separate incidents, which seemed like a stretch, she had only met with him ... two ... three ... four times, and then their wedding night would be the fifth.

Ye gods! He thinks I am a silly, bird-witted little girl!

Octavia knocked at the door, and Gwen called out for her to enter. Harried, she gestured at the wardrobe as she sponged herself clean at the washbasin. "I must find my husband!"

Her lady's maid puckered her forehead in confusion but complied, pulling out a gown, clean shift, and stockings, and then picking up Gwen's stays from the floor without comment. Gwen blushed, averting her eyes while she finished washing up. What was there to say in such a situation?

She quickly drew on the stockings and pulled the shift over her head. Octavia assisted her with the stays, which took longer than expected because Gwen was panting with the anxiety to depart her room and ensure Aidan was not appalled with her unsolicited words.

Finally, they had her gown done up and Gwen stormed from the room without explanation for her haste and with her hair flying loose. Buttercup dropped down from the bed and chased after her, a pattering of paws announcing her company as Gwen raced down to find Aidan.

When she reached downstairs, Gwen searched through the rooms, finally finding Aidan at the breakfast table with a plate of eggs and ham. He had a distant expression on his face, and his eyes were focused on the garden outside the window, while his fork was paused midair as if he had forgotten what he was about.

"Aidan?"

He did not respond.

"Aidan?"

He started, his gaze swinging to find her.

"Good morning," he said before dropping his fork to raise a cup of coffee to his lips.

Gwen bit her lip. He seemed ... distant. "How are you this morning?"

It took several seconds for him to respond with a "Hmm?"

"How are you this morning?"

The bemused expression returned to his face. "Fine, fine. How are you?" Aidan smiled, but it did not reach his eyes and his thoughts were obviously occupied.

Gwen clenched her fists, her stomach rolling with anxiety. This was not good. She must have upset him by declaring her feelings. It was clear that things were not as they were the night before.

Panic set in. They had shared the perfect evening. Why did she have to ruin it with maudlin sentiment? Why could she not allow their new marriage to breathe and develop naturally?

She walked forward and took a seat by his side, determined to find a way to bridge the *faux pas*. Buttercup followed her under the table and sat down upon Gwen's feet. A footman brought the usual plate of cut fruit that she preferred, placing it on the table in front of her. Gwen stared at it, trying to think what to say. Should she bring up what she had said to apologize or simply pretend it had never happened?

"Shall we do something together today?"

Aidan took a moment to respond, as if his mind was elsewhere. "I am afraid that will not work today. I ... have plans."

Gwen used her fork to push a strawberry around her plate. He was so different from their night together. She had been the center of his world after he had arrived at her door, but now he was reserved. This was all so new to her, and she had no ideas on how to bring back the rapport of the night before.

"Oh."

"I might not be here for dinner. I have some things to take care of today."

Gwen was hit with a wave of desperation. Buttercup shifted about, as if sensing her agitation. Leaning over, she whispered to prevent the servant from overhearing. "Will you come to my room tonight?"

Please say yes. Please, please say yes.

"We shall see what time I return."

Gwen's heart fell. Soon Aidan rose to leave the breakfast room, leaving Gwen to consider her options. It was clear Aidan must be repulsed by her premature announcement of her feelings, but there must be a way to overcome the awkwardness she had created?

Buttercup whined from behind the tablecloth as if to commiserate with Gwen's misery.

Aidan had been wonderful while she had been ... too damn needy. It was clear that she was scaring him away.

* * *

AIDAN FINGERED the letter in his pocket. Filminster was cryptic as ever, presumably fearing to commit the details to the page, but Aidan understood what it meant. It was time for him to take action and discover what Smythe was up to.

It happened again. I have doubled the guards. - Filminster

Ridley House was still being watched, and someone had attempted to breach his sister's home again. The only consolation was that there were men there to protect her from harm.

He headed to the library, trying to think what to do. Smythe was still up in his rooms, presumably getting some sleep after being out all night, which only confirmed Aidan's suspicions he had been out.

Perhaps I could try to search his study once more?

It seemed pointless, but perhaps something new would turn up. Aidan was growing more certain that he should follow his father-in-law. Perhaps Smythe would leave his home again this afternoon and Aidan could find out what he was about?

That did not leave Aidan with many options. He supposed he could visit Ridley House to find out what had happened exactly, and then return to the Smythe home in time to see if Smythe took off on his errands again.

This seemed like the only course of action available. He could not just pace up and down in the library for several hours while Smythe was upstairs asleep.

His mind made up, he returned to the hall to order his mount prepared. When he reached the entry hall it was to find the butler engaging with two workmen. They were carefully lifting the grand painting hanging above the primary staircase, a large landscape of English ladies of the last century promenading in their finery. Lavish hats boasted ruffles and lace, perched on powdered hair while dogs ran around their feet. It appeared to be set in one of the parks of London, perhaps St. James's.

And it was clearly valuable, possibly a Gainsborough.

"What is this, Jenson?"

The butler, a slim man in his fifties with iron-gray hair, glanced over his shoulder, then quickly turned back to the task at hand as the three men slowly lowered the heavy, gilded frame to the floor. Ordinarily, a gentleman would not demand such information from another's household staff, but Aidan was the heir to a viscount, so few would have the temerity to deny him.

"Mr. Smythe has sold the painting, and these men are here to collect it."

Aidan ran a hand through his hair, fighting back a growl of fuming frustration.

Smythe must be at the bottom of this!

The ongoing liquidation of assets coincided with both the murder and the recent attempts to breach Ridley House. Both reeked of desperation. A killer who needed to hide evidence of his dastardly deeds and obtain funds for some mysterious reason. Covering up the murder of a peer would cost coin. There were men being paid to watch Ridley House, and the now-deceased footman who had attacked Lily weeks earlier had hidden quite a stash in his things.

Most of Gwen's dowry had been forfeited in light of the scandal, the Abbotts providing for her and their future progeny in the marriage contracts. Something Smythe had insisted on, and his own father had acquiesced to. Yet another indication that Smythe was obsessed with obtaining funds for some undisclosed reason.

As a result, Smythe had not been in a position to deny Aidan access to his residence because his contribution to Gwen's future had been practically non-existent.

Smythe's perfidy was on full display, and it was imperative that Aidan prove it and end this threat. If anything happened to Lily or her husband, the guilt would be too much to bear.

CHAPTER 12

"At his best, man is the noblest of all animals; separated from law and justice he is the worst."

Aristotle

* * *

Gwen paced up and down in the library, doing her best to wear a hole into the wooden boards of the floor. They once had a luxurious Aubusson rug in here, but her father had had it taken away the month before, which was why her footfalls were not dampened by its wool pile.

She was stuck in a strange netherworld. Her new life had not truly begun because she was still residing in her father's house, which was becoming unrecognizable, piece by piece. When she and Aidan moved into their own residence, surely an improved life would arise?

Stomp, stomp, stomp.

Patter, patter, patter.

Buttercup evidently thought the pacing was some sort of game, chasing along behind Gwen.

But they were not to move for several more weeks, and Gwen needed to find a way to repair her error soon or their marriage would begin poorly. Aidan must be repelled by her naïve statement, but there had to be something she could do to return them to the state of bliss from the night before.

She walked toward the towering shelves, then turned.

Stomp, stomp, stomp.

Patter, patter, patter.

She headed back toward the spindly library table where she preferred to work. Gwen mused that she did not sound like a spotted giraffe when she walked back and forth. Rather, she was a herd of elephants trampling the undergrowth in her frazzled state.

"Lady Moreland is here."

She halted so quickly she nearly lost her balance. "What?"

Octavia repeated herself. "Lady Moreland's here."

Gwen glared at her, but Octavia just threw up her hands as if to say she had no more information to impart—a viscountess had come to call and Octavia could do naught to change it.

Huffing, Gwen considered the news. Truthfully, she had nothing useful to do but worry over where Aidan was. How could she mend matters between them, while waiting for the time when they would leave to start their new life together?

Perhaps a distracting visit was just the thing to occupy her agitated thoughts. Perhaps Lady Moreland might provide some insight that would assist Gwen in understanding Aidan better. Perhaps she had no choice but to receive her new mother-in-law, so why was she still standing about considering her lack of options?

"Where is she?"

Octavia scowled, as if talking to a fool. "In the drawing room, of course."

"Bring a tea tray?"

The servant nodded. "Come, Buttercup." She patted her leg to encourage the dog to walk with her, the two of them sweeping out of sight.

Gwen drew a fortifying breath, smoothed her hair and then her gown, and when she was certain she was not a sight, she left the library. Out in the hall, she stopped in front of a gilt-framed mirror, one of the few left in their home, to verify she was put together, then headed into the drawing room.

Lady Moreland was standing by the fireplace, evidently lost in thought. Her mother-in-law was an astute dresser, wearing fashionable colors that suited her complexion and coloring to perfection. Saffron, Egyptian Brown, Carmelite ... all perfectly matched to an impeccable woman of fashion.

The older woman had been confident and composed in all their earlier encounters, but she seemed to be woolgathering at that moment.

"Lady Moreland?"

Aidan's mother started, then turned to Gwen. A smile spread over her handsome face. "Gwen, please. Call me Mama Abbott. We are family, dear."

"I have a tea tray coming, Mama Abbott."

"Then I suppose we shall sit and talk."

Gwen smiled politely, not sure what she was doing here, but she moved to take a seat across from her.

"I am not sure what I am doing here."

Gwen blinked. It was like having her thoughts pulled out of her head. She waited.

"Lord Moreland and I are leaving London, and I have been thinking about you and Aidan."

Gwen nodded in acknowledgment. She was aware that

Aidan's parents were headed to their country seat now that the wedding was a *fait accompli*.

"Perhaps when I return to London, you will have good news for me." Lady Moreland gestured to her belly. Gwen felt the heat of a blush spreading over her face.

"It is just that since Lily's attack, I feel that my family is keeping secrets from me and I cannot stop thinking about what the future might bring."

Gwen straightened, certain she had misheard her mother-in-law.

"Lily's attack?"

Lady Moreland had been staring down at her hands as she spoke, smoothing her skirts in a distracted manner. She raised her head at Gwen's question. "Last month. Lily was attacked by one of the footmen after she discovered his involvement in the baron's murder."

Gwen surreptitiously pinched herself on the leg. Just to be certain that she was awake, and this was not some strange bad dream. The creeping suspicion that she was asleep was a common manifestation since her first meeting with Aidan, it would seem.

"The baron's murder …" Gwen sifted through her memories. "You mean the late Lord Filminster, who was found dead last month?"

Lady Moreland nodded. "That is correct. One of the footmen was hired by the killer, and Lily figured it out, so he attacked her. If it were not for the butler, she could have been killed."

Gwen gasped. "I have heard nothing of it."

Her mother-in-law dabbed at her eyes with her forefinger. "It was all rather shocking, but only the family knows of it. It is only right you be aware because you are family now, dear."

Gwen nodded in awe. "Thank you."

"It is a frightening prospect, to think of losing a child. I find myself thinking of you this morning. I wanted to assure myself ... that you would take care of my boy. He has carried such a burden of guilt since Lily was ruined. He feels he should have been with her that night, you see."

Gwen did not see. She had no clue what her mother-in-law was speaking of. Aidan was burdened with guilt over Lily's ruin? Was that why he had offered to marry Gwen when they had been discovered together on the terrace?

"Which night?"

"The night of the coronation, when Lord Filminster was murdered. Lily stepped forward as an alibi to Brendan Ridley, stating she had spent the night with him. She did not, of course. Lily is a young lady and would never do such a thing, but she said it because Ridley's paramour would not come forward. Lily ruined herself to prevent his arrest."

Gwen's eyes nearly popped out of her head. What bizarre intrigue was this?

She had been vaguely aware of the murder, and the ensuing scandal with Lily and her husband when Lily had informed the coroner that she and the new Lord Filminster had spent the night together. Apparently, that had been a lie.

Did that mean that Lily's husband, Gwen's new brother-in-law, could have murdered his father?

But no, Lady Moreland had implied that there had been a legitimate alibi who would not risk her reputation, so Lily had taken it upon herself to step forward. Gwen took a moment to marvel at the young woman's courage.

What, if anything, did that have to do with her and Aidan?

"It is very odd that Aidan managed to ruin a woman so soon after Lily's scandal. I am still at a loss why this happened to both my children. Do you think I raised them correctly?"

Lady Moreland was staring at her with brimming eyes. Eyes that reminded her of Aidan. Gwen's heart twinged in sympathy to see her mother-in-law so troubled. "Of course! Aidan is a perfect gentleman. What happened between us was an aberration. We were overcome by the majesty of the moon, and such exquisite poetry ... so now we are married. He did right by me."

"I am glad it is you, my dear. You seem resilient. Intelligent. You are a good match for my boy. When I first learned of this, I did not know what to think, but after meeting you, my mind has been at ease. At least ... regarding your suitability for my scholarly son."

Musing over the revelations, Gwen stood to move around the table and place herself on the settee next to Lady Moreland. "Lily and Aidan are honorable people. Lily stepped forward to help Lord Filminster, and Aidan did not hesitate in offering for me. Your children are a credit to you, La—Mama Abbott. You raised them to stand by what they know in their hearts to be right, and they did so. The fact that their scandals were so close in time is ... a coincidence."

"You think so?"

"I do."

It was not altogether true. Gwen wondered if Aidan's proposal was because he did not want to see a young woman ruined as Lily had been. Perhaps his resolve to marry her had not been so much about their mutual attraction, but merely his conscience driving his actions. He certainly was in a strange and distant mood now that their wedding night was over.

Yet ... their wedding night had been sublime. Something from a gothic novel or a poem by Lord Byron. Surely he must entertain feelings for her if he could spend so many hours in her company? It had been like they were marooned on a remote island, the only people left in the world. The way he had spoken to her had implied a deep regard.

One thing was certain. There were secrets to Aidan that he was not disclosing. His sister had been engaged in a scandal just a few weeks earlier, and this was the first she knew that he had blamed himself for what had happened.

And one more thing was certain. Gwen had been so absorbed by her own issues, her own needs and wants, that it had not struck her to think what Aidan might need.

Learning he was shouldering guilt over his sister made her realize her own selfishness over the past two weeks. What of her husband's needs?

He had stepped in to save her from scandal when he could have walked away. His family had been generous in negotiating financial terms because her father did not have the funds for a large dowry.

Instead of moping around, she needed to forge a true connection with Aidan. To become his partner and assist him with his burdens. They were to traverse life together, so she must stop feeling sorry for herself and demand her place at his side.

"You are a good girl, Gwen. My son and my future grandchildren are fortunate to have a woman like you to steer their lives."

Gwen was touched. When she first met Lady Moreland, she had thought the viscountess would be like the other mamas of the *ton*, dismissive of Gwen and her appearance. But from their first meeting, she had been warm and welcoming, embarrassing her and Aidan with talk of babes.

"You are a good mama, Mama Abbott. Watching over your children."

Lady Moreland sighed. "I do wish they would not keep secrets from me. They think I cannot handle the truth, and I confess it has been a trying time, especially after Sophia's troubles last year. I will allow them their privacy for now, but it does not prevent me from visiting you to secure your promise that you will take care of Aidan while we are gone from Town. He is a true gentleman, but he needs you. He attempts to carry his burdens without assistance, but do not allow him to do so."

Gwen took hold of Lady Moreland's hand and squeezed. "I promise to assist him."

Lady Moreland nodded. "Then I shall leave you to it. I hope to hear news of a prospective grandchild soon."

Gwen smiled, not precisely sure what came next, but determined to figure it out somehow. She must convince Aidan to talk to her about his problems.

* * *

REACHING RIDLEY HOUSE, Aidan discovered it was in chaos. Servants were rushing about with trunks, and Michaels only nodded toward the drawing room at the top of the stairs before striding off to address some unnamed household emergency.

A terror in his chest propelled Aidan up two steps at a time to race into the room where he found his sister and Filminster in an embrace.

"Lily!"

Her elfin face rose from her husband's chest to peek at him. "Aidan, please do not panic."

The terror he was feeling only grew. "What is happening?"

Filminster dropped his arms and stepped back. "We had another attempt to breach Ridley House."

"Your letter informed me of that. Why are the servants packing?"

Lily fluttered her eyes, walking away to stand at a

window facing the street. "We have determined it is too dangerous to remain in residence. I ... went into the library this morning to fetch a book before breakfast. It was still rather dark. I was in there for several minutes before I realized that there was a draught in the room. When I looked over to the window, I saw a man climbing in and screamed for help."

Aidan winced, realizing her voice was hoarse. Lily must have screamed bloody blue murder if it had inflamed her throat so. Unless ...

"Did he ... hurt you?"

His little sister, his tiny, barely five-foot sister, who had been lifted by her throat by a hefty footman at the beginning of the month, shook her head. "He jumped down and ran off as soon as I started screaming."

Aidan's eyes burned as he ran forward and swept her into a hug. "I am so sorry, Lily."

"It is not your fault, Aidan. You must not blame yourself."

"How can I not?"

She pulled back, staring up at him from a pale face. Lily had experienced far too much danger in a short span of time, and the strain of it was evident. "I am happy. I love Brendan. This is the fault of the madman who killed the baron."

Aidan swallowed, nodding. "If anything happened to you ..."

...it would kill me.

"What happens now? Are you finally leaving for Somerset?"

Lily shook her head. "Briggs still believes that traveling out on the roads will leave us too exposed. Whoever is hiring these men is becoming more brazen."

Filminster coughed into his hand, clearly reluctant to interrupt. "Lily and I have been invited to stay with the duke and my sister at their London home. They have hired guards so that our servants and the Johns can remain on duty to defend Ridley House."

For some reason beyond Aidan's grasp, Filminster referred to the guards as Johns. Lily had told him it was because they were all named John, which he supposed was possible but not likely given how many Filminster had hired.

"Thank God. Lily must be protected at all costs."

"Agreed."

Aidan let Lily go, raking a hand through his hair while he tried to think. "Surely at this point, if the killer is becoming so bold, we should report what we know to the authorities? Then he will lose interest in Ridley House if his secret is out."

His brother-in-law sighed. "I have thought of that. That we could end his interest in us if we simply disclose the matter to the Home Secretary. But the perpetrator still believes that there is a possibility that he can cover this up, and that the baron's letter has not been found. Which means we can continue to lure him out and eventually catch him. If we report the matter, the killer could vanish to avoid arrest."

Lily interjected. "I agree. As long as the killer believes the letter is in Ridley House, and that we do not know why the baron was killed, we have a chance to discreetly investigate. If the Home Secretary opens an investigation, it will all be over. The killer would likely make a run for it, and we will never find him if he leaves England. He must be brought to justice. The more desperate he becomes to protect himself, the more mistakes he will make."

"But what if he suspects that you and Filminster have found the letter?"

She shook her head. "I do not know, but he still believes there is a possibility to maintain his inheritance, so we must act as if that is the case."

Aidan was impressed with Lily's resolve and resilience. "When did you become so clever?"

"I am not a girl anymore, Aidan Abbott. While you were away, I grew up. I improved my French and read books on military strategy. Much happened in the past few years."

It was true. Aidan had returned home to find his cousin married to a notorious rogue, and within weeks his little sister had ruined herself to save Filminster from the gallows. The Abbott women were a force to be reckoned with.

This brought Gwen to mind, along with a wave of heat, as he recalled their activities in bed the night before. Gwen was an intelligent woman with thoughts of her own, but would she prove to be as resilient as Lily if Aidan was forced to bring her father to justice?

"Faugh! This is such a tangled web!"

Lily and Filminster burst into unnerved laughter. Even Aidan managed a chuckle. It was incomprehensible what a farce this entire matter had become.

CHAPTER 13

"Whosoever is delighted in solitude is either a wild beast or a god."

Aristotle

* * *

When Aidan hurried back to the Smythe home, riding his mount around to the mews in the back, he found that a carriage was being prepared. As he had hoped, Smythe was on his way out. This might be the opportunity he needed to learn more about what Smythe had been doing.

Waving off the groom, Aidan turned to ride back out.

Finding a discreet position out on the main road passing the front of the house, he waited. Anticipation sang through his veins that finally he could take some sort of action. Where was Smythe heading to?

What if he is merely visiting his clubs?

Aidan hoped not. The frustration of not doing anything

to move this investigation forward was driving him quietly mad.

Valor snorted, pawing the earth with a heavy hoof.

"Easy." Aidan stroked the gelding's withers, composing himself to reduce his internal tension. It would not do to distress the beast with his own calamity when he needed to remain hidden.

Soon Smythe hurried from the front door, dressed in a dark and disheveled overcoat and his blue eyes flashing in the sunlight.

Aidan frowned, noticing for the first time that the black carriage had no markings. There was no reason to expect them because Smythe did not currently possess a rank, but along with the skirted coat he wore, it was practically impossible to recognize who was being driven.

Scanning the driver and footman, Aidan realized that they were not dressed in their usual livery. They, too, were *incognito*.

What fresh intrigue was this?

Aidan's spirits lifted, the thrill of the chase racing through his body. Finally, he had something to pursue. A tangible clue. He knew in his very bones that Smythe was on the move, ready to engage in some sort of dubious activity. This was not to be a routine errand to his solicitor or man of business. Smythe was hiding his identity to pursue his dark ends.

As the carriage drew off, Aidan carefully tightened his calf. Valor immediately broke into a trot, and they kept pace with the carriage as it moved down quiet streets. After a while they joined Strand Street, which was bustling with carriages, mounted riders, and pedestrians going about their business. St. James's Park was well behind them, and Aidan was careful to keep Smythe's carriage in sight, noting that they were heading east as the traffic grew more congested.

Turning off Fleet Street, Aidan followed the carriage

which turned onto Thames Street, near the river, and the carriage kept heading west. Smythe appeared to be heading toward the London Docks, but who knew if they would just keep moving west beyond that point?

The closer they came to the docks, the more difficult it grew for Aidan to keep the carriage in sight. Merchants and dock workers mingled in congregation on the roadside, while wagons piled high with crates and barrels clogged the streets. Aidan pressed his mount forward, and just as he turned a corner, another rider came flying through a gap in the traffic.

Valor was startled by the sudden motion and proximity, rearing up and bellowing out a loud whinny. Aidan was caught off guard, attempting to keep Smythe's carriage in view, and next he knew, he had been bucked from Valor's back. As the earth flew toward him, Aidan hit the road with a roll, barely missing the large wheels of a passing wagon.

Bruised and shaken, he sprang to his feet and grabbed hold of the panicking Valor's reins, quickly tugging the gelding's head down and walking him back several steps to disengage his hindquarters. Valor acquiesced, panting in quieting agitation but relaxing his panicked stance.

Once his horse was secured, Aidan threw a glance over his shoulder and cursed loudly. Several passersby flinched and tossed him glances of reproval, but he paid them no mind.

Smythe's carriage was gone.

Leading Valor, Aidan limped to the side of the busy street and discovered his buckskins were torn above one knee. Inspecting his coat, he found several tears. Feeling about carefully, he perceived that he had badly bruised his upper arm and shoulder, but it seemed he had not broken anything. What he *had* done was lose his quarry and nearly gotten himself killed.

Disappointment burned through him, as hot as the passion he had shared with his bride the night before. Brushing the dirt off his clothes and swiping at his face, Aidan seethed with a fury he had never experienced before as he spat out the dust in his mouth.

Once he had fully caught his breath, he remounted Valor, who was now calm. They made their way gingerly down the street as Aidan searched for the vanished carriage.

People, horses, and vehicles were milling in every direction and he knew it was a pointless task, but he spent the next hour riding the cross streets and searching for Smythe, even dismounting to peer into the dim interiors of shops and taverns.

Eventually he gave in and turned Valor's head to return home.

He had failed. They knew nothing new about what Smythe was up to. All he had achieved was to acquire himself numerous abrasions and wreck his favorite breeches. Meanwhile Lily had been chased out of her new home by a thug, and he would need to hide these bruises from Gwen to avoid questions.

The low growl he emitted was drowned by the sounds of the street, but he did not give a damn if someone overheard him. This entire matter was out of hand. The best he could hope for was that Smythe would return to the vicinity, which meant that Aidan would have to follow him again.

It took some time to reach the Smythe home where Aidan left Valor with a groom in the mews. Ordinarily he would have taken the time to rub the gelding down, but during the ride home, his muscles had made their protests known along with the contusions on his knee, upper arm, and shoulder, which had hit the street first and taken the brunt of his weight. He wanted to get out of his ruined clothes and bathe away the nameless grime that had become embedded under his fingernails.

Crossing the back garden, he entered the house and prayed he would not encounter Gwen. Once he was in his room, he would summon his valet and get some assistance to clean up. Perhaps his man had some sort of ointment to alleviate the accumulating pains. Climbing the steps to the next floor, Aidan kneaded his neck, which he must have wrenched in the fall.

Bloody hell! I could have been killed.

Aidan was thankful he had had enough presence of mind to drop into a roll as he had. Fortunately, because of the traffic, he and Valor had been traveling at a slower speed, or he might not have avoided tragedy—it did not pay to be distracted when riding.

Finally reaching his room, Aidan slipped in. He rang the bell, which he hoped would result in his valet showing up. Then he proceeded to tug the clothes off his body impatiently. Once he was naked, he walked over to the mirror by the wardrobe to inspect his leg, arm, and shoulder. Livid bruises were already discoloring his skin in dramatic hues, as if to testify just how dangerous the fall had been.

Aidan rubbed his hands over his cheek, which was thankfully unmarred except for the grime that came off under his fingertips.

As he had suspected, he would need to avoid Gwen catching sight of these. He did not wish to lie to her any more than necessary because he had their future marriage to consider. It would be better if she did not know.

The thought of his bride, now that he had not the distraction of Smythe to worry about until the man reappeared, had Aidan shiver with hot memories of their night together.

He was afraid the concerns weighing down on him this

morning had made him act in an aloof manner when they had last seen each other at the breakfast table.

It was time for him to make amends to her once he was bathed and dressed once more, for he suspected it would be many hours before Smythe made a reappearance.

* * *

GWEN WAS WRITING in her notebook in the library. She was working on a translation of Propertius, the Latin poet. It was a project that her mother had wanted to do before she had become ill, and Gwen had taken it up recently after a scare of her own had made her realize how short life could be.

Following her dreams while she had her health and youth was a lesson she was eager to engage with. It was important to pursue one's goals and to live free of regrets.

It was why she had planned to convince her father to allow her to bring a foundling into their home, but now a babe of her own was an imminent possibility—if she could recapture her husband's attentions.

Which was why, when Aidan finally returned home, she was going to take their marriage in hand and find out what burden Aidan might be bearing. It was time to forge a true partnership.

In the meantime, she needed to remain busy. Waiting for Aidan to return home, or for her new life to begin, she would keep herself occupied.

Pausing her quill, she ran her finger over the poem.

Cynthia prima suis miserum me cepit ocellis,
contactum nullis ante cupidinibus.

She returned to the notebook, tapping the quill on her

lips as she considered how to capture the essence of the elegant words.

"Cynthia first captivated wretched me with her eyes, I who had never before been touched by Cupid."

In her chest, Gwen's heart swelled, and she smiled with the sheer joy of shared appreciation.

"*Cuncta tuus sepelivit amor, nec femina post te ulla dedit collo dulcia vincla meo*," she responded, holding her breath to hear what would come next.

Aidan chuckled. "Thy love has buried all others, nor has any woman after thee put sweet fetters upon my neck."

Gwen sighed in raptured awe. "You put me to shame, husband. What need is there for my efforts if you translate with such poetic skill?"

He had been peering over her shoulder, and it was with such sweet loss that Gwen watched him move away to take the seat next to her. Her gentle lover from the night before had returned, and her heart was too tight to contain the happiness at his arrival. It threatened to burst with the overflowing feelings it must contain.

"I am naught but an ordinary man with a muse of great grace to lift my voice." His gaze drew lovingly over her face, leaving no doubt to whom he referred.

Gwen blushed even as her smile spread wider to make the muscles of her cheeks ache. "You are home."

His lips spread into a broad smile. "I am home."

Gwen noted his coat was a different color from breakfast, and his white linen was pristine. He should smell like horse if he had been about Town on his mount, but he was fresh. He smelled like clean laundry and leather. "You changed?"

His smile slowly dissipated. "I thought it would be dinner soon, so I scrubbed Valor's sweat from my skin so I may find you."

Gwen leaned back in her chair and twisted her neck to

peer at the casement clock in the corner. "I shall have to prepare for dinner myself, I suppose."

"Or we can have a tray brought to your room?" His tone was suggestive, purred at a low volume as he reached out to gently caress the back of her hand, which was bare for writing.

"Truly?"

His eyes grazed over her appreciatively, lingering on the swell of her breasts. "Oh, yes."

Gwen grinned, pushing her chair back and rising with enthusiasm. "Yes!"

Aidan made to rise, but then Gwen remembered the conversation she had planned.

"Oh, wait!" She plopped back down in her chair.

Aidan settled back, a quizzical expression crossing his face.

"Your mother paid me a visit."

He blinked in surprise, not saying anything at her announcement.

"She informed me what happened with Lily."

Aidan cocked his head, narrowing his eyes. "Lily?"

"She thought that as a new member of the family I should be aware of the attack on Lily by the footman."

"Indeed?" His face did not alter, but Gwen sensed tension in the air.

"I was utterly horrified to hear that anyone could try to harm your sister. She is such a sweet and tiny thing. What kind of monster would attempt to hurt her?"

Aidan's lips flickered into a smile, but it seemed forced somehow. "Lily is stronger than she looks. I am proud of how well she has handled herself."

"Of course. When I met her, I would not have guessed that something so distressing had occurred recently. Still, it was a shock to learn of it."

Her husband nodded, but an echo of the distraction he had displayed that morning had returned to his features. "Was there any more to the conversation?"

"Well ... she seemed to believe that you blamed yourself for the scandal with Lily. The fact that she was forced to marry Lord Filminster, and she told me how Lily lied to provide him with an alibi."

Aidan straightened in his chair. "Huh! That is quite a bit of family secrets to reveal in one afternoon." He raked a hand through his hair, appearing quite unhappy. "You do understand that word cannot get out that Lily lied? Filminster was under tremendous suspicion, but he could not have done it. My sister witnessed his arrival and departure, so she did not exactly ... lie. She simply ... altered some of the specifics to ensure she was believed. I would hate for Filminster to be unfairly accused if word got out about what she had done. And if Lily were to be punished for perjuring herself ... I dare not contemplate such horrors."

"Her secret is safe with me. I do not like to gossip and I do not have anyone to tell, even if I wanted to. But was your mother correct? Do you blame yourself for Lily's scandal?"

Aidan's brown eyes stared at her, and he was obviously disconcerted by such a direct question, but Gwen truly did not know how to raise the subject other than directly.

"I have felt remorseful that I chose to go out that night to carouse with my friends. If I had been there, perhaps I could have stood as his alibi instead."

"So Lily does not want to be married to Filminster?"

A grimace was the only reply for several seconds. He appeared to be debating his answer. "Lily and Filminster are deeply in love. She assured me she has no regrets just this afternoon."

Gwen smiled. "Oh, I am glad to hear that. I was not sure what to think. Is it why you insisted on marrying me?"

Aidan blinked, astonishment chasing across his features before he shook his head. "No! You and I have naught to do with Lily and Filminster. You are my Venus. My very own Cynthia. The fetters upon my neck are sweet, Gwen Abbott."

Gwen held her breath in wonder. The words were too melodious to process. It was almost as if he were saying ... that perhaps he loved her?

She wanted to ask, but it was too forthright, and she had suffered too many disappointments in her past. The words were stuck on her tongue, and she had not the confidence to voice them. Instead, she clung to the sentiments he had stated and assured herself that was what he would say if he were to speak plainly.

Do not push him.

Gwen remembered how she had declared her feelings in a moment of drowsy weakness, only to regret it this morning. She did not want to ruin their developing affinity with neediness, as she had suspected she had done earlier, so instead ... she smiled. "Thank you."

Aidan raised his eyebrows, his expression hopeful. "Now to bed?"

She nodded, standing up.

They left the library to run up the stairs, hand in hand, and Gwen felt the bittersweet love for Aidan cascading from her heart into every inch of her body. Would he still be here when she awoke tomorrow and not vanish into his thoughts as he had done that morning?

Tonight, he seemed almost carefree.

When they reached her room, she fumbled with the door and they stumbled into the room with their lips fused together.

"Uh ..."

Gwen yanked her head away. "Octavia!"

The lady's maid was standing by the wardrobe, her eyes averted to the floor as she fiddled with her skirts. She dropped into a curtsy, her face ruddy. "I shall ... just ..." She pointed awkwardly at the closed door behind Gwen and Aidan.

Gwen felt her ears warming in embarrassment. She resolutely stared at the wall beyond the other woman's shoulder. "Could you arrange a dinner tray?"

Octavia nodded, sidling closer as she tried to reach the door. Aidan relinquished his hold on Gwen, stepping aside with a bow of his head. Octavia leapt for the door, hurriedly pulling it open to depart the room.

The decisive shutting of the door was all the cue needed for Aidan and Gwen to burst into nervous laughter.

When Aidan had recovered his composure, he swept around the room, closing the curtains. Gwen blinked as the room fell into deep shadows. What strange turn of events was this? Was Aidan shy?

He returned to her side, placing his hands on her hips to tug her forward against him. She could barely make him out in the dark, but he was staring down at her and he was breathing hard.

Gwen reached up to curl her arms around his neck, reveling in the sensation of her breasts pressed to his chest.

"I have been thinking about last night." He had leaned forward so his lips brushed against her temple, tickling her skin with the delicious promise of more to come. "How you felt beneath me ... around me."

Gwen exhaled, desire slowly flickering to life in her lower belly as she pressed ever closer. "I ... have thought about it, too."

His hands were caressing up and down her waist. At her confession, he groaned, reaching lower to cup her buttocks and tug her against his groin. Feeling his rigid length in his falls caused her intimate muscles to tighten in instinctual response. Evidence of his arousal was ... so arousing.

Aidan lowered his face to capture her lips, and their mouths came together as if they were one. Her passion flamed up as he explored her with hungry abandon, his tongue and hands moving in tandem to ratchet up the blaze in her belly until she was certain that there must be actual smoke enveloping their entwined bodies.

She gyrated her hips against him, attempting to alleviate the building tension between her legs, and moaned in relief as his fingers found the buttons of her bodice and began to release her from the constriction of her gown.

It was strange making love in almost complete darkness, with no lamps to light the room, but she had no time to worry about it. Her hands swept down to dig into his shoulders and upper arms with clawing passion.

Aidan flinched, gasping as if he were in pain, which Gwen could only commiserate with. The sensations he raised in her body were a sweet agony, building up and up at the feeling of his lips and his hard body against hers.

He reached up to tug her hands down to his chest, which she willingly rediscovered with her fingertips.

CHAPTER 14

"The energy of the mind is the essence of life."

Aristotle

* * *

Aidan grunted in pain, pulling Gwen's hands down to his chest lest he yell out loud. Her fingers had found the worst of his bruises, digging in so he felt dizzy from the sharp pang.

Thankfully, the ache dropped to a dull throbbing, and the fire of lust rose once more. Aidan ransacked his thoughts on how to make love to Gwen without hurting himself and alerting her to his injuries.

His fingers fumbled with the buttons of her bodice as he tried to recall the illustrations in the Sanskrit book that Trafford had lent him.

Inspiration hit as Aidan finished unbuttoning her gown and pulled it away from her, down her arms. Gwen moaned when he brought his hands back up to cup her breasts, kneading through her stays while he plotted a course to her bed.

He pulled on the tapes of her stays and dropped them over her arms to the ground while Gwen turned her head to nuzzle his neck with soft lips.

His heart pounded with the force of his passions as he ripped at his coat to drop it to the floor. His waistcoat followed quickly.

Seeking her lips, he used one hand to pull her into another searing kiss while using his free hand to unbutton his falls. Once his breeches were hanging loose, he grabbed Gwen by the hand and led her to the bed.

Yanking the coverlet and sheet back, he nudged her to sit before joining her to take his boots and stockings off. Gwen's arms were tendrils, her hands exploring his body without pause as he struggled with the excess clothing.

He rose and kicked off his breeches and small clothes, before dropping into the bed and hauling Gwen over him. It made his bruised muscles protest to lift her so, but it was over shortly and then she was straddling him with her slick crease pressed against his erection. Aidan grabbed handfuls of her shift and pulled it up, up, up her gyrating body before tossing it away.

And then his Venus was rising above him. In the darkened room, he could yet make out the expanse of pale skin and the bared roundness of her breasts hovering above him in a tempting manner. Reaching up roughened hands, he caressed soft skin. The jutting tips of her nipples erotically pressed into the palms of his hands as he kneaded and plumped.

Gwen moaned loudly, her head dropping back to lift her breasts in his grip, and Aidan was overcome.

Gently, he ran a hand down her undulating belly to search through her nest of curls and find the center of her pleasure, using a fingertip to brush over the little nub at the apex of her crease. Gwen gasped loudly above him, pushing her hips up as Aidan swirled over the pearl that Trafford had emphasized the importance of.

Botheration! Do not think of Trafford!

Aidan's pleasure was mounting immeasurably as Gwen moved over him. He had to bring her pleasure quickly, as his own peak approached, so he focused his attention. Spreading the honeyed wetness of her excitement over plumped folds, he continued his ministrations with Gwen bucking forward and over him in a frenzy as if riding a mount.

Soon she was keening, chasing her peak until she moaned loudly above him. As she slowly relaxed onto his chest, Aidan guided his cock to the entrance hidden within her moistened cleft and thrust up to bury himself in her wet heat.

Gwen shifted in his arms, moaning as he joined with her and finding his lips to kiss him with fervor. Aidan growled in the back of his throat, her tight channel clasping him firmly as he bucked and thrust to his own completion, dizzy with the pleasure of feeling her lithe body in his arms as his lust reached a crescendo and he spent his seed deep into her writhing body.

His bride collapsed over him, draped across his body in the manner of linen clinging to sweat-soaked skin. Aidan leaned up to kiss her damp cheek. His gratitude that he had found such a woman knew no bounds as he wrapped his arms around her to bury his face in her citrus-scented hair. He prayed he could somehow sort out this muddle with Smythe while holding on to Gwen's affections, which had become essential to his future happiness.

* * *

AUGUST 27, 1821

Aidan made love to her a couple more times throughout the night, all in peculiar positions that she had not been aware of. She had wanted to caress his body, but the ecstasy of their lovemaking had swept all thoughts from her head as Aidan had taught her new ways to bring them both pleasure in the dark.

After the first time, he rose to don his shirt and had lit only one lamp on the far side of the room before collecting their tray of food from the hall. It was barely enough light to see what she was eating, but it had been a romantic interlude only heightened by the deep shadows shrouding the bedroom.

They had finally fallen asleep close to dawn, their arms wrapped around each other as if they were afraid to let each other go.

Gwen fell into a slumber so deep, she did not even dream, nestling into Aidan's warm embrace and unwilling to release him, even for a second.

She awoke to cool sheets. Aidan had left her side yet again. Gwen groaned as Octavia pulled the curtains open and gray light entered the room. Buttercup raised her head to give a curt bark as if she, too, was astonished to be disturbed so rudely.

"What fresh hell is this?"

Octavia giggled. "It's the afternoon. I decided it was time to wake you up, or you'll struggle to fall asleep tonight."

Gwen sat up, clutching a sheet to her bare body. "Afternoon?"

"Indeed. Lord Abbott is committed to siring an heir straightaway, it'd seem."

Despite her embarrassment, Gwen laughed. She reached

out a hand to scratch Buttercup, who tilted her angular head in blissful supplication. "Where is Lord Abbott?"

"He left some time ago. No word when he'll return, I'm afraid."

Gwen fell back on her pillow with a heavy sough. "I planned on forging a true connection with him, but he turned my head with sweet words and ..." She gestured vaguely to indicate the mattress.

The lady's maid walked up to tower over her. Gwen suspected Octavia liked to do this because Gwen was so much taller. It was the only time that the woman was in a dominating position. Buttercup rose on her short legs, baring her teeth with a low growl to warn Octavia she was encroaching on her territory.

Octavia ignored Buttercup's posturing.

"What do you mean, true connection? I thought things were progressing well with your husband."

"I do not know. His mother told me he has been keeping secrets and I agree. One minute he is all soulful sighs and poetic words, and the next he is a hundred miles away. He does not tell me anything about himself or his day. Where does he go? What does he do? Whom does he spend time with? Why did he not tell me of Lily's troubles?"

Octavia's eyes widened. "Lady Filminster? What troubles does she have?"

Gwen recalled Aidan's warning to keep the details of Lily's marriage to herself or risk endangering Lord Filminster's reputation and freedom. She winced.

"I cannot say."

Octavia swung an open hand up to her forehead, palm up. "For shame, Gwendolyn Abbott! Do you not trust me?"

Gwen grinned. "Not a bit. You are an incorrigible gossip, so I will not share a word about Lady Filminster with you."

Octavia burst into laughter, her bony shoulders shaking

with mirth. "If it's to remain a secret, I'd rather not bear the burden, then."

The lady's maid moved away to collect Gwen's clothing. She sat up in her bed, staring out the window at the bank of iron-gray clouds until she finally ventured the question.

"How was he? This morning?"

Octavia paused in the open door of the wardrobe, licking her thin lips. "I'd say ... distracted."

Gwen nodded. When Aidan was in her presence, she quite forgot her concerns, just wishing to glory in the glow of burgeoning love. But when he was away, that was when her worries set in. What did she truly know about her new husband?

Aidan had quickly captured her heart, but Gwen could not quite grasp his thoughts or his feelings. He seemed genuinely interested in her, but beyond that, she knew nothing about him.

What burdens did he shoulder, and how could she convince him to confide in her so they could form a true marriage?

Outside, the sky darkened with ever more glowering clouds, and Gwen was startled out of her wits by a great clap of thunder followed by the roar of rain falling from the heavens.

Buttercup whimpered, burying her head under a pillow and shaking in fear. Gwen made a comforting sound, stroking the trembling dog to calm her. "It is just some weather, Buttercup. You will be fine, girl. You will be fine."

* * *

RAIN ROARED down upon the roof of the hackney.

Aidan yawned widely and carefully kneaded the bruised shoulder he had landed on the day before. It was aching something fierce, and he was pleased with his decision to hire a driver rather than attempt to ride. Grabbing more than three hours of sleep would have been welcome under the circumstances, but he could not afford the time.

He had taken a page from Smythe's book, having decided that he could follow the Smythe carriage with less fear of being spotted if he was in a hackney that was indistinguishable from the next.

The rain made it more difficult to see, and his driver wore a battered hat and large, black overcoat with the collar raised to defend him from the elements. It further obscured any possibility that Smythe would notice he was being followed.

Aidan stretched his legs out, grimacing at the state of his damp boots, and hoped that Smythe would make a move again this day. He and the driver, Old Fred, had been observing the Smythe mews—he pulled on his fob to check his timepiece—for the better part of two hours.

Occasionally, they would traverse a block or two before taking up a fresh position to prevent rousing the suspicions of servants from the neighborhood. It was a boring and arduous process that made Aidan appreciate the tedious work of runners hired to retrieve stolen goods.

He rolled his shoulders, stretched his neck from side to side, and lamented that he had not brought a book to read while he waited inside the dim interior of the aging carriage. The thin squabs were flattened with the imprint of thousands of buttocks, and the upholstery had been mended dozens of times. The neat repairs spoke to the fastidious nature of Old Fred.

He did not envy the aging man—sitting out on his box seat while the heavens poured water down in buckets. Even now, Aidan followed a trail of rainwater slipping down the interior of the aged carriage windows. He was grateful the driver had been persuaded to aid him for the day.

There was a knock on the window, and Aidan felt the pull of the carriage. Peering out the window, he saw the Smythe carriage exiting the mews. This was it!

Old Fred followed at a snail's pace, drawing to a stop at the corner to wait. The front door of the Smythe home opened and Aidan's father-in-law exited. At least, Aidan assumed it was Smythe, given the general size and gait of the cloak-covered gentleman running forward to climb the steps into the carriage interior while a figure dutifully held the door ajar. The steps were raised, the door was shut, and the servant climbed aboard.

Aidan's heart hammered in anticipation. He was prepared to see this to the end, having spent the morning catching hackneys until he had discovered Old Fred.

Today, there would be no reckless riders to cause him to be tossed from his mount.

He had instructed Old Fred to stay close when they reached the more congested streets. Aidan could not afford to lose Smythe again.

His only consolation on this dreary day was that Lily was in residence at the much larger townhouse of the duke, who had more footmen than Filminster in addition to the brawny guards that Halmesbury had hired to protect his guests.

Nevertheless, this investigation needed to progress before someone else was hurt... or worse.

Old Fred nudged his horses forward, and soon they were following Smythe. Both carriages moved slowly as the wheels churned up mud from the puddled streets. Smythe was determined to reach his destination if he chose to brave such hard weather.

They trundled down empty streets, the citizens of London dissuaded from venturing out. When they reached the Strand, the traffic picked up. Riders were not to be seen, but carriages clogged the road as they moved tentatively through the downpour.

The journey to the London Docks took considerably more time than the day before. Pedestrians stood shivering beneath shop awnings and, on one corner, a wagon was mired in the slopping mud. Other drivers yelled impatiently from their perches, while the teams of men and horses toiled to unstick it, but Aidan only had eyes for Smythe's carriage.

Old Fred did an exemplary job of keeping it in sight, and Aidan felt proud of finding the man to assist him. It seemed that this would work!

Aidan caught sight of the London Docks down the street just as their quarry stopped to pull into an alley. Old Fred dutifully drew to a stop half a block away, and Aidan quickly pulled his hat down over his ears and raised the collar of the great overcoat he had borrowed from one of his father's grooms.

Opening the door, Aidan dropped to the ground, his riding boots squelching in inches of mud. Running forward with his hand holding his hat to his head to defend himself from the rain, Aidan reached the alleyway and carefully peered around the corner to see Smythe disappearing into a doorway.

Aidan studied the distance to where the carriage stood, then ran back down the block to the street parallel to the alley and found that the building was a tavern. He strode through the front entryway.

Inside it was dark, barely any daylight to shine in from the street and a few flickering oil lamps on the walls. Aidan carefully navigated through a maze of scarred tables and chairs, searching for Smythe. Dock workers in colorful linens, jerkins, and hardy boots sat in groups while sailors dressed in their merchant blues drank and talked loudly among themselves.

With great relief, Aidan spotted Smythe at a corner table. He was seated across from a rough man dressed in the style of a dock worker. He had the shoulders of someone who was accustomed to lifting great burdens of weight, and several days' growth of black beard on his unshaven cheeks.

Aidan quickly located a free table nearby and took a seat, careful to keep his hat down low and tugging his collar up to ensure it obscured his face.

He could not make out what they were talking about, but Smythe was leaning forward with an intense expression. He was knocking his hand down on the table as if his temper were piqued. The other man raised his hands in a gesture that implied he did not have an answer to what Smythe had said.

Aidan's heart hammered loudly in his chest. There was no doubt that Smythe was up to no good. No gentleman met with dock workers and, as if to confirm his thoughts, Smythe reached into his coat and pulled out a small purse.

He placed it on the table and pushed it forward to the unknown conspirator. A hand covered in coarse black hair reached out to take it, and the rough chap swept his gaze about the tavern before peering inside. He nodded, putting the purse away in an inner pocket.

A tavern maid came up, interrupting Aidan's surveillance. He ordered an ale to get rid of her, relieved when she walked away quickly to serve another who had hollered out.

The meeting continued for a while, and Aidan wished he could overhear what they were discussing, but the tavern was engaged in a roaring trade because of the heavy rain, and Aidan could barely hear himself think in the chaos. He nursed his drink and observed what he could, waiting for the next development.

Fumbling about in his overcoat to find the pocket of his waistcoat, Aidan checked the time and realized he had been observing them for near an hour.

There was no more to learn from the position where he sat. He wondered if he should wait it out and follow Smythe to the next destination. When he looked back up, it was to find that his father-in-law had finally risen to his feet, gesturing.

Aidan tossed a coin onto the table and quickly made his way out of the tavern. Swiveling his head around, he managed to pick out the figure of Old Fred bent over his reins. The rain had eased, but the day was still gray and dreary. Racing over to the hackney, the mud sucking at his boots, Aidan yanked the door open and embarked, knocking on the front glass.

Old Fred drove the carriage to the alleyway, where they waited on the main road. Then, slowly, the hackney entered the alley to follow Smythe's carriage out onto the opposite street.

Within three blocks, the Smythe carriage pulled into another alleyway. As before, Aidan assessed the position of the back door Smythe entered. Running out onto the parallel street again, Aidan found the corresponding door.

He hesitated, perplexed, before entering yet another dock tavern. This tavern was more shadowed than before, with no maids and only a man behind the bar serving to a thin crowd of brooding men.

Aidan hunched his shoulders down to appear shorter and ensure his figure was not recognizable. With fewer men patronizing the establishment, it would be easier for Smythe to spot him if he was not careful.

The table and chairs close to Smythe and his new cohort were not occupied, but Aidan did not dare approach lest he be spotted.

As before, Smythe gestured adamantly and leaned in to talk with yet another beefy dock worker. This one appeared to have not bathed in a week, nor any of the other patrons. Aidan breathed through his mouth to avoid the sour odor hanging about like an evil omen.

At the bar, a drunken argument broke out between two slovenly men, slurring as they gesticulated wildly. The sullen proprietor behind the bar came out, grabbing both men by the scruff of their collars to escort them out crudely. Aidan shook his head in amazement that he was sitting in such a place. He still could not overhear anything from the table where he sat, so instead he observed and seethed.

Smythe was a blackguard deeply involved in sinister schemes. There was no other explanation for why he would be visiting such blighted spots to converse with a criminal element.

Were these the ruffians who had attempted to break in to Ridley House? Had one of these men scared the wits out of his little sister? What gave Smythe the right to behave this way?

It was becoming more and more obvious that his father-in-law had visited the late Baron of Filminster on the night of the coronation and bludgeoned Brendan's uncle to death before running away into the night like a pathetic coward.

Aidan needed to find the evidence to end this farce.

Which means I will be forced to hurt Gwen when she learns of her father's perfidy.

This reminder of what lay ahead was unwelcome, so Aidan forced his attention back to the present.

After thirty minutes, Smythe took his leave and Aidan left the tavern to rejoin Old Fred. Once again, they trailed the Smythe carriage down the alleyway and onto the opposite street.

It was with some disappointment that Aidan realized they had turned and were headed back east.

Smythe must have completed his errands for the day, or the weather had dissuaded him from further activities, because they were headed back to the Smythe home across London.

If only Aidan could have caught him in the act of something. Frustration sizzled through his veins as he rubbed his hands up and down over his breeches and thought about how to bring this to a resolution. It was obvious that Smythe was guilty, as Aidan had thought from the beginning. But how to prove it?

It was excruciating to be this close to discovering the truth, yet not know what to do to finish it and prove what he knew in his gut. He thought about the day Lily had been attacked, the marks on her neck from when the villainous footman had held her by the throat. He thought about how his little sister could have been killed.

And the more he thought, the more he seethed that Smythe could behave like an ordinary gentleman to his face, all charming grins and polite talk, while behind the mask was a cold-blooded murderer. He had hosted Filminster and Lily in his home, along with their family, and pretended to be a friendly face and a new relation, yet hurried about Town daily to plot his dastardly conspiracies.

It was up to Aidan to stop him.

CHAPTER 15

✤

"The ultimate value of life depends upon awareness and the power of contemplation rather than upon mere survival."

Aristotle

* * *

When Aidan reached the Smythe home, ensuring he came in a good half hour after Smythe, it was to be met with another letter. Stalking over to the little drawing room off the entry hall, Aidan quickly unfolded the note to see what hellish report he was to receive.

> *After we left RH last evening, it happened again. Michaels is injured, but the doctor assures me he will recover.*
> *Filminster.*

Aidan's vision turned red as rage rushed through him.

The butler had saved Lily's life! And if Lily had been at Ridley House, she could have been hurt or killed, being such a tiny little thing!

Smythe was behind it! Aidan knew this was the truth. There was no other explanation for what he had witnessed this afternoon nor for the bills of sale he had found in Smythe's desk.

Aidan's hands were shaking with fury as he crumpled the page in his hand, attempting to quell the hot emotion causing his heart to race. He was panting with the sheer outrage that the killer was only dozens of feet away and he could do nothing about it.

It was beyond the pale! Completely untenable!

He stood here, helpless, while his family and their close connections were under attack.

The more he tried to hold his temper at bay, the hotter it simmered—*boiled*—until the appalling dishonor of this disastrous farce caused his feet to turn toward the door. In a blinding anger, Aidan stormed down the hall to throw open the door to Smythe's office.

His father-in-law's head shot up in surprise, then he frowned in confusion when he saw Aidan standing in the doorway.

"May I help you, son?"

Aidan stepped in, closing the door behind him with deliberation. It was time to end this, but there was no need for Gwen to overhear this confrontation.

"I know what you have done."

Smythe blanched before his eyes, and Aidan knew he had him cornered. He walked forward into the room, coming to a stop midway to glower at Smythe over his desk.

His father-in-law got to his feet. "I can explain."

Aidan could not believe his ears. The reprobate was

admitting it yet thought that Aidan would stand by him. "You can explain! Have you gone mad, sir?"

Smythe raised shaking hands to run them through his graying hair, his blue eyes stark in a face that had lost all color. "I beg of you, there is no need for this to get out. Not yet."

Aidan again could not believe what he was hearing. The man had no conscience. "I am afraid there is no delaying the news that you killed a man."

Smythe's jaw dropped open. "I did what?"

It was then that Aidan heard a rustle behind him.

Turning around, the horror of finding Gwen standing at the terrace doors swept through him in a wave. Seeing her red hair lit from behind, the sun peeking through the clouds for the first time that day, she was a glorious angel, and Aidan realized in that moment that his Venus had stolen his very heart from his chest the very first night he had met her. Which was unfortunate because her face was hard and pale as her expression firmed into a ferocious glare.

"What is he talking about, Papa?" Gwen's glare never wavered, even as she addressed her words to Smythe.

"I ... do not know. Who is it that I am supposed to have killed?"

Aidan swallowed. Losing his temper, and storming in here without a plan, just might be the costliest mistake he had ever made.

Ever.

He was supposed to have handled this with finesse. To ensure Gwen was not heartbroken in the process. To be here to support her when she learned the truth about her father.

All of which was currently a moot point.

He turned away to look at Smythe. There was no honor to how Aidan had reacted to this muddle, so all he could do was proceed with his accusation. One step at a time.

"You killed the Baron of Filminster to secure your inheritance."

Smythe blinked his intense blue eyes before collapsing into his leather swivel chair. "I ... most certainly did no such thing."

"You just admitted it!"

Smythe's brows drew together, a heavy scowl marring his face. "I most certainly did not."

"What were you confessing to, then?"

"Not that! Why do you think I would kill the baron?" Smythe shook his head. "And why would killing him secure my inheritance? I did not even know the man that well."

Gwen's skirts rustled as she walked up to Aidan from behind. He was too ashamed to look at her, so he stared resolutely at Smythe, watching him like a hawk that had spotted its next prey. But it was he who was the prey to his bride's menace.

"When was the baron killed? Was it the night of the coronation?" Gwen's voice was melodic steel, and Aidan's chest tightened in response. If he had wrecked their marriage before it had even begun, he would never recover. He raised a hand to rub at the pain in his chest where his heart refused to beat.

"Yes."

"Then Papa could not have done what you accuse him of."

Aidan could scarcely breathe as he slowly admitted to himself, as if from a great distance, that he may have made a mistake. It never paid to lose one's temper. How many times had his own father repeated those words?

"How would you know that?"

"Because last month I contracted a terrible fever. Octavia and Papa were at my side night and day. The day of the coronation was when the doctor informed my father that I might expire before the night was over, and Octavia can attest that he kept vigil at my bedside all night long until my fever finally broke in the early hours."

Aidan blinked in horror, struggling to breathe at the awful accusation he had made. His gaze found Smythe's, who had an expression of sympathy on his face. "It is true, son. I do not know why you think I killed the baron, but I was at Gwendolyn's side all day and night. I could not bear to walk away lest she die while I was absent. It was such a blessed relief when her fever broke."

Behind Aidan there was once again a rustle of skirts, a hint of citrus teasing his senses, and the sound of a door opening and closing, then racing footsteps in the hall.

Aidan spun around to find he was alone with Smythe. Buttercup was at the door, pawing and scratching to be let out. She sat back and howled in distress, much as Aidan wished to do. Gwen had left without a word, taking his very heart with her so that he stood with his chest cracked open to reveal the gaping hole where it had once resided.

Aidan strode across the room to allow the distressed animal out, giving her a pat on the head, before whipping around to glare at Smythe.

"What the hell were you confessing to?" Aidan's cry was one of pure despair, his hopes for his marriage cracking into a thousand shards of glass as he realized he had ruined everything.

"Not that."

"Then what?"

"Take a seat, Aidan. I shall explain, but first you must calm yourself."

It was an excellent suggestion because Aidan felt as weak as a kitten. Lily Billy herself, his petite little sister, could overpower him in his current state.

He walked over to drop into one of the plump armchairs. He would race after Gwen if he had any notion of what to say. Given that he did not, he welcomed any assistance he could gain from Frederick Smythe to repair his egregious mistake in accusing his father-in-law of murder in front of his bride.

"Gwen thinks I married her because of this."

Smythe sank farther into his chair and nodded. "That is likely what she is thinking."

"But you did not kill the baron?"

"I did not. I find myself a little overwhelmed that you believe I am capable of such a vile action."

Aidan ran a trembling hand through his hair, an echo of Smythe's earlier distress. "It was all the assets you sold, and the fact that you were meeting with ruffians at the docks. It made perfect sense."

Smythe exhaled heavily. "There is an explanation for that which is far more innocent." He stopped, raising his gray brows. "This is such a muddle. I think we should sort this out one bit at a time. Let us begin with ... Why would I kill the baron?"

***

Gwen kept her composure up until the moment the study door was shut behind her. And then the stream of tears could no longer be held back.

It had all been too good to be true.

She had known that, but had dared to believe in her father's prediction that the right man would come along and fall in love with her. Gwen could scarcely see as she ran down the hall, brushing past their butler, Jenson, before colliding into a figure in the entry hall.

Looking up, she gazed into Lord Filminster's eyes. His brows lowered as he caught her. "Are you well, Lady Abbott?"

Gwen stared at him, crushed. Did all of Aidan's family

know what he had been up to? That he had married her so he could investigate her father?

"I ... really liked you. And Lily. But you were all here to deceive us!" Gwen whipped her arm out of his reach and ran for the stairs.

Her wonderful wedding day had been a lie.

None of Aidan's family, except for Lady Moreland—Mama Abbott—had been sincere in their attentions to her that day. It was just like before, when she had gone to school, only to find that everyone there hated her.

A sob escaped, and she nearly fell to her knees, but Gwen clenched her fists and kept scrambling along until she finally reached the family wing.

Lifting her skirts, she ran for her life, one of her slippers flying off, but she did not stop. She reached her room and slammed herself in, before dropping into a sobbing heap on the floor.

She had really begun to believe.

Gwen, Gwen the Spotted Giraffe had actually thought that a handsome, intelligent gentleman was falling in love with her!

Outside, Buttercup scratched at the door, whining to be let in. Gwen reached up to unlock the door, letting the dog in before shutting and locking the door once more.

Gwen sat back against the wall and wiped her face. Buttercup watched her with those big brown eyes, before settling her head down on Gwen's foot to stare up at her with a worried gaze.

"Do not worry, girl. You and I will be all right," Gwen whispered, but despite the reassurance, tears began to drip from her swollen eyes yet again. She reached out to rub Buttercup's head. Anything to assuage the pain in her heart now that she had learned her husband did not marry her for ... well ... her.

She had thought Aidan was the right man, but it had been an illusion. A cruel trick of the moonlight.

* * *

AIDAN WAS STILL TRYING to figure out what he could say to Smythe when the butler knocked on the door to announce that Lord Filminster was here to see Lord Abbott.

His heart, which had only just begun to tentatively beat once more, stopped in his chest at this news.

Something has happened to Lily! Why else would Filminster visit me in Smythe's home?

Aidan's imagination ran riot. Was his sister injured? Dead? Had Michaels succumbed to his injuries after heroically saving his sister?

Smythe must have read his distress on his face.

"Show Filminster in."

Jenson nodded and bowed to leave the room.

"I shall step outside so you can speak with your brother-in-law."

Aidan nodded, numb to everything except the dread that something terrible had happened.

Shortly, Filminster entered the room and Smythe departed.

"What is it? Has something happened to Lily?"

Filminster walked over to the armchair next to him, taking a seat and shaking his head. "It is not Lily. But something may have happened to Trafford."

Aidan shook his head in confusion. "Trafford?"

His brother-in-law nodded, pulling out a folded page from his coat pocket. "A woman delivered this to the duke's home a little while ago. The butler could tell me nothing about her other than she had blonde hair, and he thought she was young. A cape and hood covered her almost completely. She left this for me."

Aidan reached out and took the note which had been written with a lead pencil. Bloody hell! If he never received another letter again, it would be too soon.

It is not Smythe. 1 of the other 3. Do not inform Peel until you hear from me. - Traf....

The writing was a sprawl, and Trafford had trailed off as if he had not the energy to complete his own name.

"Is this ... blood?"

Drops of reddish brown marred the page, and Aidan considered the worst—that his clownish acquaintance and occasional mentor might be mortally wounded ... even dead.

Filminster wearily ran a hand over his face. "We think so. Briggs and his men are searching for Trafford. I came to learn if you know anything about his whereabouts because no one has seen him in several hours and his father's home was locked up except for the servants. Apparently, the Earl of Stirling left for the Continent on Crown business this morning."

"By George! What the hell happened?"

Filminster sighed, falling back in his seat to stare at the crown moldings above them. "Trafford was most unhappy to learn of Lily's encounter yesterday. He vented his frustrations that the investigations were moving too slowly and there must be a way to draw the killer out. I think ... he did something, and it did not go well."

"But he is alive."

"Alive enough to write the letter, and send the girl to deliver it. But I am deeply concerned. Trafford is a good friend."

"Do we inform the authorities? Meet with Peel?" Aidan did not personally know the Home Secretary, but perhaps he could assist.

"I discussed it with Halmesbury. The duke believes we must proceed with caution. Without knowing where Trafford is, or the danger he is in, we must respect his wish to wait for word from him."

"Devil take this farce! I just accused Smythe and Gwen overheard me."

"I gathered as much. Your wife bumped into me in quite a state. She accused me and Lily of deceiving her, which I suppose is fair enough considering ... Dammit! I am sorry to have brought all this strife into your lives. When I found my uncle lying dead on the floor, I knew there would be trouble, but I never dreamed of involving so many people."

Aidan shook his head. "You are family now ... Brendan. You did not involve us, we involved ourselves to protect you. And, no matter your troubles with the late baron, he still deserves justice. Someone murdered him in his own study." It was still difficult to call his brother-in-law by name, but considering the bizarre circumstances, Filminster needed the reassurance.

"I keep wondering if we made a mistake investigating this matter ourselves. Should I have gone to Peel as soon as I read the letter from the baron?"

Aidan stood up, wandering over to the window to stare out at the gray afternoon. It was still drizzling rain, but there was a glimmer of sun through a thin bank of clouds.

"Perhaps, but we are committed to this course, so there is no time for regrets. Trafford said we must wait for word from him, so while your men try to find him, I shall sort out this crisis with Smythe and my wife."

"You will let me know if you need anything? Lily and I remain entrenched at the duke's home, so anything. Anything at all. You have risked much to assist us."

Aidan nodded. "I shall send word if I need assistance.

Keep me apprised about the search for Trafford. He is … more than I initially realized."

Filminster chuckled. "Trafford grows on you. Then one day you realize you cannot live without him in your life."

Huffing, Aidan nodded again. Trafford's tutelage on love-making had been as effective as he had promised on Aidan's wedding day. He shook his head. The scoundrel had better survive whatever he was doing. The world would be a worse place without his antics.

"I shall leave you to it. There are places I want to check for Trafford. Send for me if you need me."

Filminster left, and Smythe returned.

Aidan and he stood and stared at each other in deep silence until Aidan eventually broke the impasse.

"I cannot inform you about the baron's death and why I suspected you. There are too many lives involved. It is best if you do not know."

Smythe crossed over to his desk to retake his leather swivel chair. "Very well, but my daughter is in great distress, according to the servants."

Aidan had never experienced such guilt, knowing that Gwen was upstairs and he did not know how to approach her to explain what she had witnessed.

"What have you been doing?" Aidan could not help himself. He had to know. Even if it was not fair to ask when he refused to answer Smythe's questions.

Smythe grinned, his blue eyes mischievous as he leaned forward to answer in a conspiratorial whisper.

"Ships! Very fast ships!"

Aidan blinked in surprise. "Ships?"

Smythe nodded, his grin spreading wider. "Around the docks, they call them clippers. I have been selling off anything that I can to invest. Ships that can move commodities faster than before. Souchong and Congo teas, for instance. I aim to profit."

Shaking his head to clear his thoughts, Aidan attempted to understand. "Why were you meeting with those brutish ruffians in the taverns?"

"I have been gathering information about the conditions of the ships and crews. Information I can use to negotiate the best arrangements for myself. I have limited funds, so I cannot afford to make any errors."

"Mr. Smythe ... I mean ... you have behaved most oddly for something so ... mundane."

Smythe straightened up, gazing down at his hands resting on his mahogany desk. "Ah, but Aidan, I am the lowly third son of a baron. My claim to the peerage is tenuous at best. When word gets out that I divested myself of land to invest in trade ... do you know what polite society will say?"

Aidan shut his eyes, accepting he was the worst kind of fool. Far more foolish than the clownish Trafford. He had suspected Smythe of murder because of discretion over actions that were simply explained while Trafford had pursued real suspects.

"It will be a scandal. Many will shun you when they learn you are no longer an idle gentleman of pleasure supported by the income of your estates."

Smythe bobbed his head slowly in assent. "I will be, horror of horrors, *a man of trade.*"

Aidan rolled his shoulders. The aches of his fall were pronounced, probably because he was tense as hell trying to calculate how to make things up to his bride. "Why are you doing this?"

Smythe pushed his chair back to stand. Clasping his hands behind his back, he walked over to the fireplace to stare into the hearth.

"My estate income was declining. When I inherit the title from my brother ... he is a man stuck in the past. His estates are out of date, run with the same methods as our father and our grandfather before him. The Americans have unlimited lands for growing and export. I have seen the future, and it is grim unless I take steps to build a secure future for my son. Gareth will have nothing left unless I take action."

Gareth. Gwen's little brother at Eton. Suddenly it all came together, and Aidan realized that the naked ambition he had witnessed on his wedding day had been Smythe's delight in securing Gwen a marriage before fresh scandal broke when his move into business became public knowledge. "You wanted Gwen to make a good match before word got out?"

Smythe turned from the fireplace, his grin back in place. "Precisely! She is married to a future viscount. Connected to the wealthy Earl of Saunton and powerful Duke of Halmesbury. My daughter's future is secure no matter what transpires. The *beau monde* will never mock her again because she is somebody of consequence."

Aidan groaned. "Mock her? What does that mean?"

And so, Smythe explained. How Gwen had left for school after her mother's death, Smythe believing that being in the company of other women would be a blessing for a grieving girl. How she had her confidence shattered by her fellow students when they teased her mercilessly.

That Smythe had been unaware until she had permanently returned home two years later, because Gwen had tried to be stoic in the face of adversity and not trouble him while he worked to pick up the pieces after the death of his wife.

How those same students had become debutantes along with her, and Gwen had suffered their condemnation each Season.

"Gwen is a lovely girl, and the older members of the *ton* mostly adore her. When you told me you were overcome, and offered to marry her, I thought this was her chance to become the confident woman she was destined to be." Smythe sat in his chair and watched Aidan, his blue eyes sad. "Did you lie? Did you marry her to investigate me?"

Aidan was pained to hear the troubles she had experienced. To realize how lonely his Venus had been until he had found her on the terrace. How devastated she must be to learn of his investigation and to believe he and his family had been disingenuous.

His hubris that he could manage the situation—manage her—when the time came to accuse Smythe was revealed to be pure idiocy. Gwen must be deeply wounded by his betrayal, believing that all the worst things she had been told about herself were proved true.

"Never. Gwen was an unintended consequence. The moment I laid eyes on her in your receiving line I was bewitched. Then, when she quoted Manilius, I knew that I had found the other half of my very soul."

Smythe huffed. "Aristotle. You two are a perfect match."

Aidan cocked his head. "I was thinking Plato, but certainly."

"Are we settled, then? You believe I am not a killer?"

Aidan nodded. "I do not believe Gwen would lie, but I received confirmation that you are innocent from another whom I trust."

"Then we find ourselves in a pickle. Gwen has developed a skeptical attitude regarding her attractions. You will find that it will not be easy to convince her of your sincerity after witnessing your accusation earlier."

Aidan rolled his shoulders and slumped back into his armchair, trying to think what came next. He needed to win her trust back, and a simple apology would not be sufficient. "She is more than I deserve after all that has happened."

Smythe shook his head. "That is the lot of all men, but you will have to find a way to make this up to her, son. She needs to know you are the man you presented yourself to be."

CHAPTER 16

"Suffering becomes beautiful when anyone bears great calamities with cheerfulness, not through insensibility but through greatness of mind."

Aristotle

* * *

Gwen caressed Buttercup on her lap in a state of numbed pain. Out in the hall, footsteps approached, coming to a halt outside her locked door.

"Gwen?"

It was him. Lord Aidan Abbott. Her husband. The man who now controlled her future while keeping dark secrets. He who had pretended she was beautiful while he plotted to destroy her father.

A tear slipped down her cheek. Gwen raised a hand to swipe at it. She had the urge to rise and let him in. To hear some sort of explanation, but she did not wish to see him yet. She needed to grieve for all the dreams that had been smashed, and she was not ready to talk. At some point she would need to pick up the pieces, but she had not the energy or will to do it yet.

"I am so sorry, Gwen. Please ... let me in so we can discuss what happened."

Buttercup raised her head to stare at Gwen with sad eyes, noticeably worried about her mistress, but Gwen shook her head as if to say, "Not today, girl. Not today."

"Gwen?"

His deep voice sounded concerned, but it was probably a lie. Aidan was adept at deceiving her, it would seem. He was Hades with his poetic verses and lying lips. And she was the worst kind of fool for believing a man such as him could ever be attracted to a spotted giraffe.

Heavy footsteps announced his departure, and Gwen resumed watching the storm clouds from her chair. The somber mood outside perfectly matched how she felt inside.

Ever so slowly, in time with the beat of her broken heart, the storm gradually departed to reveal the oranges, purples, and pinks of a sunset, which was all the more dramatic for the puffy clouds lit by the sun's dying rays.

There was another knock on the door, followed by someone turning the handle, but Gwen paid no mind. She had no thoughts in her head, and no words to say. Not to anyone.

"Gwendolyn Smythe, are you in there?"

Octavia sounded worried, but Gwen was disinterested. She remained silent, stroking Buttercup's silky ears.

"Are you well?"

The handle rattled again.

"Let me in. Please. I wish to know you're well."

Gwen ignored the plea. She did not wish to provide reassurance to others when she had none for herself. It was going to be a challenge to work out how to salvage something from the wreckage, but mourning what she had believed she had found took precedence. She could decide what she wanted to do in the morning, but tonight was for nursing the gaping wound in her chest.

After a few moments Octavia gave up, footsteps in the hall announcing her departure.

The sun finally vanished and Gwen was left in the dark with only Buttercup to warm her cooling body. The little dog emanated heat in her lap, for which she was grateful.

She thought about rising to light a lamp, or undressing herself so she could climb into bed, but all seemed so much effort, so she turned her cheek to feel the velvet upholstery and remember a time when she was a girl with a wonderful mother, and with a hope that she would grow up to marry a man who loved her as much as Papa and Mama had loved each other.

Thinking of her mother was the jolt she needed to depart her melancholy. Tonight the moon was absent, and there were only stars to weakly light the night. The madness brought on by the moonlight had finally passed.

Mama would tell me I cannot hide in my room forever.

Gwen gave a heavy sigh, admitting the truth of it, and lifted Buttercup to place her on the floor. She supposed she might need to rouse herself. No point in feeling sorry for herself any longer—it was time to take care of eating and whatnot. The time for grieving had passed.

She found the bell and rang for Octavia before crossing the room to unlock the door. Then she moved around the room to light the lamps. The universe did not care about the deceitful nature of Man. It was time to return to living her life. It was time to plot a new future.

* * *

AIDAN STOOD in Smythe's study, rolling his stiff shoulders while he contemplated the blazing sunset through the terrace doors. The bruising had been particularly bothersome since the incident with Gwen. After his attempt to talk to her, he was planning out his amends.

He was waiting for a final knock on the door, turning on his heel when he heard it.

Jenson entered. "The Duke of Halmesbury and Lord Filminster are here."

Smythe stood up at his desk, gesturing. Jenson stepped out of the way to let the duke and Aidan's brother-in-law in, before slipping out and shutting the door behind him.

Additional armchairs had been brought in from other rooms. Aidan scanned the faces of Smythe's guests. His father had been the first to arrive, sitting closest to Smythe. Then the Earl of Saunton had shown up just ten minutes earlier in response to Aidan's hastily delivered requests and was leaning against the mantel, eschewing his seat for the time being. The duke's exaggerated height dwarfed the plump chair he had settled into, and Filminster perched on the edge of his seat, appearing rather solemn and throwing glances at Smythe.

"For those of you not yet aware, Mr. Smythe did not kill the baron."

Lord Moreland swept a hand over his face. "Thank the Lord! The notion of informing your mother ... it was ..." His father simply shook his head in explanation.

Evidently, his father was the only one who had not yet heard the news about Trafford and the other three suspects, but there had simply not been time to brief him. Saunton, Halmesbury, and Filminster merely nodded in agreement. Filminster must have gotten word to Saunton earlier in the day. Aidan supposed the earl might even be assisting in the search for Trafford, the earl's brother being a close friend of Stirling's heir.

Aidan paced, not accustomed to speaking to so many important members of high society at once. He was still growing to know his new relations, and what he was about to ask them to do—it was a lot to ask.

"My wife informed me that Mr. Smythe was at her side the day of the coronation. All through the night, in fact, due to a severe illness. Of course, we have received a note from … that confirms this." Aidan glanced at Smythe, realizing he had been about to reveal Trafford's involvement.

With the number of people who were already privy to the details of the murder, it seemed in Trafford's best interests to not disclose the information. Especially while they still awaited word on his whereabouts.

He raised a hand to swipe at his brow. Worry about Trafford had impinged into his mind regularly, even while he had urgently planned out the evening ahead to assist both Smythe and his daughter.

"Mr. Smythe has informed me of what he has been doing, why he has been selling his assets. Once I learned the truth, I felt it was my responsibility to arrange this meeting before the ladies arrive."

Smythe was tense, his grin absent as he fidgeted with the items on his desk. It had taken much for Aidan to persuade him that this meeting would be successful.

"Aidan assures me that I can trust all of you. That word of what I say tonight will not prematurely get around, and that you gentlemen might be of assistance."

The duke leaned forward. "I assure you that anything you have to say will be held in the utmost confidence. We are all family in this room."

Smythe nodded before taking a seat. "I knew the day would come when I would eventually have to inform others of what I am doing, but I find myself ... more nervous than I expected."

Aidan stepped forward. "Mr. Smythe plans to engage in trade. And I wanted to ask for your assistance."

Silence fell over the room at the announcement. After a few seconds, Saunton, still standing at the fireplace, cleared his throat and fidgeted with his cravat as if it had tightened around his throat. "I ... have to confess that I already engage in trade."

Aidan's brows shot up in surprise. "What?"

Noblemen and landowners did not sully their hands— their very reputations—with anything as lowering as work. Nay, the mark of a true gentleman was that he had a steward to manage his estates and that he lived an idle life of pleasure. Not that any of the men in this room were idle, but they managed to navigate the constraints of polite society with success.

Saunton threw his hands up. "What choice did I have ... I inherited a title on the verge of bankruptcy, along with neglected estates. My blighted father, the Lord of Satan as his tenants affectionately referred to him, was addled in the head, and he certainly did not manage his properties correctly. When my time came, I needed funds to modernize the estates, so I engaged a proxy to involve myself in trade. Mills, steam, whatever would make a profit. How do you think I tripled my wealth in so few years?"

The duke rubbed his thigh, tugging at his coat, before speaking. "When Saunton told me what he planned to do, I engaged a proxy of my own to do the same. It has greatly diversified my interests. I have a stake in businesses as far as Scotland."

"A gentleman is permitted by the rules and wisdom of our polite society to invest outside of his estates," Aidan replied, pacing in agitation.

Saunton grimaced, tugging on the collar of his shirt. "I—we—are considerably more active in our businesses than elite investments made through our retainers."

Aidan was dumbfounded. He shot a glance at his father, who immediately looked away. "Father?"

Lord Moreland rose from his chair, crossing to the windows to peer out over the garden and clasping his hands behind his back. "I have been discussing the possibility with my solicitor and man of business. Baker has been looking into possible businesses on my behalf, but I have not yet chosen which to pursue. It is ... intriguing that these gentlemen have successfully navigated these paths. It is not a subject one can freely discuss."

"Halmesbury and Saunton have been advising me on where to begin," Filminster confessed when Aidan turned to inquire.

Smythe rose from his desk, crossing to the cabinet across the room. Picking up a decanter, he poured a finger of brandy into a tumbler. Lifting it to his lips, he swallowed it down and smacked the glass back on the cabinet. When he turned around, he had a huge grin in place and his eyes were twinkling. Smythe might be the shortest man in the room, but he had found his footing and was brimming with confidence. "Well, then you are the right group of men to hear my proposal."

Aidan chuckled. "It would appear so. I thought this would be more difficult to discuss, but ..." He waved a hand at Smythe to proceed.

"Aidan and I have discussed the possibility of forming a syndicate. A business arrangement to purchase fast ships. I have already obtained a list of clippers in sound condition with reliable crews, and I plan to approach the owners with an offer to purchase."

Lord Moreland took his seat with an expression of interest. "You want to own the means of transport rather than manufacturing the goods. Which would mean being more versatile to the public's demand. What is your plan?"

Smythe tugged at his lapels. "I plan to form a shipping company that specializes in fast journeys—less than one year to the Orient and back. We would specialize in profitable goods, such as Chinese tea. If we invest together, we could purchase the fastest ships available while ordering more to be built to specification."

"What of the East India Company? They have a monopoly on trading with India."

Smythe nodded. "I have connections within the company and have privately discussed my plan with them. There are underserved trade routes that can be taken advantage of. Our strength would be speed and versatility. When you have been in business as long as the East India Company, it is difficult to shift strategy. As a new venture, we can take advantage of the changes in demand and trade since Napoleon's defeat."

Halmesbury leaned forward in his seat, his elbows on his knees. He looked over to Saunton, who gave a nod, clearly approving of the scheme. The duke looked back to Smythe and said, "We are interested. I would want to see the routes and understand the opportunities you have uncovered, of course."

"Could you work through a proxy, Mr. Smythe?" Aidan wondered if it was necessary for Smythe to ruin his reputation, given what had been revealed about Halmesbury and Saunton's secret business dealings.

Smythe shook his head in dissent. "I have decided I must be the headman to make this venture a success. There are connections I have cultivated these past few years, in Parliament, within the shipping companies themselves, and I have cousins in the navy, so I know the right men. High society might be scandalized, but the men I do business with will be impressed to work with me."

Halmesbury stood up and walked over to hold out his hand. Smythe hesitated, clearly surprised by the gesture, but took it and shook hands vigorously with the duke.

"You have an excellent reputation for forging deals at Lords on behalf of your brother, Smythe. Saunton and I will review your proposal. If all is in order, we will be willing to provide finance, along with connections and advice, if we remain undisclosed parties," Halmesbury announced.

Saunton strode over to shake Smythe's hand in turn. "It sounds like an exciting new chapter."

Lord Moreland cleared his throat, remaining in his seat. "I am interested, too, once I see the details of the proposal."

Filminster nodded. "I will follow Halmesbury and Saunton in whatever they advise. They know what they are doing while I am still learning about managing my estates."

Aidan felt one weight lift off his shoulders. The first part of his plan was a success. Smythe had a pledge from powerful peers to back him as he moved his interests into trade. Their support would be invaluable over the coming days, especially within the *beau monde*, where Smythe would need support once he made his scandalous move into business dealings.

After the meeting concluded, the gentlemen stepped out onto the terrace to converse while they waited for their wives to arrive. A short recess before they assisted Aidan with his plans for Gwen.

Filminster and Aidan walked away to stand near where the ball had taken place, where they could not be overheard.

"Is there news of Trafford?" Aidan was almost afraid to ask. Somehow he had become fond of Julius Trafford and his wild antics, despite Aidan's resolution to maintain his distance.

Filminster nodded, tapping his hand on the stone

balustrade. "Yes. Lady Astley is apparently missing someone, too. She was meant to collect Stirling's ward this afternoon, but she was delayed by rain. When her carriage arrived at Trafford's family home, the ward was nowhere to be found."

Aidan thought about the bloodied note. "The woman who delivered the letter to Halmesbury's home?"

Filminster lifted his shoulders. "It could be her. Miss Audrey Gideon. No one seems to know too much about her, but it cannot be a coincidence that two people residing in the same home disappeared in the same afternoon. The trouble is we have to be discreet so we do not endanger Trafford or Miss Gideon any more than they already are, so our inquiries are hampered."

Aidan could tell that his brother-in-law was worried. "Trafford is ingenious in his schemes. He will work it out to get word to us soon."

"I hope so. It is difficult knowing that a friend has endangered his life to assist me. I have been trying to think how I could have handled the whole matter differently."

Aidan shook his head. "What is done is done. All that remains is to deal with the present. Trafford was adamant about helping, and he is no fool."

Filminster burst out laughing despite his anxiety. "That is not true. Trafford would be the first to insist that he is, indeed, a fool."

Chuckling, Aidan shook his head at the ridiculous assertion he had just made. "I meant to say ... he is an enterprising and gumptious fool."

The two of them stood in silence, thinking their private thoughts about the odd fish, Trafford.

Aidan eventually shifted. "What news of Michaels? You said he had been injured."

"My butler is a hardy and cantankerous old devil. He was

meant to rest on doctor's orders, but he is already up and about terrorizing my household staff."

"What happened exactly?"

Filminster rubbed a hand through his hair. "The stubborn bastard tackled a man half his age when the ruffian breached my study through one of the windows. Michaels heard the sound of glass breaking and instead of calling for the guards, he ran in and threw himself at the blackguard and got a good whack in the face for his troubles. Apparently, he then thunked the ruffian with the same sculpture that was used to kill the baron before hollering for help. Unfortunately, the reprobate got away."

Aidan shook his head. "Michaels is a good man, even if he is a belligerent old goat."

His brother-in-law groped the stone balustrade and peered into the night. "I owe Michaels everything for saving Lily that day. I could not imagine what I would ..." Filminster broke off, unable to complete the sentence.

Exhaling sharply, Aidan lifted a hand to pat Filminster on the back. "I know ... Brendan. Believe me, I know."

"Do you suppose ... that Trafford will be all right?"

Aidan's gut clenched in anxiety. "He has to be. If anyone can take care of himself, it is Trafford."

Filminster nodded, but his face was wreathed with concern as he stared into the shadowed garden.

* * *

Gwen sipped a cup of tea and tried to think about recent events from a new point of view. The warmth of the aromatic leaves was a boon to her wounded heart and helped lift her spirits. The ache in her chest could not be denied, but at least she could think to explore her options.

She recalled Lady Moreland's visit, and the revelation

that Lily had been attacked in the aftermath of the baron's murder.

Gwen supposed, given the circumstances, she could understand that Aidan would take extreme measures to protect his family. It was unfortunate that she had been embroiled in his plans, and it hurt that he had used her so. But she could place herself in his shoes and comprehend how desperation had driven his actions.

Sadly, none of this abated the pain that she had merely been a pawn in his game to seek vengeance against Papa. But thinking about that would only lead her back to tears. She took another sip, enjoying the sensation of the beverage spreading heat through her veins to warm her icy fingers and toes. Sitting at the window in the chill of the storm had allowed the cold to seep into her very bones, but now she was slowly warming up.

"This is a good cup of tea." Octavia sighed from the bench at the foot of the bed, holding her cup and saucer close to her flat bosom.

"That seems rather self-congratulatory."

The lady's maid shrugged. "A fact is a fact. Just because I made the tea doesn't mean it's not true."

Gwen huffed a weak laugh. "I wish I had an ounce of your confidence."

Octavia frowned, staring down into her cup. "You do, Gwendolyn Smythe. In everything except yourself."

Sighing, Gwen put her cup down on the side table next to her mother's armchair. "It is clear Aidan did not marry me because of an interest in me, but rather to get closer to Papa."

"I don't think that's true." Octavia's tone was belligerent. "I've seen how he looks at you. That's not a man who's been forced into an unwanted marriage."

"Come. Let us not quarrel. I need to think about what comes next. I did not wish to trap Aidan in this marriage, but

I think we are stuck with each other now. Annulment will not be possible, considering we have consummated the marriage."

Octavia snorted in surprise, spewing drops of tea. "You certainly have done that!"

Gwen blushed. She could feel the heat and guessed her ears were a deep red. After a few minutes, when the heat had subsided, she continued.

"I do not know what comes next. It is our duty to sire an heir, but I have been thinking that perhaps I should remain here in Papa's home. Allow Aidan his freedom. Perhaps he could visit me here until we confirm that I am increasing and then he can move out."

Octavia shook her head. "He'll not agree to that, I tell you. Lord Abbott is in love with you."

It was Gwen's turn to snort. One would think that it was her lady's maid who liked to read. She certainly had the imagination of someone who did.

"I refuse to contemplate things that will make me sad. It is time to be realistic."

Octavia slapped the bench with her open palm. "I'm being realistic. It's possible that Lord Abbott had reasons for attending the ball that night that had to do with Mr. Smythe, but there was no reason for him to kiss you ... unless he wanted to."

Gwen scowled. "Perhaps he needed to gain access to our home! Perhaps he decided the most expedient method to investigate Papa was to ruin his only daughter!"

Octavia swallowed down her tea and put the cup and saucer down with a thunk on the bench. "You must fight for your happiness, Gwendolyn Smythe!"

"If my husband is so distressed by our rift, why did he make one frail attempt to talk to me several hours ago? He knocked at my door for only a few minutes. Buttercup is more persistent at scratching to be let in than he was in attempting a reconciliation. He probably found something to do this evening while I sit here grieving over moonbeams and poetry!"

Octavia smacked her hand down again, causing the cup and saucer to jump and clatter. "Mr. Smythe's not up here either, but you don't complain about that!"

"My father is likely defending himself against unjust murder accusations, so he hardly has the time to visit! He will speak with me when he has the opportunity. His regard is far more resilient."

They glared at each other across the room until Buttercup stood up from where she had been lying in the middle of the floor. The dog raced over to the window and began to jump and bark at the night, her short tail rigid.

"What on earth is she up to?" Gwen's question was almost impossible to hear when Buttercup increased the volume to snarl and bark even louder.

Octavia and Gwen looked at each other in consternation, their earlier argument forgotten as the little dog turned into a slavering guard dog, trembling with frenzied excitement.

* * *

AIDAN GROWLED IN FRUSTRATION. "The ladder will not remain in place! The ground is far too muddy! See what it has done to my boots?"

Smythe was panting from his exertions. "Burn my buttons!"

The Earl of Saunton started laughing hard, bending over in fits of glee. "Did I tell you about how my brother attempted something like this to win his wife's hand last year?"

Filminster started chuckling in response. "I was there! We were stuck in the mud for nigh a week."

Aidan scowled at the offending device, gesticulating at the other men to hush. "Keep your voices down! Buttercup is yapping something fierce up there. Gwen will discover us."

Halmesbury sighed, his back against the wall while he observed the antics. "I think we must revisit this plan. Your wife deserves our support, but this …" Halmesbury waved his hand in the direction of the wet ground at the foot of the ladder. "This is not going to work."

Aidan straightened up. "Agreed." He released the ladder which thunked against the side of the house. "Let us go back inside and rethink this before we alert Gwen to what we are up to."

The men filed back up the steps to the terrace, wiping their boots carefully to enter Smythe's office. Aidan had had a vague notion of climbing up to Gwen's window to recite the lines of Romeo, but it had not felt quite right and the mud had put the flimsy idea to its permanent rest.

Taking their seats, they went over the details of the plan once more. Several suggestions were offered, but they did not seem fitting to Aidan. He shook his head, dismissing them each in turn while raking through his mind for an idea. Any idea.

* * *

JUST AS SUDDENLY AS she had begun, Buttercup stopped midbark. Huffing in smug victory as if she had conquered a great villain, the little dog walked back to her spot on the rug and flopped down. Her eyes found Gwen as she settled her long jaw back onto her paw and stared.

Octavia and Gwen frowned at each other, neither offering any explanation for the strange behavior. The lady's maid shrugged and picked up the threads of their disrupted conversation. "I think you should allow Lord Abbott to explain the situation to you so you can sort this muddle out."

"And I think that my husband has a strong sense of obligation. He will convince me of the veracity of his feelings just to make me feel better. All the while resenting this marriage he tangled himself in only to find that Papa was not the murderer he sought. He made a huge error in judgment, and over time he can only grow to hate me for this trap he put himself in."

Octavia shot up to pace the room. "Confound it! Why can't you believe he might have genuine regard for you, you obstinate girl?"

Gwen shoved down the pain that threatened to boil over and drown her in a vat of tears if she allowed herself to consider the hopes she had had for their future. "There is no evidence to support that theory!"

"What of passion I saw in his eyes? What of the sweet words he spoke?"

Gwen hardened herself to not think about that. Thinking of that led to deep disappointment. "It was an act."

Octavia came to a stop. "Have you no faith?"

Her lip quivered, and the sting of tears blurred her vision. "Not in this."

Octavia swung around, narrowing her bulbous eyes into a sharp glare. "Not in you!"

Gwen averted her eyes, rising to her feet to stand by the window. The night was black without a moon to light the way. A fitting allegory for her obliterated dreams of love and happiness at Aidan's side as his true partner.

Partners do not keep secrets from each other.

"I have plenty of faith in me as an individual, but I am not a great beauty to inspire the love of someone like Aidan. I just do not believe that a man would find me attractive after all these years. I was practically on the shelf when I met him."

Octavia grunted in exasperation. "The men you met were pompous idiots who were too terrified of a tall, intelligent woman. You are too original for those men."

"Will you help me discuss my options, or must we end this conversation for the night?"

Octavia sighed, her bony shoulders drooping in defeat. "Perhaps you will view this differently once you sleep. Why not discuss something else?"

Nodding, Gwen took her seat. "I had high hopes. It is ever so lonely with only you and Papa to talk to."

Octavia chuckled. "What of Lady Hays and Lady Astley? They converse with you at every event you attend."

Gwen groaned, dropping her head into her hands. "I wish they would not. Lady Hays is a sweet old woman, but she quite forgets what she was speaking about, and Lady Astley is a spiteful harridan. If her husband were not so important and wealthy, she would not get away with half the things she says."

Octavia must have moved back to the bench, her tone defiant when she responded. "I think it's all going to work out and you'll have many wonderful friends if you allow yourself to believe."

The ache in her heart increased, threatening to overwhelm her with the memories of what had been and ideas of what could be.

The night before, she had been locked in Aidan's embrace while he explored her body with his lips.

Tonight she sat with Octavia arguing in her room, and the most notable thing to look forward to this evening was her dinner tray. "I gave it a chance. I opened my heart only to discover that I was still Gwen, Gwen the Spotted Giraffe."

CHAPTER 17

"The roots of education are bitter, but the fruit is sweet."

Aristotle

* * *

Aidan was still frantic for an idea of how to convince his wife of his deep regard when Jenson announced that the wives of the guests present had arrived for dinner.

He had some hazy ideas of what he might like to do, but not a solid plan. Beneath his breath, he cursed. Further interruptions to stall his thoughts! He needed to formulate a proper plan from the pieces he had gathered, but they refused to form into a whole!

The gentlemen adjourned to the small drawing room where Aidan's sister, his cousin, his mother, and the duchess were gathered. Lily stood in the middle of the room, hopping up and down while holding something unrecognizable in her hand.

The moment she saw him, she ran forward eagerly.

"Aidan! I brought something for you. Annabel had it in her attic. It took us the longest time to find it. Actually, there was a whole crate of them, but we just brought the one because we thought it might be useful."

Aidan ignored his sister's excited chatter to stare at what she was holding. "What is it?"

Lily held it up, then carefully pulled and pushed to reveal that it telescoped out into a large sphere. "It is a Chinese lantern. Annabel had them strung for a ball that she and the duke held a few months ago. See!" Lily held it up again, spinning it slowly. "We thought it would be just the thing. To show Gwen that you love her." Lily stopped, frowning at the paper contrivance before tilting her chin to glare at him.

"You do love her, do you not? That is why we are here?"

Aidan lifted his hand to chuck her under the chin affectionately. Lily's thoughts sometimes jumbled out of her mouth faster than most could comprehend. He knew the trick was to respond to the most important one first.

"Of course I do."

Lily smiled broadly. "I knew it! The day of the wedding it was patently obvious to us all, but you told us it was a matter of honor and doing the right thing and so forth. But I told Brendan you had the expression of a man in love. I was watching you closely, and you flinched ever so slightly when Gwen hesitated during her vows."

Aidan looked about to find that all eyes were on him, and he felt heat rising—to bare his soul in front of so many people. Men! His mother! They were all watching with great interest, including Gwen's father.

"I do love her. It will be difficult to convince her, which is why I asked for everyone's help."

Lily bounced on her toes, reaching out to grab him by his forearm. "This is so exciting. So what do you think? Do you see what it looks like?"

She held the lantern up as far as she could reach, which was not very high, but as Aidan contemplated it, and he cocked his head back and forth, a glimmer of a plan took root as he comprehended Lily's exuberance about the paper lantern.

Swinging his gaze around the room, he found that everyone was as focused as he. The wives were watching closely, almost breathless, as they waited for his response. His cousin, Sophia, was biting her lower lip while the earl had his arm about her. The duchess, Annabel as Lily had referred to her, nibbled on a fingernail as if agitated, with the duke towering behind her who, too, watched the twirling lantern with a small smile. His mother stood farther back with Lord Moreland at her side, dabbing at her lashes with a handkerchief as if overcome. And Filminster and Smythe looked on from the door, Smythe's customary grin wide as his gaze followed the motion of the lantern swaying in Lily's outstretched hand.

Aidan straightened up and grinned. "It is absolutely perfect."

* * *

GWEN'S STOMACH GROWLED, and she clapped a hand over her offending organ with a hint of aggravation. "Why is it taking so long for the maid to bring my dinner tray? It is late into the evening already!"

Octavia shrugged. She was pulling out Gwen's things for bed and turning the coverlet and sheets down.

"I ate hours ago."

"That is hardly helpful."

The lady's maid lifted a hand to smother a laugh. "It was to me."

Gwen pulled a face. If her dinner tray did not arrive soon,

she would be forced to leave her room, and she was not ready to bump into her deceitful husband. Not yet. Skipping a meal under the circumstances was illogical because she would just wake up in a worse mood than she was in now.

She still had no notion what to say or do when she finally encountered him, and every time she thought about it, her heart fractured and her eyes burned with unshed tears. So she refused to think about the altercation in her father's study.

Nay, Octavia's suggestion to get a good night's sleep and contend with this benighted situation in the morning was sound. Yet ... eating still needed to happen.

Gwen considered going down the back stairs to reach the kitchen directly. Perhaps she could make a sandwich. She had long since emptied the teapot of its contents. Surely she would not run into Aidan if she detoured around the back of the house.

Somehow, her feet would not obey. She was not ready to encounter anyone or talk. Octavia and Buttercup were the only company she could tolerate until she had time to sift through her thoughts and decide how she wanted to proceed.

Thump, thump.

Gwen gave out a loud squeal at the knock on the door. She had been so focused on her thoughts, she had not heard the approaching footsteps.

She threw a glance at Octavia, who shrugged. Gwen did not wish to speak with Aidan, if it was him. Octavia gestured at the door, offering to open it, but Gwen shook her head furtively.

"Gwendolyn?"

She exhaled heavily in relief before crossing to the door to open it.

Her father was grinning, his pearly teeth flashing in the

dim hall when she came face to face with him through the doorway. Papa was in good spirits, which was rather surprising considering the last she had seen of him a few hours earlier.

"Papa?"

"It is time to come downstairs, Gwendolyn."

Gwen shook her head. "I do not wish to see ... him."

Papa pursed his lips. "I would like to discuss what happened, and I promise it will only be you and I. Aidan ... is elsewhere."

"I am not ready," Gwen replied, her voice low and distressed.

Her father relaxed his smile, quirking his head in sympathy. "Time and tide wait for no man."

"It is not yet noon. I will face him tomorrow."

Her father frowned in confusion. "It was always highly frustrating to debate with your mother, and I see that you have inherited the devilish trait."

Gwen waved a hand. "It is what Chaucer meant when he wrote the line, is it not?"

"Gwendolyn, I am not the gifted scholar you are. I have no notion what you are referring to. Are you trying to be clever?"

She sighed in defeat. Being pedantic about language was not going to dissuade her father from wanting to converse. "Chaucer was referring to noontide, not the cycles of the sea. I was merely stating I would confront this muddle in the morning—at noon, perhaps."

Her father huffed in a half chuckle. "I see ... that is an amusing rebuttal, given the circumstances."

"Yet it did not work."

Her father smiled, revealing his teeth once more. "I am afraid not, child. It is imperative we speak."

Papa held out a hand palm up to indicate the hall leading

to the main staircase.

"I will not run into Aidan."

"No, I swear it. Not until you are ready."

Gwen stepped out into the hall, leaving the door open for Octavia, and linked her arm through her father's. "Well, then, lead the way."

Despite her father's assurances, Gwen looked about nervously as they walked down the hall and descended the stairs, expecting Aidan to appear any moment. Her husband had a habit of appearing unexpectedly, but she did not wish to see him.

On the main floor, they walked toward the study, and Gwen noticed that the door to the small drawing room was shut. Was Aidan in there, she wondered.

Reaching the study, Gwen dropped into a plump armchair by the fireplace while Papa sat in the matching chair. The hearth was empty, but it was still the most comfortable place to sit and talk together, rather than sit across the expanse of her father's desk.

Her father tapped his trouser-covered leg as if considering his words.

"This has been quite a whirlwind of events these past weeks."

Last month she had woken from severe illness to discover that she lived yet. Then she had re-evaluated her life and decided on her plan to adopt a foundling into their home because she wanted a child of her own more than anything. One did not get a second chance at life and waste it.

But, then, unexpectedly, she had been gazing on the most beautiful night imaginable only to have a god of a man recite poetry from the shadows before finding herself wrapped in his arms and enjoying her very first kiss. Followed by a scandal, a rushed marriage, and the discovery that her husband was an insincere liar pursuing family vengeance.

So Gwen nodded in agreement.

"I have spoken to your husband at length, and we have resolved our misunderstanding."

"Be that as it may, that does not alter the fact of his dishonesty with me."

Her father wet his lips. "I think it does. Aidan is a man in the midst of a family crisis. His sister was brutally attacked by a servant just weeks ago, and he tells me she is still in danger. He was desperate to solve a murder, and he erroneously selected me as the culprit." Papa leaned forward, resting his forearms on his knees to turn his eyes on Gwen. "Here is the thing, though. I had secrets of my own I was hiding, which entangled this misunderstanding. Honesty from me would have prevented some of what happened."

"Are you referring to the sold art and property?"

"I am. My plan is to move into business. My income was not increasing, and I found an opportunity to diversify into far more lucrative ventures."

"The shipping company."

Her father frowned, slumping back into his chair in surprise. "You knew?"

Gwen nodded. "After you sold the property up north, I needed to make sure you had not taken leave of your senses."

"How did you work it out?"

Gwen gestured to the desk. "I pried through your office and found the notebook in the bottom drawer. You had written details about the ships—load capacities, the dates of their journeys, information about the captains and officers. I concluded you were considering them for purchase."

Papa shook his head, befuddled by her confession. "Yet you said nothing?"

Gwen shrugged. "What was there to say? I approved of your plan and saw no need to bring it up. You appeared to have an excellent notion of how to proceed."

"What of the repercussions?"

"There will be a scandal when it becomes known. That was why you were so adamant that we hold the ball. Because you wanted me to marry before you lowered our status within high society."

Papa nodded. "Aidan noted there were oddities which led him to believe I might be the man he was looking for. But, now that he has learned the truth, Aidan has arranged for my new venture to be backed. The Duke of Halmesbury, Lord Saunton, Lord Moreland, and Lord Filminster have all pledged to confidentially back me, which means I am assured of success and do not need to commit too much of my funds. It means I can plan something on a much larger scale with far fewer risks. It is more than is required, and he is doing it because he is committed to this marriage with you."

"He has no choice. He is stuck with me."

Her father shook his head again. "A man always has a choice, Gwendolyn. And Aidan has chosen you."

Gwen fidgeted with her skirts in agitation. "I have reflected on what it might be like to be in his situation, and I appreciate the position he found himself in, but that does not change the lies he told me."

Her father straightened in his chair. "And I think that you have allowed your experiences at school to color your entire life. It is time to let go of the carping of others and accept your worth. It is time because those girls do not matter. What matters is now. What matters is your marriage."

Tears burned Gwen's eyes once more, and she swallowed them back with difficulty. She refused to begin crying again. "How can I possibly believe he has chosen me willingly?"

"I think you should allow him to convince you. It is time to apply that astute intellect of yours to observe what is in front of your eyes."

Papa rose to cross the room, opening one of the terrace doors and standing aside.

Gwen frowned, peering behind her father but seeing nothing but the black sky. Stars twinkled in the distance, but the firmament was very dark without a large moon to light it. Very dark indeed.

Her father bobbed his head toward the door. Gwen clenched and unclenched her fists, wanting to see Aidan, but not wanting to see him. Several moments passed as she considered her options.

"Go to him, Gwendolyn."

Soughing, Gwen begrudgingly stood up and moved across the room. Pausing in the doorway, she stared down at her slippers, searching for fortitude.

"You will never do anything in this world without courage. It is the greatest quality of the mind next to honor."

She gave a reluctant smile. "You are not such a terrible scholar, Papa. You recite Aristotle at the strangest times."

"There is always time for Aristotle," her father replied in a high-pitched voice, and Gwen giggled despite her trepidation. It was an eerie echo from the past, her mother's voice traveling down the years as if she stood in the room with them. It was precisely what she would have said had she been here now.

Taking a deep breath, Gwen stepped onto the terrace.

Her father drew the door shut behind her, and she was left alone outside. With some confusion, she looked about for Aidan, before catching sight of something very unexpected.

Down the length of the terrace, close to where she had first met Aidan, hung a lit orb in the direction of the waned moon. Searching about the terrace, she still did not find her husband, so with no small amount of curiosity, she approached the sphere.

It was a large lantern made of paper, lit from within, and

it swung above her from the eaves of the house. Gwen realized in amazement that it was a moon. With her head tilted back, she took in the beauty of the lantern in the landscape of the dark night, before noticing that many candles were lined upon the stone balustrade. Their flickering flames were much like the twinkling of the stars, and it became clear that the scene had been set to be reminiscent of the night she had met Aidan in the moonlight.

It was so utterly beautiful. Gwen raised her hands to her mouth, muffling a sob as she understood that this setting had been created for her.

> "She walks in beauty, like the night
> Of cloudless climes and starry skies;
> And all that's best of dark and bright
> Meet in her aspect and her eyes:
> Thus mellow'd to that tender light
> Which heaven to gaudy day denies."

Gwen choked back another sob, turning to find that Aidan had approached to take a bended knee behind her. Lord Byron's words had never sounded so sweet, but Aidan needed to speak words of his own. He had hidden behind the writers of bygone times for too long.

As if he had read her thoughts, he reached out, taking hold of her hand and raising it to his cheek.

"I am so sorry, my love. I am sorry I deceived you, but more than that, I am sorry I never spoke the words in my heart." Aidan drew a deep breath, gazing up at her in adoration. "You captured me from the moment you recited the verse of Manilius. I knew I had found the other half of my soul, the woman who would endlessly challenge me. Whom I would cherish for the rest of my days. It was impossible to walk away which is why I kissed you in the moonlight. I love you, Gwen Abbott, with every bit of my soul."

Tears streamed, dripping off her chin to run down her neck, but Gwen ignored them. "How can I know that is true?"

Aidan stared pensively back up at her, biting his lip. "What if I told you a secret? An embarrassing secret that a man would only tell his beloved wife …" He hesitated. "And perhaps a very close friend."

Gwen used her palms to wipe her cheeks, and nodded, intrigued to hear what he might tell her. Would she finally learn something tangible about her moonlight visitor?

Aidan rose up, peering over his shoulder before leaning down to whisper in her ear. "You are the only woman I have ever lain with, Gwen. The only one who ever tempted me to such heights of passion."

Gwen gasped, pulling back to gaze up into his face. "Is that true?"

Aidan peered about again, as if afraid of being overheard. "It is."

"You mean the other night when we …"

Her husband's brows shot up, and he swiftly raised a finger to press her lips shut. "Shh … and yes."

Gwen savored the feeling of his naked finger against her mouth while she thought about his confession. Slowly, a warmth began to spread through her body, sending shivers down her arms and legs. Even her head felt giddy. Pulling his hand away, she leaned in and whispered into his ear. "I was your first?"

He bobbed his head, murmuring close to tickle her hair with his warm breath. "I left that afternoon to receive lessons on what to do. I … did not want to disappoint you."

It was not the sort of secret a man wished to share, especially not with a lover. Gwen threw her arms around his neck, awed to be trusted with such private information. "Oh, Aidan. I love you, too!"

His lips found hers in the glow of the lantern above them, and as before, Gwen found herself being deeply kissed, as if she had brought a mythological lover to life with wishes made upon a magic moon.

Behind her, the sound of the terrace doors opening barely registered as she tangled tongues with Aidan and accepted him into her heart until, finally, they both raised their heads to look to the doors.

Gwen was taken aback to find much of Aidan's family gathered there. The duke and duchess stood arm in arm at the back. Lily and Filminster stood at the front, with Lily's elfish face beaming in the light of the white paper lantern. The earl and countess watched from the door, while Aidan's parents respectively stared down at their hands, presumably embarrassed to see their son engaged in a passionate embrace.

Slowly, they each raised their arms toward her as if they wanted to hug. "Welcome to the family, Gwen Abbott!" Lily cried.

Aidan coaxed her forward to meet their guests, and one by one they embraced her, tugging her close to buss her on the cheek and welcome her in their own words. Even the duke, who tended to be more reserved than the others, drew her into a quick hug with a thick, muscled arm. "Welcome, Gwen. My apologies for any deception, but the duchess and I will make it up to you, I swear it. We are proud to have you join us."

Gwen was overcome by incredible warmth. Outside of her own family, she had never experienced such emotion, and from such important members of society. Soon she was openly weeping again.

Lord Moreland handed her a handkerchief to dab her

face. "I am so relieved to learn your father's true plans, young lady. I look forward to a successful future with Frederick Smythe."

Gwen nodded, using the square to blow her nose as she finally admitted her father had been correct—Aidan was the right man.

Her stomach growled in loud agreement, and Gwen's eyes widened in horror. Papa had come up behind her to give her a quick hug, and chuckled. "I think it is time to eat, everyone. I am afraid my daughter has been expecting her supper for some time, but I instructed the maid not to bring it to her."

Lily grabbed her by the hand, yanking her toward the open door. "I am hungry, too! I have not eaten since breakfast, and that was at eight in the morning. Annabel and the duke like to rise early, so I am acquiring the habit, too, but it takes getting used to—such long periods between meals."

Gwen giggled, clasping the hand of her loquacious sister-in-law as they walked in together. How much fun it would be to form a connection with each of Aidan's family. Her brother, Gareth, would enjoy getting to know them and their children. Little Ethan was a delight and had mastered the game of chess far beyond his years. He and Gareth would enjoy many fierce battles in the future, was her prediction.

Glancing back, she found Aidan right behind her. "Are you going to tell me why you thought my father murdered a man?"

He grimaced. "I suppose if I must."

Gwen thought about it for a second, and decided then and there that it was time to stop retreating. It was time to learn how to stand up for herself and demand her place in this world. This was the perfect place to begin.

"You must." She was proud of the firmness in her voice.

CHAPTER 18

"Wishing to be friends is quick work, but friendship is a slow ripening fruit."

Aristotle

* * *

Aidan watched as Gwen sipped her soup with gusto. She might not like it under normal circumstances, but she was certainly ravenous enough to be enthusiastic this evening.

It was a joy to finally be honest with his wife. The day of their wedding, they had enjoyed a convivial afternoon with their guests, but tonight spirits were high. Their guests were markedly more relaxed when they were not anticipating the potential tragedy of destroying Gwen's little family in the pursuit of justice.

It was a pleasure to observe her coming into her own, her countenance unstrained as she listened intently to the anecdote that the earl and Filminster were retelling.

A story about how the earl's brother had won his wife.

Under the table, Aidan reached over to cover Gwen's free hand. She threw him a sideways glance with a half-smile before turning back to listen to Saunton's tale. The only thing marring his enjoyment of their family dinner was thoughts of Trafford.

Where was the clownish heir? Was he well? Or was he fighting for his life as the blood on the note had implied? Worry was gnawing at Aidan.

The fool had grown on him, and Aidan admitted ... Well, it seemed callous to sit here enjoying dinner together when they did not know where Trafford was. He had apparently risked his life in pursuit of Lily and Brendan's safety.

Listening to Saunton's story, Aidan realized that others around the dinner table, too, were thinking of their missing friend.

"Then Trafford said he could attest that Perry was an irreparable idiot to all who were present."

Next to him, Gwen giggled, raising a hand to cover her mouth. "Little Julius has always been a bit of a scoundrel."

Silence fell and their guests turned to stare at Gwen in amazement. Smythe did not notice, continuing to spoon his soup until he realized that something was amiss. He looked up with a quizzical expression to look about the table and stare at Gwen when he realized she was the focus.

Aidan cleared his throat. "Do you ... know Lord Trafford?"

Gwen raised her head, her brow furrowing as she noted that she was the center of attention. "No, but Lady Hays tells stories about Little Julius all the time. He frequently sneaked into her home to wreak havoc on her household as a boy."

Saunton raised a hand to fiddle with his cravat. "Lady Hays?"

Gwen bobbed her head. "Her townhouse is near her

niece's in Mayfair. We are talking about the heir to the Earl of Stirling? Little Julius was a regular visitor in her home."

Aidan shot a look to Filminster who met his eyes and gave a subtle shake of his head. So no one had thought to search for Trafford at the home of Lady Hays. Then a spark of memory teased Aidan.

"Do you mean ... Aunty Gertrude?"

Gwen smiled. "That is correct. Lady Gertrude Hays. She was just telling me a story about him at the ball the night we met. After we announced a betrothal, she cornered me for some time. She thought it was a great pity that I had not met her great-nephew. I think she had hoped ... we might enjoy each other's company."

The euphemism was clear. Lady Hays had hoped for a match between Trafford and Gwen.

"She told me he needed an intelligent woman such as myself to bring him up to scratch."

Aidan and Filminster made eye contact once more.

"And is Lady Hays in London now?"

Gwen shook her head. "She left London with her husband a day or two after the ball. She will not be back for several months. Lady Hays mentioned she would invite us to a house party for Christmastide."

Aidan sat back in his chair, hope surging through him. Perhaps Trafford was in Aunty Gertrude's home with the missing girl!

It makes sense if her home is close to Trafford's home! It could shed light on how Miss Gideon has vanished.

But they could hardly just ride up the street and knock on the door. Not if the killer was searching for Trafford and might be following their movements or surveilling the nearby family townhouse. And not if they did not want to bring undue attention to where Trafford might be hiding.

Near the head of the table, the duke coughed into his

hand. "Smythe, this wine is excellent. What vineyard is it from?"

Glancing down at the duke's untouched goblet, Aidan realized Halmesbury was changing the subject before they gave themselves away. There was fidgeting around the table and then Saunton raised a goblet with a wide smile. "Indeed, it is very good." He, too, had barely touched the wine. Aidan's cousin, Sophia, had suffered at the hands of men addicted to hard spirits, so none of her immediate family imbibed to show her support.

Conversation shifted to the meal that was being served, but when Aidan turned his attention back to his soup, he could see from the corner of his eye that Gwen was gazing at him in curiosity.

She leaned over to whisper into his ear, heating his blood with her sweet scent of citrus and the shadow of cleavage revealed to his vision by her position. "When we are alone, I expect to be informed what that was about."

Aidan licked his lips, his mind engulfed with thoughts of peeling Gwen's gown from her slender body. His pulse quickened at the notion of taking her to bed once their guests left for the night. "When we are alone, there might not be much time for talk."

Gwen raised her chin to look at him, her blue eyes blazing with mirrored passion. She appeared a little breathless as she stared back at him. Gwen shook her head as if to clear it. "We will make time for both."

He smiled, lowering his free hand to knead her thigh under the table as Gwen turned back to her meal. Aidan noted the blush creeping up her neck with smug satisfaction and thought about witnessing the rosy red washing over her naked body when he ...

Aidan shook his head before he lost track of where he

was sitting, in full view of his entire family, including his parents nearby.

* * *

"WHAT WAS THAT ABOUT?" Gwen wasted no time getting to the point once they reached her bedroom. Buttercup must have sensed the tension, dropping down from the bed to scamper across the floor. She planted her paws and began to bark at Aidan in bristling outrage.

Aidan and Gwen looked at each other, and despite her resolve to insist she be included, Gwen burst into laughter.

"The trials and tribulations of being the beloved mistress to a protective pet," remarked Aidan, his lips quirked into a crooked grin. Gwen shook her head, laughing too hard to respond but pointing at the door as she sought her composure.

Aidan opened the door he had shut seconds before, and Gwen caught her breath to sweep the offended little dog gently into the hall before quickly shutting Buttercup out.

Gwen rose and placed her fists upon her waist in the best menacing pose she could assemble. "I want to know what is going on, Aidan! Between you and Papa, there have been too many secrets. I am part of your family now!"

Aidan bit his lip. Leaning forward, he pressed a slow, firm kiss to her lips before raising his head. "You are my family now, Gwen Abbott."

His voice was low and deep, sending a thrill through her body. She shivered in delight, stepping closer so that they were toe to toe, her breasts brushing against his chest as she tilted her head back to stare deep into his eyes.

"Obfuscation will not work, husband. Why was Lord Trafford of so much interest?"

Aidan stared down at her, before slowly lowering his

head to press another slow kiss to her lips. Then he straightened up and stepped away.

"Trafford has run off to investigate the other three suspects on our list. Something has happened to him, we do not know what, but he has disappeared. There is a note from him declaring your father's innocence, but ... there were indications of violence. Trafford might be injured."

Gwen bit her lip. She had followed the words, but they did not make much sense. "I think ... you must start at the beginning."

Aidan nodded, beginning to pace up and down her room as he described the events of the past few weeks. How the baron had been killed. How Lily had been attacked. How Filminster had found a note revealing the motive for the murder, but not the culprit. How they had narrowed a list of suspects to Smythe and three others, and the subsequent events at Ridley House.

Gwen listened in quiet anguish until, finally, Aidan fell silent.

"You have all taken so much risk," she eventually exclaimed. "Did you know the baron?"

Aidan shook his head.

Gwen leaned back against the door, feeling pensive as she tried to sort through her thoughts. "Trafford could be at Lady Hays's home. She and Lord Hays leave their oldest retainers to take care of it in their absence. Servants that would have known Little Julius for many years."

"I hope he is there. It will be difficult to confirm because we cannot simply walk up to the front door and knock. There might be people watching us, hoping we will lead them to him."

"Do you think he uncovered the truth? Do you think he knows the identity of the murderer?"

"There is no way to know. Until we speak with Trafford, we are in the dark as we were before."

Gwen shook her head. "That is not true. From what you have told me, the list of suspects is confirmed. You now know it must be one of those three men. Any resources that were committed to searching for other suspects can now be redirected to these specific men."

Aidan cocked his head in thought, frowning slightly as he considered what she had said.

"I suppose you are right."

She rolled her eyes, folding her arms over her stomach to glare at him. "I know I am right. The evidence is before you. And the letter from Trafford was clearly stated. One of the other three. No perhaps or question about it. Why else would he now be hiding? Your investigation has been successful, and you have narrowed it down to a finite number of men who could have committed the crime."

Aidan's expression turned into one of admiration. "You are making me regret not speaking with you on the matter before. You offer a fresh perspective."

"I am a scholar. I consider the facts."

Aidan approached her, wrapping an arm around her waist to pull her close and gaze down into her face. "And what about you? Have you finally accepted the facts about you?" He raised a hand to brush her hair back from her face, his eyes staring deeply into hers, and Gwen's skin tingled in helpless delight.

"Gwen, Gwen the Spotted Giraffe?" Her father had confessed after dinner to revealing her youthful secrets earlier that day in the interests of reconciliation, so she knew Aidan was aware of her past troubles.

Aidan leaned in to brush his lips over her freckled cheek. "I happen to like your spots, Gwen Abbott." He rose to nuzzle at her temple, teasing her hair with his hot breath to make her shiver. "And I appreciate your height." He raised his head to stare deep into her eyes. "And your name is exquisite poetry." Aidan stroked her mouth with the pad of his thumb. "Gwen." He leaned in to steal a kiss. "Gwen." He tilted her chin with his forefinger to gaze into her soul with impassioned chocolate brown eyes. "Gwen."

Then he paused, waiting for her to respond while she weakly attempted to recall what they had been discussing before he had laid waste to her with his ardent attentions. Aidan's whispered words weaved a spell on her senses, making her finally accept that his adoration was genuine.

"I"—her voice was thready as want rose from her belly to consume her with its flames—"have realized that those girls ... might be wrong about my attractions."

"Very wrong," Aidan muttered, lowering his head to capture her mouth with his. Gwen moaned in the back of her throat as their tongues entwined, lifting her arms to grip him by the shoulders.

Aidan cursed, breaking their kiss to step back with a pained expression.

Gwen's brows came together. "What is it ... never say it ... is this another secret?"

Her husband moved back another step, guilt painted on his features. He rubbed at his forehead, clearly reluctant to answer her. "I may have been thrown from my horse when I was following your father."

She gasped. "May have?" Gwen stepped forward.

"I did ... get thrown. Valor was startled and panicked in a congested street."

Gwen stepped forward again. "That sounds serious."

Aidan reddened, not willing to meet her eyes and making her grow suspicious.

"When did this happen?" she demanded.

Aidan rolled his shoulders, as if to shake off the pain. "Yesterday," he replied in a small voice.

She sighed heavily. "Of course. That is why you closed the curtains and insisted we remain in the dark!"

He nodded.

Gwen bit back her irritation. "Let me see, then." She gestured at his coat.

Aidan rolled his shoulders once more, then removed the coat to lay it out neatly on the bench at the foot of her bed. Next, he unfurled his cravat to lay it down beside the coat. When he yanked his shirt from his breeches, Gwen grew fiery in anticipation. She had only seen his naked body that first night, the night of their wedding, and it was still an unusual experience to watch a man undress. Her chest rose and fell in agitation as her blood heated up. Only for her to exclaim in horror when he whipped the shirt over his head to reveal his upper body.

"Aidan!"

His upper arm and shoulder were mottled with livid bruising. Reds, blues, and purples formed grotesque patterns upon his bronzed skin. Gwen quickly circled him with her hand held over her mouth. The hind part of his shoulder was even worse, with angry contusions covering almost a quarter of his back.

Which was the moment she realized that Aidan could have been lost to her forever. "You could have been killed!"

Aidan threw his shirt in a pile on the bench, coming back to take her in his arms and hold her to his bare chest. "Would that have been a bad thing, Gwen Abbott?"

Gwen's vision was blurred when she looked up at him through the tears that had gathered in her eyes. "A very bad thing," she whispered.

"Then I shall take far more care in the future." Aidan lowered his head to capture her lip between his teeth, nibbling gently before he traced the edge of her mouth with his tongue.

"Hmm ..." she breathed. "Is it true you have never lain with a woman before me?"

Aidan purred an affirmation, his mouth trailing kisses along her cheek to breathe softly against her temple.

"You demonstrated competency ... for a man who was new to the activity," she mumbled, finding it difficult to keep a thought in her head when hot sensation was pulsing between her thighs and up her belly.

"Little Julius instructed me in painful detail," he admitted, before suckling her earlobe into the wet heat of his mouth.

"Well ... we better save Little Julius ... from his pursuers, then ... because we owe him a ... great debt of gratitude." Gwen's head fell back to expose the line of her neck, and Aidan quickly took advantage to trail his hot mouth down the curve of soft flesh to nip gently at her shoulder.

Fingers fiddled with the buttons of her bodice, desire strumming in every direction at his warm touch. Soon it was undone, and Aidan was tugging the gown from her body. It dropped to pool around her feet, but she had no time to be concerned when his large palms came up to cup her through her stays. He growled in frustration, moving to tug her tapes and rip the garment away and throwing it aside.

Gwen thrilled at the evidence of his lust for her, reaching up to stroke his bared chest and revel in the sensation of the dusting of crisp curls and the hard muscles below her fingertips. He reached up to take hold of her hands, moving them to his waist so he could lean in to wrap his mouth around a jutting nipple, pleading for his attentions under the fabric of her shift.

She moaned loudly, tugging at his waist to pull him closer as his tongue flicked over the turgid tip. Next she knew, he had his arms about her and was lifting her up off her feet, their bodies pressed together tightly, so he could walk her over to the bed where he gently lowered her down.

While he towered over her, his eyes on her nearly naked body, surveying her slender form through the transparent cotton, Gwen watched with wide eyes as he undid the buttons of his falls. Taking a seat on the bed, he quickly pulled off his boots and unrolled his stockings before shrugging out of his breeches.

She was less shy this evening. It was their third night together, so this time she watched in open fascination as he revealed the engorged appendage which announced his desire for her. She reached out to grasp it, enraptured by the feeling of satin skin over hard steel, but Aidan growled and pulled her hand away.

Gwen was startled, her head cocking back to question him.

"I am still rather new to this, Venus. Touching me might lead to a disappointing finish."

She smirked, sitting up to remove her shift so they were both naked together. "We would not want that!"

Grabbing him by the waist once more, she tugged him over, falling back onto the bed so he fell over her. Catching himself on his elbows, he watched her from an inch away, their heated skin rubbing together in the most delicious manner. Gwen gazed back, her heart thudding faster and faster in her chest as his hand slipped down between them. A finger found the crease between her legs, and Aidan explored her folds. Gliding over her slickness, he found the apex and swirled.

Gwen threw her head back and moaned, her legs parting to give him access as he settled his knees between hers. Aidan continued to stroke her, and her body writhed with the pleasure of it as her hips rose and fell rhythmically beneath his. Her movements became frayed, fractured, as sensation rose in waves to engulf her in a keening release.

Aidan quickly brought his hand back up to enter her with one decisive thrust, filling her with his blazing flesh. As he pulled back and thrust into her once more, Gwen moaned and gripped the coverlet with both hands as her desire mounted once more.

Together they chased the peak of oblivion before they both cried out and rode the wave together, crashing back to the earth in each other's arms.

Aidan fell to his side next to her, wrapping his arms tightly around her body. "It is better with no secrets between us."

Gwen giggled breathlessly, boneless from their mutual passion. "Much better."

"Shall we ... pledge to never have secrets again?"

She winced. "If that is how it is to be, then I suppose I better confess ... The night you asked me about Papa selling his property ... I told you the truth that he did not discuss it with me, but the truth is ... I suspected what he had planned and did not disclose it."

Aidan raised his head, peering at her in the dim light. "Gwendolyn Abbott! You misled me!"

She grinned, blushing with guilt. "To be fair, we were not yet married, and I did not know you all that well."

His lips curled into a smile, and he leaned down to brush them over hers. "No more secrets in the future?"

Gwen nodded. "No more secrets, nor half-truths, nor carefully worded answers intended to misdirect. Unless I am planning a surprise."

Aidan settled back down, holding her close. "When this is all over with Trafford and finding the killer, shall we take that trip to Italy together?"

Her heart fluttered in her chest. "You meant that? That you would take me to Florence?"

"Of course, but at the rate we are going, we might want to leave soon. If you are with child, we will have some time limitations to contend with."

Gwen purred in the back of her throat, overcome that her moonlight visitor was placing all her deepest wishes at her feet. Great art. A child of her own. Deep in her soul, she finally acknowledged that he was not a visitor at all, but the other half of her soul, and their entire future was before them.

"Then we have no choice but to solve this murder swiftly," she replied.

EPILOGUE

"Well begun is half done."

Aristotle

* * *

AUGUST 29, 1821

Gwen pulled the edge of her hood down, careful to hide any evidence of her red hair beneath it. Her unusual height could not be helped, but she would keep her knees slightly bent and her shoulders hunched as she walked down the street.

Old Fred brought the hackney to a stop by the main square, and Gwen carefully disembarked, keeping the hood down and holding her skirts so she would not tumble. Old Fred had been told not to assist her, or do anything out of the ordinary.

The men had argued at some length against involving her, but she had stood her ground and reasoned it out.

If there were ruffians about, searching for Trafford or his father's ward, they would not think twice about a woman walking by.

It was the only way to safely approach Lady Hays's townhouse without rousing suspicion, considering how close it was to Trafford's family home.

There could be men watching, so it must be a woman.

It had been three days and still no word from Trafford.

Something had to be done.

Aidan had finally acquiesced when she had agreed that Old Fred would be the driver and remain within a few feet of her. The hackney driver had apparently been in the army, so her husband had provided him with twin pistols to hide within pockets of the massive overcoat he wore.

Gwen reached for the large covered basket on the passenger bench. She was pretending to make a delivery, and they hoped that no one would be aware Lady Hays and her husband had already left London. Nevertheless, the remaining servants on duty might receive a delivery in the owner's absence.

Hoisting the basket up, she turned and headed toward the townhouse, making for the tradesman's entrance.

She rang the bell and waited. It might take some time to attract the attention of the old couple who took care of the house when the household packed up and left for the country.

After a few minutes, Gwen rang the bell again, gnawing on her lip while she waited with bated breath.

Trafford could be right there, dozens of feet away. And he could know the identity of the man who had murdered the baron.

She wanted so much to help. To bring home good news. Any news.

Her new family was so worried, waiting for word of Little Julius.

But despite her eagerness to help, all Gwen could do was wait for someone to come to the door.

* * *

Next in the Inconvenient Scandals Series:
Lord Trafford's Folly
A daring lord and a young woman find themselves in peril, igniting a possible romance as they escape to stay alive.

AFTERWORD

While gentlemen of the Regency were certainly permitted to invest without sullying their reputations, engaging in trade was an entirely different matter.

In fact, if a man built up his wealth and wished to become a gentleman, he did so by purchasing estates and then severing all financial ties to the business that helped him achieve his wealth.

This was to remove the stain of trade from his family so they would be accepted within the new social strata they had ascended to.

Frederick Smythe's choice to pursue trade would have been insightful from a financial standpoint, but would certainly lower his family into a different class.

Hence, the willingness of Halmesbury, Saunton, Filminster, and Lord Moreland to assist on the condition that their involvement was to remain a secret. To be fair regarding their discretion, by remaining unknown parties, they would offset the damage to Gwen's status, so Frederick would want to keep their involvement unknown.

The Kama Sutra was available in many versions across the

Indian subcontinent. However, it was not published in Britain until 1883, when Sir Richard Francis Burton found a way to circumvent censorship laws. It soon became one of the most pirated books, being copied and reprinted and even republished.

Trafford is the sort of enterprising man of leisure who would know the right people and be able to obtain a copy of the notorious book in its original Sanskrit sixty years earlier.

Speaking of Julius Trafford, he is missing along with Miss Audrey Gideon. There is quite a scandal brewing, not to mention risk to life and limb. If he manages to survive this murder investigation, Trafford will be faced with doing the right thing to save the young woman who has been inadvertently ruined by his misadventures.

Find out what happens in *Lord Trafford's Folly*, the third book in the Inconvenient Scandals series of Regency mystery romances.

* * *

Join Nina's Newsletter at NinaJarrett.com for free books, fun Regency content, announcements, and exclusive discounts.

Follow Nina Jarrett on your favorite platform.

ABOUT THE AUTHOR

Nina started writing her own stories in elementary school but got distracted when she finished school and moved on to non-profit work with recovering drug addicts. There she worked with people from every walk of life from privileged neighborhoods to the shanty towns of urban and rural South Africa.

One day she met a real life romantic hero. She instantly married her fellow bibliophile and moved to the USA where she enjoyed a career as a sales coaching executive at an Inc 500 company. She lives with her husband on the Florida Gulf Coast.

Nina believes in kindness and the indomitable power of the human spirit. She is fascinated by the amazing, funny people she has met across the world who dared to change their lives. She likes to tell mischievous tales of life-changing decisions and character transformations while drinking excellent coffee and avoiding cookies.

Join Nina's Newsletter at NinaJarrrett.com for free books, fun Regency content, announcements, and exclusive discounts.

Follow Nina Jarrett on your favorite platform.

ALSO BY NINA JARRETT

INCONVENIENT BRIDES

Book 1: The Duke Wins a Bride

Book 2: To Redeem an Earl

Book 3: My Fair Bluestocking

Book 4: Sleepless in Saunton

Book 5: Caroline Saves the Blacksmith

INCONVENIENT SCANDALS

The Duke and Duchess of Halmesbury will return, along with the Balfour family, in an all-new suspense romance series.

Book 1: Long Live the Baron

Book 2: Moonlight Encounter

Book 3: Lord Trafford's Folly

Book 4: The Trouble With Titles

Book 5: Lord of Intrigue

* * *

BOOK 1: THE DUKE WINS A BRIDE

Her fiancé betrayed her. The duke steps in. Could a marriage of convenience transform into true love?

In this spicy historical romance, a sheltered baron's daughter and a celebrated duke agree on a marriage of convenience, but he has a secret that may ruin it all.

She is desperate to escape...

When Miss Annabel Ridley learns her betrothed has been unfaithful, she knows she must cancel the wedding. The problem is no one else seems to agree with her, least of all her father. With her wedding day approaching, she must find a way to escape her doomed marriage. She seeks out the Duke of Halmesbury to request he intercede with her rakish betrothed to break it off before the wedding day.

He is ready to try again...

Widower Philip Markham has decided it is time to search for a new wife. He hopes to find a bold bride to avoid the mistakes of his past. Fate seems to be favoring him when he finds a captivating young woman in his study begging for his help to disengage from a despised figure from his past. He astonishes her with a proposal of his own—a marriage of convenience to suit them both. If she accepts, he resolves to never reveal the truth of his past lest it ruin their chances of possibly finding love.

* * *

BOOK 2: TO REDEEM AN EARL

She planned to stay unmarried, but Lord Richard Balfour is determined to make her his countess.

In this steamy historical romance, a cynical debutante and a scandalous earl find themselves entangled in an undeniable attraction. Will they open their hearts to love or will his past destroy their future together?

She has vowed she will never marry...

Miss Sophia Hayward knows all about men and their immoral behavior. She has watched her father and older brother behave like reckless fools her entire life. All she wants is to avoid marriage to a lord until she reaches her majority because she has plans which do not include a husband. Until she meets the one peer who will not take a hint.

He must have her...

Lord Richard Balfour has engaged in many disgraceful activities with the women of his past. He had no regrets until he encounters a cheeky debutante who makes him want to be a better man. Only problem is, he has a lot of bad behavior to make amends for if he is ever going to persuade Sophia to take him seriously. Will he learn to be a better man before his mistakes catch up with him and ruin their chance at true love?

* * *

MY FAIR BLUESTOCKING: BOOK 3

A rebellious young woman. A spoilt buck. When passions ignite, will opposites attract?

She thinks he is arrogant and vain ...

The Davis family has ascended to the gentry due to their unusual connection to the Earl of Saunton. Now the earl wants Emma Davis and her sister to come to London for the Season. Emma relishes refusing, but her sister is excited to meet eligible gentlemen. Now she can't tell the earl's arrogant brother to go to hell when he shows up with the invitation. She will cooperate for her beloved sibling, but she is not allowing the handsome Perry to sway her mind ... or her heart.

He thinks she is disheveled, but intriguing ...

Peregrine Balfour cannot believe the errands his brother is making him do. Fetching a country mouse. Preparing her for polite society. Dancing lessons. He should be stealing into the beds of welcoming widows, not delivering finishing lessons to an unstylish shrew. Pity he can't help noticing the ravishing young woman that is being revealed by his tuition until the only schooling he wants to deliver is in the language of love.

Will these two conflicting personalities find a way to reconcile their unexpected attraction before Perry makes a grave mistake?

* * *

BOOK 4: SLEEPLESS IN SAUNTON

A sleepless debutante. A widowed architect. A lavish country house party might be perfect for new love to bloom.

In this steamy historical romance, a sleepless young woman yearns for love while a successful widower pines for his beloved wife. Hot summer nights at a lavish country house might be the perfect environment for new love to bloom.

She cannot sleep ...

Jane Davis went to London with her sister for a Season full of hope and excitement. Now her sister is married and Jane wanders the halls alone in the middle of the night. Disappointed with the gentlemen she has met, she misses her family and is desperate for a full night's sleep. Until she meets a sweet young girl who asks if Jane will be her new mother.

He misses his wife ...

It has been two years since Barclay Thompson's beloved wife passed away. Now the Earl of Saunton has claimed him as a brother and, for the sake of his young daughter, Barclay has acknowledged their relationship. But loneliness keeps him up at night until he encounters a young woman who might make his dead heart beat again. Honor demands he walk away rather than ruin the young lady's reputation. Associating with a by-blow like him will bar her from good society, no matter how badly his little girl wants him to make a match.

Can these three lonely souls take a chance on love and reconnect with the world together?

* * *

BOOK 5: CAROLINE SAVES THE BLACKSMITH

She helps injured the blacksmith on Christmas Eve, leading to a romantic attraction despite their aversion to love.

She has a dark past that she must keep a secret. He has a dark past he wishes to forget. The magic of the festive season might be the key to unlocking a fiery new passion.

She will not repeat her past mistakes ...

Caroline Brown once made an unforgivable mistake with a handsome earl, betraying a beloved friend in the process. Now she is rebuilding her life as the new owner of a dressmaker's shop in the busy town of Chatternwell. She is determined to guard her heart from all men, including the darkly handsome blacksmith, until the local doctor requests her help on the night before Christmas.

He can't stop thinking about her ...

William Jackson has avoided relationships since his battle wounds healed, but the new proprietress on his street is increasingly in his thoughts, which is why he is avoiding her at all costs. But an unexpected injury while his mother is away lays him up on Christmas Eve and now the chit is mothering him in the most irritating and delightful manner.

Can the magic of the holiday season help two broken souls overcome their dark pasts to form a blissful union?

* * *

BOOK 6: LONG LIVE THE BARON

After she clears his name of murder, a marriage of convenience is the only way to save her reputation! Will their uneasy alliance spark a lasting passion?

A steamy historical suspense romance, about a young woman driven to do the right thing, a lord who does not quite appreciate the gesture, and a murder investigation that could end their new relationship before it begins.

Her conscience drives her to act ...

Miss Lily Abbott knows the new baron is innocent because she saw him entering the widow's home next door at the time of the crime. But when the widow refuses to assist him, this young woman who hoped to marry for love cannot stand idly by when she knows the truth. Lily risks everything to provide an alibi for the glib gentleman who barely remembers her name.

He can't believe he has to marry her ...

Lord Brendan Ridley stands accused of patricide to gain the title he now holds. Not even his close family connection to the powerful Duke of Halmesbury can help him. He prays his paramour will come forward to clear his name, but honor dictates he not reveal his whereabouts that night without her consent. When help comes from an unexpected quarter, he finds himself forced to marry an annoying chatterbox to save her from scandal.

When these two mismatched people are forced to marry, will they find a way to work together to reveal an enduring passion before the real murderer strikes again?

* * *

BOOK 7: MOONLIGHT ENCOUNTER

Lord Aidan Abbott investigates Mr. Smythe but compromises his daughter, Gwen, at a ball in front of a crowd of important guests.

In this steamy historical romance, the heir to a viscountcy is determined to protect his sister, accidentally ruining a young woman while searching her father's home. Now he will need to choose between his crusade and the growing love between them.

He feels guilty for failing his family ...

Lord Aidan Abbott neglected his duties as a chaperone when his parents left his little sister in his charge. Because of him, Lily was forced to wed under a cloud of scandal. Now Aidan must solve a murder to keep his sister and her new husband out of danger.

She is caught unawares ...

A mysterious lord interrupts Miss Gwendolyn Smythe while she is taking air on the terrace. Unfortunately, they are discovered together, so she is forced to marry a man she has never met before to quell the scandal. Now Gwen is determined to make the best of their new marriage, with or without his cooperation.

While Aidan continues to secretly investigate Gwendolyn's family, he realizes that the scholarly redhead now holds his heart in her hands. How can he reveal what he has been doing without shattering their only chance at love?

* * *

BOOK 8: LORD TRAFFORD'S FOLLY

A daring lord and a young woman find themselves in peril, igniting a possible romance as they escape to stay alive.

A steamy historical suspense romance, about a lord who agrees to help his friends with their quest to solve a murder. Now he must fend for himself while protecting the young lady he has endangered with his choices. Can he keep her safe from harm from both the enemy pursuing them, and his urge to kiss those plump lips?

He thought it would be a lark ...

When Lord Julius Trafford, the heir to an earl, agrees to help his friends in a quest to solve a murder, it was mostly because he was bored. Now he is in hot water, and he has dragged his father's delectable ward into danger with him. Together, they are forced on the run, and Lord Trafford must engage his wits before it's too late.

She is determined to keep him alive ...

Miss Audrey Gideon feels compelled to care for Lord Trafford when he is attacked by a murderous assailant. As they make their escape from London in search of safety, Julius begins to demonstrate his true potential and Audrey wonders if there is more to the foppish heir than meets the eye.

Can this unlikely pair rise to the challenge and discover true love along the way?

* * *

BOOK 9: THE TROUBLE WITH TITLES

She has loved him for years. In his darkest hour, she is determined to save him by uncovering the real killer.

In this steamy historical romance an heir stands to lose everything unless he can find the truth, and the girl next door is the only one standing by his side while danger lurks in the shadows.

He could lose his title and his life ...

Simon Scott is set to inherit a title and a fortune until powerful lords accuse him of murder. Now his betrothed has broken ties with him and he could be arrested at any moment. Trouble is he knows he is innocent, but who will believe him when all the evidence points to him?

She knows he is not a killer ...

Madeline Bigsby has been in love with Simon since they were children, but he was too self-absorbed to notice. In his darkest hour, she is determined to save him by uncovering the real killer.

The stakes are high and love has never been such a dangerous game. Can Simon accept help from the girl he left behind to discover who has framed him and perhaps learn the value of true love along the way?

www.ingramcontent.com/pod-product-compliance
Ingram Content Group UK Ltd.
Pitfield, Milton Keynes, MK11 3LW, UK
UKHW041420180225
4646UKWH00010B/49